Finch Books by Britt Cooper and Erin Dulin

The Chronicles of Fayble
Queen of Shadows
Mistress of Blades
Daughter of Neverwoode
Rose of Ruin

Chronicles of Fayble

ROSE OF RUIN

BRITT COOPER &
ERIN DULIN

Rose of Ruin
ISBN # 978-1-80250-708-9
©Copyright Britt Cooper & Erin Dulin 2024
Cover Art by Kelly Martin ©Copyright October 2024
Interior text design by Claire Siemaszkiewicz
Finch Books

Published in 2024 by Finch Books, United Kingdom.

Finch Books is an imprint of Totally Entwined Group Limited.

ROSE OF RUIN

Dedication

Thank you to our husbands and families who
stand in the gap when we are up to our ears in
deadlines. We will learn someday. Maybe.

Chapter One

It was inevitable that Ffion would be forced to face his demons sooner or later, though a not insignificant part of him wished for later never to come.

The road home from Neverwoode was fraught with perils — creatures of lore and circumstances befitting only the darkest of nightmares. The woodlands had become an unexpected refuge, serving as his home despite their fabled terrors, and providing a respite from an altogether different sort of monster.

Most largely steered clear of the once-hidden kingdom while faithfully denying the existence of the mythical beings and tales of legend that originated within its borders.

How easily the human mind was manipulated, conceiving of such things as quickly as it dismissed them.

Fools.

He'd been among them for a blissful period of some three-odd years. In Neverwoode, it had been easy to forget and even easier to pretend. He'd been devoted to causes and people outside of himself with great satisfaction, even as a small voice within him accused him daily of running. *Hiding.*

He had. There was no sense in denying it. Yet while his conscience might see fit to berate him for his cowardice, Ffion had no doubt his detour into not one but two strange realms fulfilled a higher purpose still.

But that didn't alleviate the gnawing guilt. For if there was one thing he'd learned throughout the whole of his misadventures, it was that duty trumped all. His unwitting companions had taught him that, with more than their fair share of patience and an urgency to serve that had put him to shame.

His wrongs couldn't right themselves. Would that his father might forgive him.

With a resigned sigh, Ffion climbed, picking up his pace as he reached the fertile terrain blanketing the outskirts of Calaise.

Home.

Nothing quite compared to the rolling splendor of their lush green meadows, even as they were overrun by scores of ruby red poppies and seas of deep blue irises. The crush of colors might've taken his breath away if it wasn't such a stark reminder of his absence.

Ever higher, he hiked, grateful for the burning in his lungs providing a distraction from his racing thoughts. The uncertainty he'd faced within Wylewoode Forest paled compared to what awaited him on the other side of the bluffs.

Disappointment. Anger. Fear.

In truth, he hadn't wanted to leave, but it seemed the only way at the time. With his mother's and brother's insistence, he'd fled, making for the anonymity of Neverwoode. Obscurity had suited him well, ushering him into a state of contentment as he relinquished his memories in favor of simply forgetting.

Oblivion could only be realized for so long, however, once the dust of the enchanted woods settled. Remembrance had flooded back, catching him out and sending him barreling toward his kingdom without regard for his safety or anybody else's.

All the time he'd had to think along the way had been a double-edged sword, with regrets and inexplicable hope welling within his spirit, damn him.

Your true nature will consume you.

The thought plagued him still, leaving him grappling with his humanity. Nothing had been the same for him since, with a few brash words having transformed him from a king in wait to a pauper on the streets, running for his life — to save his own and protect the lives of others from his newly discovered appetite for revenge.

His desire was strong, driving him into the woods neighboring Calaise. Escaping Marin's errant curse had been his aim, but he'd run headlong into immediate distress, drawn toward the very thing he wished to destroy.

Ffion had scented her long before he laid eyes upon her. She'd sat amongst the fronds and bracken, her head cradled in her hands. White-blonde hair beset with thistles and bits of leaves had fallen about her shaking shoulders, her slight form breathless as she'd wept. She'd smelled of earth, of illusion — all the things he now despised.

Her blood had called to something feral buried deep within his soul, demanding he eliminate her.

Any will to ignore her presence had been quickly overcome by the basest of instincts — a beastly quest that had grown out of that handful of uttered words from the pixie tinkerer, fating him to the role of hunter against otherworldly prey he hadn't known existed before Marin had shown his face within the palace walls.

She was an easy target, and he a more practiced huntsman than he'd ever fathomed possible. Indeed, the sporting pursuits of his youth were less than nothing by comparison. His heightened senses and newfound lust made him a veritable brute, a predator with no discernible morality left to his name.

Yet a captivating refrain had drifted into his heart, sung into his being without a single word articulated. The melody had stopped him cold as he'd watched the pixie woman, her vulnerability nothing short of disarming. Only then had he realized what made her so different from the others he'd hunted.

Her goodness was too real, too raw to be lost. In her, he'd sensed profound decency, bewildering him and bringing him to his knees. Never before had he perceived such virtue from a pixie or a human.

In a sudden rush of awareness, Ffion had let go, relinquishing the mighty creature that had outstripped his control. He'd given in to the overwhelming calm that had seized his mind, forgetting his roots, forgetting his passions and ambitions.

He'd *breathed*. Deeply, for the first time in what felt like months. Rising to his feet, he'd collected himself, making for the one he'd come to know as Petra. For years he'd followed her like a pup does its master, eagerly joining her on adventures through reveries in Otherlande and freeing the people of Wylewoode from the mind-altering clutches of pixie dust they'd known as sift.

It was then that his world had come crashing down around him. The eradication of sift had led to an immediate loss of peace, sending him spiraling toward the vulgar instincts that had disappeared in Petra's presence.

Ffion willed away the ache that always accompanied his regrets as he stepped onto the precipice overlooking his realm, the toes of his boots sending a scattering of pebbles tumbling over the cliff's rim.

Calaise came into view — a glimmering commonwealth set within the fruitful valley that saw their nation to abundant prosperity. Gilded spires jutted from the castle domes, reaching like fingers toward the sky while crimson blooms ran the length and breadth of the grounds, covering the iron ramparts surrounding the palace. The sight of it had his insides roiling alongside an equally unsettling presence he hadn't been able to shake for the whole of his journey home.

For more than half his travels, he'd denied the reality, keeping his distance and altering his path to create space. His control had been minimal at best, slipping further out of his grasp with each passing footstep. The nearness of his kingdom beckoned to his inner beast, challenging his restraint. He lifted his head, closing his eyes as he scented the breeze blowing at his back.

Her.

"You're not very careful. One swift push would see you over the edge, plunging to your demise. Wouldn't that be a tragedy, Prince Ffion?"

He turned to find Bellamy, the renegade half-breed who'd afflicted him with her presence throughout his duties in Neverwoode. "You'd love to try that now, wouldn't you?"

"I only need one go of it." She prowled toward him, her lips quirked in a haughty smirk, taunting him to the bitter end of his patience. Confidence had never been a struggle for the spritely vixen, which only aggravated him more.

He stepped within a breath of her, meeting her defiant gaze. The depths within her eyes might've been intriguing, had he not been so distracted by the darkness lurking beneath the surface. "At least Petra fought the otherwordly side of herself. Too much to expect, I suppose."

"Perhaps she should've embraced it." Bellamy wrinkled her nose, her features pinched in disgust. "But you. Just…don't."

Her comment startled him. Did she well and truly know?

She backed away without an ounce of fear, a suspicious look upon her face. Yet her heritage gave Ffion pause. Pixies were known for their trickery, more so for their rudeness. A mind game wasn't out of the question. Likely, even, given her hatred for him.

Ffion shook his head, dismissing her ruminations. Better to ignore than engage. He'd done as much since he'd had the misfortune of meeting her in Wylewoode, choosing instead to focus on the tasks at hand, though she seemingly did her best to distract and annoy.

Would that she might finally let him alone.

"Brave of you to try," Bellamy continued, turning her back to him. So much for being on her way. She glanced over her shoulder, narrowing her eyes. "I wonder who will reach him first."

"Who?"

"You know very well. I could smell him on you in Neverwoode." Striding toward Ffion, she looked past him to the kingdom lying beyond with a brief spark of uncertainty in her gaze. "Safe to say I know him better than you, though you're likely more wounded than I. Humans are so sensitive."

There was no question in Ffion's mind as to who *he* was, for the prince detected the foul odor of the pixie Marin upon her as well. "My business with him is my own, and doubtless more urgent than yours."

Bellamy scoffed. "You'd like to think so, wouldn't you? Yet all my brothers and sisters are dead, and I'm my own last chance to avoid the same fate."

That brought Ffion up short. And while he thought he saw a glimmer of fear cross her face, it passed as quickly as it came.

"My father's despised amongst his people," she continued. "And who better to see him to his end than his halfling children? We're no better in their eyes — worse, in fact — though failure will surely see me to the same fate as my siblings."

"Your father —"

"*Yes*," she hissed. "So tell me again how your business is more urgent than mine, beast."

Her callous disposition grated, swiftly erasing any sense of compassion he might've felt, irritating him just as she had in the heart of Neverwoode. Ffion folded his arms across his broad chest, ignoring the thrill he felt standing in the presence of one every bit as wicked as he. "A bounty hunter this whole time. Just when I thought I couldn't dislike you any more."

"It's my life or his, and I choose mine, such as it is."

She was as predictable as the tides, and he couldn't help but grin. "Of course you do." He took a deep breath, already regretful of the words on his lips. "If it's his legacy you wish to undo, you'll never pull it off alone. You, of all creatures, should know that pixie trickery will sustain him. We may fair better if we track him together."

If he'd thought her frosty before, it was nothing compared to the animus he saw in front of him now.

She pinched her lip between her teeth as if to guard the secrets of her mind while she mulled his proposal. Everything about his circumstances was suspect, and working with one so manipulative, so *dangerous*, gave him pause. But the mad side of himself buried deeply within demanded a reckless venture.

Bellamy watched him, her long auburn hair swirling around her as the light wind picked up speed, giving her an ethereal air entirely at odds with her sullen demeanor. "It doesn't matter as long as he's dead."

Chapter Two

Death stalked Bellamy everywhere she went. Even now, she was stoking its flames, inviting it to ruin her in all her callous disregard. Not that she wished for it, but somehow, an advanced departure felt eminent.

When she was young, she'd fought daily for survival. It was easier amongst humans, given their vulnerabilities by comparison. Yet, some instinctive part of them never fully received her, and the same was true of pixies. Egregiously so.

Thus, Bellamy bothered with neither, save for the occasions when such interactions couldn't otherwise be avoided.

It had been the case with her mother, killed by a handful of pixies when she was a small child of three or four. Bellamy had long since forgotten the details of her face. She couldn't recall her voice or manner, but remembered well that her hair was just the same shade of auburn. Nevertheless, she'd cried over her loss and was left wholly alone.

For his part, her father had watched everything from afar, like a parody sourced from poignant tragedy. His kin were all awful, but he was the worst.

After a lifetime of observing the deviant inclinations of her folkloric relations, Bellamy craved authenticity. She wasn't kind, nor was she sympathetic or gracious, but she was honest.

It was the one thing she appreciated about her new companion.

Bellamy knew Ffion was a threat for as long as she remained in his presence. He reeked of her kind, but not in the way of a halfling or a full-blooded pixie.

Ffion bore the scent of every wretched life he'd taken.

"I can smell them on you, the ones like me you've killed." Bellamy watched him moving ahead of her, his strength evident in the way he confronted the fragments of crumbling earth before him with impassive precision like the seasoned predator she suspected he was, even if he was holding back.

Ffion snorted in response—an irreverent huff for the expired souls he wore like a choice perfume.

"How many?"

"I don't know." His gaze darkened as he descended over the cliff's razored edge. "I remember little once it's done, but they all find a way to leave their mark, as you've discerned."

At that, Bellamy raised a brow. He couldn't be much older than she, even if his build suggested the discipline of a conditioned assassin, not to mention his stealth. She was well-practiced. Quick. But so would have been the pixies her companion had already put to rest, and they were more agile, their veins flowing with pure, glittering liquid gold.

"I wonder if you don't revel in their stench forever branded upon your flesh. If you don't celebrate your victories like any other proud warrior. We are a perverse plague over these lands, after all." Bellamy watched as Ffion's shoulders tensed in response to her words. Rolling his head to either side, he lowered himself further down the rockface, his gaze meeting hers with near-feral delight.

"If only." He scoffed, moving deftly toward the earth below, his smile marred with unbridled contempt. "But you're not one of them, no matter the nuisance you've proven to be. Unlike them, you can choose to be different, though I doubt you will."

She hated him for his discernment. A war for Bellamy's soul was waged each morning, and she chose not to engage most days. Pixies were horrid, selfish beings, but humans were rarely better. Often, she pretended she was neither, thriving in solitude where nothing could disturb her precarious assembly of peace.

Reason tempted her to acknowledge that, in many ways, the nothingness in which she cloaked herself made her worse than both, and it seemed the pauper prince agreed.

Before Bellamy could hear another word, she leaped from the towering ledge where Ffion clung, and it was freedom, if only for a moment. She would never fly, not like the pure-born, but neither would she take for granted the gift of embracing a gentle current guiding her feet to solid ground, especially when it meant leaving him behind.

From their first meeting in Neverwoode, she'd known who he was, but it hadn't mattered. He'd been remarkable even then, manipulating the deceptive merits of sift to conjure a more youthful visage until his true identity mattered even less. Few would've known or cared who he was in that forsaken kingdom regardless — not in a territory so afflicted with oblivion. But Ffion was calculating and alarmingly shrewd.

At the moment, Bellamy was convinced that their mutual interests were all that prevented him from killing her, and it was a simple matter of time before his patience ran dry.

She need only survive him until Marin was dead.

It was madness to work alongside the savage in the first place, with her only hope being to ensnare and eliminate her father before the others got to him. Bellamy had no qualms about delivering Marin to his maker. He deserved that much and worse. Still, her duty as his progeny was to finish him herself, even if he took her with him.

She didn't know her father well, apart from the thorn he was in every living creature's side. He was toying with her, which was only part of what had kept her from reaching Calaise sooner. Everything was a game to Marin, a meticulously curated gambit meant to entertain him and him alone, to the whole of Fayble's detriment. In every step of her journey, it crossed Bellamy's mind that she could walk directly into one of his traps.

The man was a tinkerer — an ingenious one at that — who seemed to favor muddling his youngest's mind over holding her captive. He'd commonly revealed contraptions and tools beyond Bellamy's wildest imaginings throughout their limited contact, almost childlike in his fervor. At times, she saw much of herself in Marin, and that was far more troubling than any of his brilliant creations.

If ever there had been a nefarious mind to fear, it was his, for eleven of her siblings had tried and failed to do what she intended to do herself. They, too, were halfling atrocities.

Were.

Marin killed his own offspring for sport. One by one. While not by his own designs, he championed every effort to see them into an early grave. It was in his best interest to do so, Bellamy believed, as putting his children down was possibly the one thing that could earn him the pixies' pardon for sullying their line.

And yet, true to their character, she was nearly as sure that promising her the liberty to live outside their prejudice in exchange for her father's life was a ruse. A great seduction, it was. Pixies were deceivers at best and profoundly wicked at worst.

Bellamy didn't resent the man behind her for wanting to destroy them. It was every bit as likely that she might survive the task at hand with him, only to assuredly die by his.

Ffion wasn't surprised to see the ease with which Bellamy regained her footing at the ridge's base. He'd assumed she possessed similar abilities as her relations, but it was still disconcerting to watch. He'd known only a fraction of what his dearest friend Petra was capable of, and that considering she'd been unaware of her genuine nature until recently.

She and her sister, Wendolyne, were the only half-breeds the prince had encountered before Bellamy. Wendolyne, however, had displayed a keen grasp of what they were. With Marin's aid, she might have lured the entire continent into a listless delusion wrought with horrors its inhabitants would never perceive until they were well beyond saving. Neverwoode nearly claimed that fate, doubtless much to the destructive pixie's delight.

And while Bellamy sought to rid society of her father, she was no ally. Ffion had made the mistake of crediting her with a conscience when she'd agreed to assist his friends in their journey through Wylewoode, but there was no trust between them. Not now or ever.

He'd never witnessed Petra's goodness in Bellamy, nor her captain's fortitude, and he would never forget her desire for their efforts in Neverwoode to fail. Further proving her destructive halfling nature was each attempt she'd made to goad Ffion into all he meant to abandon, and worse was the undeniable desire that lurked beneath his flesh.

He wanted to.

And what a twisted irony it was that he could do so while he was with her. His soul craved the barbarity of his inner beast, eager to make itself known, to hunt and destroy. His body ached for the strength he'd spent the last few years trying to forget.

Bellamy moved faster than any person ought, her gait one of fluid, feline grace. Both beautiful and perfectly unnerving as every other like her. But hers was a fire he would not smother just yet. Not until he could determine what hope there was for her humanity, if any.

She was already fostering the chaos of his still small voice by reminding him how good it could feel to let go. He saw it in the way her eyes had closed before her feet found purchase on the forest floor, that she felt most herself when she didn't hide her wicked essence. It was enviable, and he hated himself for it.

Yet, some impulses weren't meant to be mastered, and the longing to release the strength rising within him beckoned.

He could suppress it for a time and track her from a distance, remaining several meters behind. Hell, he could trail her from miles behind and never lose her scent. *That* was the sort of lifeblood Bellamy spoke so facetiously about, and hers, perhaps the most intoxicating of them all.

Chapter Three

Ffion's pulse thrummed in tandem with his noiseless tread as he decided his course, the blood pumping wildly through his veins when he finally scrambled down the cliffside with effortless precision.

Before that moment, every step, every interaction and decision he made had been calculated, and never had his methods changed. Being meticulous was a necessity, with his efforts to suppress his inner beast too challenging to allow for any flexibility. He was rigid in his approach, knowing that any mistakes could lead to him starting over. It was either that or bitter regret.

It had been years since he'd afforded himself his current level of exhilaration, and in a way, loath as he was to admit it, it felt like freedom. There was no other way to describe it, even as it provoked the living nightmare he'd worked so hard to keep at bay, and he hated her more for it.

Bellamy made no attempts to disguise the bane she was. If anything, she embraced it. She was everything he feared he might become if he forgot himself, even for a moment. It had already begun, with Ffion falling in stride beside her, his breathing steady despite the speed that brought him to her side.

"That was neat." Bellamy acknowledged his presence with a pretty twist of her lips as she spoke, nodding toward the mighty overhang at their backs. She was nothing if not condescending, but it was of no consequence to him. Marin was not far if the thick, cloying air around them was any indication.

Once he was dead, all would be right. Right enough, anyway, and he would never have to see her again.

Ffion wanted to be good, to be the man his father, the High King of Calaise, had raised him to be, but Bellamy drew from him his darkest desires. Yet, she was not to blame. Her father, the cursed patron of his malady, had set this derangement into motion, and Ffion had proven worthy of his torment.

"It's no wonder they're all dead," Bellamy huffed unceremoniously, all the while maintaining an abiding calm.

She surprised him with that. It was a near compliment to acknowledge his aptitude at all, much less to grant he might hold an advantage over pixies in their cunning and skill. Still, he knew better than to believe Bellamy would think anything of him apart from their vested interest.

"They deserved it." Ffion felt no need to defend his actions. His kills. It was no less than the truth.

"We all do," she uttered, and he felt her gaze on him for a moment. Perhaps it was how she said it, but behind her words was an acute revulsion Ffion knew well.

He merely grunted in response. What else could be said, for Bellamy was right. That reality fostered a deep-seated bitterness, with Ffion's spirit darkening a bit more each night he gave in.

When he hunted.

He wasn't good — or not good enough, else his affliction would've ceased to preoccupy him. So said his puppet master, Marin, when he'd cursed him to his depths. *Your true nature will consume you,* said he, on that forsaken night four years past.

And so it had.

Under a canopy of starlight each night, Ffion was lost to himself, overwhelmed by an insatiable need to end the immoral blight plaguing the land. It was never enough, and he was beginning to believe it never would be, despite the reprieve given him in Neverwoode. He, too, was a walking calamity, making him no better than the halfling keeping him company.

In the end, this was why he understood Bellamy, and she, him. It was why they could not abide the other's company.

Traveling in the day was easier to bear, making it possible to ignore her wicked core. Like Petra, the half-breed bore the trademark stench of their ancestors, if it could be described as such. A tantalizing aura had drenched Ffion's consciousness just before he'd seen her there with Petra and the Captain on the shores of Altanys Cove. It was familiar, like each of their kind, but... *more.*

Unsettling.

Injudiciously bold and provocative, Bellamy's intrinsic essence was one of arrogant command. Where Petra had been broken when he'd first chanced upon her, the fury beside him was ruinous in her certitude.

Daylight would soon slip away, but they had reached their destination. The environment around them had shifted into something sickly that was distinctly Marin. Ffion would have recognized it anywhere, and apparently, Bellamy did as well.

Her entire demeanor altered in an instant as her elegant posture turned hostile. Ffion knew as well as she that Marin was not there. He had been, likely very recently, but he had led them on a wild goose chase that would not end well. Bellamy groaned when she turned to meet Ffion's darkened stare, her features filled with contempt.

He wondered how often she'd experienced that very same letdown before, but he couldn't quite bring himself to feel sympathetic. They were learned creatures, and she no less, even if she were the daughter of a bedeviled soul.

Not far in the distance, the woods rippled before his eyes — a faint, iridescent shimmer peeking through the undulating brush and pine.

Ffion despised sift.

"How thoughtful of my father to prepare a place for me to stay while I plot all the ways to end his life." Bellamy closed her eyes, pursing her lips as she drew a fortifying breath before meeting Ffion's gaze once more. "Games... always with the games."

Ffion ignored the tears pooling at the edges of her eyes, enhancing the warm earthen tones staring back at him.

He was restless, he realized, under her study. It was growing darker by the minute, the shadows around them deepening with the setting sun. He knew what would happen once they swallowed what remained of the day's amber glow. The twilight was much the same as the mesmerizing flecks in Bellamy's eyes, only hers favored honey and ginger at once.

Even the sun, in all its splendor, could not compare.

He shook his head, driving away the damned reveries. This was how it happened when he lost himself, his musings driving him to distraction, then dissolving into the golden hour when he would abandon all control night after night. It wasn't a curse but a disease that sent him into fits that would not end until the light returned.

Bellamy examined Marin's deceitful snare. "Shall we burn it?"

Ffion saw an inferno blazing behind her spiteful gaze, for beyond sift's illusory façade lay a charming little cottage like those of so many legendary tales. Picturesque though it was, it had been the pixie bastard who'd brought them there, and it could be nothing more than a trap.

The man was a devil in every sense of the word. He'd cursed Ffion and, in turn, the future of his kingdom through his birthright. How could he ever rule when each day, once dusk settled, his muscles began to twitch and searing pain shot through his bones? It was driving him to distraction — all the more reason to not be in Calaise.

To not be king…

"We need somewhere to bed down," Ffion decided. He pressed on toward their lodging for the evening, and Bellamy followed closely despite her ambitions to reduce it to ash. Retrieving the sling looped through the belt of his trousers, he slipped a hand into his satchel, taking a round stone from it, though he would not need a weapon.

"You know as well as I do that it's a trap. My father went so far as to shroud it from other wanderers to preserve it for my sake." Bellamy strode past Ffion, twisting her long mahogany waves into a knot at her neck as she swept by.

She was tense and visibly leery when she reached for the brass knob, testing to see if the door would open freely. The hinges did not protest, nor did the air move as the door opened, as if the cottage had held its breath awaiting their arrival.

"It's not a gift but a means of plaguing me with the knowledge that he's one step ahead." Her words were steeped in venom. And some part of him felt for her and the hollowness of her sentiments. Hers was a lost, burdened soul. Maybe as haunted as his.

Ffion approached her from behind, fixing his sling over his forehead. "If he sets you off balance, he's already won. We'll stay here. And then we will kill him when we wake." He whispered the words into her ear, unwilling to participate in whatever unknown ploy was at play. Perhaps Marin possessed some means of observation within the small shack. Bellamy's nod was nearly imperceptible, but an understanding was established, nonetheless.

It wasn't long before the veil of eventide fell, and they ate together in companionable silence, Ffion glancing toward the window with a frequency he was sure Bellamy hadn't missed. His limbs were growing tender, and his hand shook under the table between them as he struggled to hold himself together.

He could endure until bed. He had to.

Much to his relief, neither wished to converse. It was a welcome silence—whether due to a mutual apprehension of their surroundings or simply their distaste for one another, it made no difference.

Time passed slowly, and before long, each sought other means of biding their stay. Ffion paced, warding away the musings of his beast, even as one of the very creatures he wished to exterminate had become his associate. For her part, Bellamy spent much of the early evening searching the vast library within their shelter, muttering profanities as she went.

"Did you think you could surround me with books, and I would forget that I want you dead?" Ffion heard her say as she plucked a thick novel from one of the shelves, thumbing through its pages. He couldn't help but smirk when she did so, for it seemed altogether contrary to what he expected of her.

"I'm not surprised he would mock me this way," said Bellamy, her fingertips running over the spines of neatly stacked titles. She carefully extracted a leather-bound chronicle Ffion knew well, beaming as she admired its fine craftsmanship.

The book in her hands had been his favorite as a boy. Bellamy couldn't have known. Unless she did—like somehow she knew he was, indeed, Ffion, crown prince of Calaise. One day, his birthright would see him seated upon his father's throne, though it could have just as easily been his brother Gierson's misfortune to inherit the realm. Younger than Ffion by a handful of minutes, had Gierson been born ahead of his unstable likeness, Calaise would be better off.

Twins. Identical, at that. How fortunate for their parents to have born only one disgrace between the two boys alongside a stroke of ill fate that the wayward brother should lead.

Ffion moved toward Bellamy, standing beside her with his hands clasped behind his back as they stared at the shelves before them. "Did you know who I was when first we met?"

"Your name alone is not exactly common," she replied. The young prince didn't trouble himself to look but felt her scrutiny. Bellamy turned to him, reaching a delicate hand toward his temple, tracing the jute cord secured above his brow before curling a fallen lock of his hair around her fingertips. "And all of Fayble knows of the flame-haired twins. Though, I admit I'd not imagined it to be quite so bronze with the way many speak of it."

"Why not mention my title sooner?" Ffion tried in vain to ignore her nearness and her off-putting hold over him as she challenged his gaze when, at last, she averted her eyes. He released a breath, watching as Bellamy slipped the book she'd retrieved into her satchel.

She shook her head, her lips puckered in apparent disgust before responding. "You're more self-important than I realized, Prince Ffion. I would have thought you, of all royals, would understand how much more consequential this world is than your feeble little monarchy. Tell me, why *did* you flee Calaise?"

An interrogation was the last thing Ffion needed when he was so near to forfeiting control over his body. His instincts to hunt would no longer settle for dormancy, especially with what his appetite demanded so excruciatingly within his grasp.

Bellamy despised him for the enduring stain her kind left upon his soul, failing to recognize it for what it was. She knew enough of his secrets without him further explaining himself, and he owed her nothing.

"You forget yourself, *Belles.* I am familiar with your sort and won't hesitate to blot you out if the need presents itself." Ffion felt the monster under his flesh pleading to be loosed as the threat dripped like poison from his tongue.

Bellamy rolled her eyes before making her way over to the singular bed. "You'd do better to use me as bait for the one you truly wish to destroy. Perhaps you're the forgetful one." Removing the satchel from her shoulder, she tossed it aside before pulling back the plush duvet. Ffion's bones despaired for a slumber they would not greet, but if Bellamy would sleep, that was mercy enough. "Do not be so puritanical as to claim you wish to sleep on the floor."

There were worse lots than lying abed on a goose feather mattress beside a contemptible beauty. So, he did, and as Bellamy's heart found a newly sedate rhythm next to him, Ffion's thundered in his ears.

It was time to leave.

Chapter Four

The bastard was nothing but a bloody liar.

It wasn't a surprise, really. While Bellamy had perceived some semblance of honesty in Ffion's assurances that they were in their bid for Marin's life together, she'd never admit as much to anyone, least of all herself.

She'd done her life alone for a reason. It was the only way forward for one with no truly heartfelt connections or aspirations beyond general survival. Relationships had been fleeting at best, with siblings and friends coming in fly-by-night fashion, departing as quickly as they'd arrived.

And Ffion's betrayal only reinforced her determination to continue that same way.

Never had their arrangement been ideal. On its face, it was making the best of a bad situation, seeming more advantageous than the alternative, pitting them against one another in an adversarial endeavor. Regardless, traveling with the ruffian would keep him near, under her watchful eyes as she worked her way closer to her con artist of a father.

In her most delusional moments, she'd even entertained the possibility that Ffion could be an asset, with his keen senses that tied him to Marin every bit as much as herself, if not more so. But in the end, it wasn't worth it.

She knew better. She always had.

He'd lain beside her, his posture rigid. Almost anticipatory. She'd written that off quickly enough, stupidly reasoning that he, too, was unaccustomed to the nearness of the opposite sex. It wasn't long before she caved, giving in to her weariness as she finally slept, admittedly more peacefully than she ever did alone.

The warmth and companionship were unexpectedly intoxicating, luring her into slumber only to wrest her from its comforting embrace when he'd left her cold in the dead of the night.

The ass.

Bellamy rose from her bed, dressing as she shook the enduring sleepiness from her body. Her head was cloudy, but not enough to keep her from the task that lay ahead. Still, with each moment she lingered, Ffion moved farther off, his pace nothing shy of absurd. Before long, she'd lose her sense of him, only to leave her fending for herself once more.

Not that she'd mind.

Stuffing her feet into her buckskin boots, she hastened her steps, cursing under her breath as she collected her belongings from a nearby table. The whole cottage felt designed to taunt, mocking her with every book, every bauble a reminder of how well Marin understood her, though he knew so little about her.

With more time on her hands, she'd have loved to take advantage of the surrounding library, but that was, no doubt, the intent. It seemed that Marin's mind games never ceased, which only made her more determined to succeed.

Bellamy reached into her satchel, rooting for the scrap of hide covering a possession she both loathed and loved. She slipped the covering from her hand mirror, exposing its curves and gilded edges. Never would she look upon her form, refusing to so much as glance at the polished glass within its golden borders.

Her appearance did not itself offend, for she was blessed with the physical graces that branded any pixie. Long, lustrous hair, glowing skin and radiant eyes. Doubtless, she was a beauty, but all she perceived was foul.

A cursed vestige of her inventive father's own design, the mirror was the only item she'd been gifted by the man, making it meaningful in a way that she couldn't quite describe. How fitting, then, that he'd managed to afflict the hand glass with a new angle altogether, revealing the crude instincts of its beholder, exposing her most reviled traits.

Denying her pixie impulses was a constant effort and had her in a regular state of discontent. How did one reconcile innate selfishness with a desire to serve? Or a tendency toward deceit and manipulation with any hope of forging friendship?

She'd watched Petra accomplish such feats, awing her as quickly as it had caused her jealousy. The pirate captain James Much had readily fallen prey to the woodland royal's charms, though Petra hadn't seemed to influence him directly in any way. Ffion, likewise, had followed her about like an acolyte, annoying Bellamy to no end with his mindless loyalty.

She turned her mirror over, taking the narrow handle in hand, carefully unscrewing the haft from the head. With a gentle tug, she removed the hidden weapon from within—a tapered length of barrel-shaped metal with a wicked point at its end.

Tucking the stiletto into her belt, she rewrapped the looking glass, ignoring the little voice within her mind demanding to know why she treasured it so.

Bellamy made for the woods, leaving Marin's trickery behind as she pursued Ffion from afar. He moved with fiendish speed and tracking him with any certainty was out of the question. It would require a more precise approach.

The evening was pleasant enough, with the whispers of fall evident in the mild breeze. She pulled her cloak a little tighter around her shoulders, taking to a subtle trail left behind by the careless brute. Bent twigs and shuffled earth led the way through the trees while a sliver from the lambent moon filtered through the branches overhead, illuminating her path with fractured shards of light.

She picked her way through the woods at a brisk pace, easily navigating roots and bushes with her infernal pixie senses—one of few occasions she was grateful for their benefit. Her surroundings were unknown to her, never having spent any time in Calaise. She'd lived the balance of her life in Wylewoode before doing an exhaustive search of Llundyn for her wayward father, hoping to locate him in the kingdom of her birth.

It was not to be.

Rather, it seemed, he'd lived his life much on the run, making brief forays into her presence to provoke her. One occasion had her thoroughly convinced she would lay eyes upon a half-brother he'd often mentioned, and she'd been eager to make his acquaintance in the aftermath of her mother's death.

In the end, it was a fallacy that saw her into the mines on the outskirts of Wylewoode—a place that would come to feel like home despite its utterly foreign character. She never did meet her half-brother, but there were other boys. Many, in fact, and though there was no blood relation between them, they were as close as brothers in her heart. Leaving them had devastated her, but she'd been left with little choice after her pixie kin had come calling.

Marin would die by her hand, or her life would be forfeit in his stead.

It had been the fate of so many of her unknown brothers and sisters before her—eleven, to be exact—and she was determined to end her wicked brethren's reign of terror upon her family. Their halfling nature made them a disgrace, both within the human realm as well as the supernatural one she knew so little about, and her only deliverance from the evil machinations of her pixie kinsfolk was the promise of solitude if she completed her mission.

She'd made for Llundyn in the dead of night, leaving the lost boys within the mine without notice as she set out. Getting to Llundyn had been the easy part, with a world filled with confusion and dead ends awaiting her upon arrival.

Her hopes of sacking her father had begun to wane when her fortunes had changed at long last. By all appearances, the people of Llundyn were oblivious to pixies and willfully naive of the possibility of something otherworldly at work, save for one. News from the mysterious quartermaster, Smee, who served the pirate captain James Much, had brought her some sort of a lead to pursue, though his musings were largely to his detriment.

Indeed, his countrymen all thought him mad, but perhaps that was for the best, for it emboldened Bellamy in her pursuit. The man was happy to spill his knowledge in exchange for an understanding ear, which she provided unequivocally. Only then did she begin to view her journey to Llundyn as less than a total waste of time, even as she found herself swiftly returning to Wylewoode.

The vague rustling of nearby leaves drew her from her reveries, reminding her of the danger lurking before her. Ffion didn't frighten her, didn't cause her to fear for her life, though he could undoubtedly claim it if he wished to. She simply didn't know what to expect of his beast—a form she'd never had the displeasure of witnessing despite her very real understanding of its presence within him.

Another crack, this one nearer. A shiver skipped down her spine, and she stood stock still, suppressing the urge to run. Pixies didn't run. They wouldn't fear the unknown. Hell, they *were* the unknown, and stars only knew how much of their *essence* she had running through her veins.

Bellamy scanned the brush hemming her in on all sides. With her stiletto in hand, she ventured a step forward before picking up speed, but she wasn't alone. A vague shadow paced her at her left, followed by another at its heels. To her right were more of the same, their numbers increasing with each passing stride.

Blazes. She *was* afraid.

Sprinting through the woods, she didn't pause when the dry boughs from low-hanging branches scratched her face, even as a deep growl echoed all around her, bouncing from one dark form to the other in a haunting refrain that promised her demise.

She pushed until her lungs burned, making for a sparse clearing when her foot caught on an exposed root, sending her flying headlong into the dirt. Scrambling to her knees, Bellamy crawled before recovering her footing, only to be well and truly set upon.

The shadow creatures emerged—a pack of wolves with shiny yellow eyes, their intent plain as they crept toward her. Whatever mastery over wildlife a pixie supposedly possessed had skipped her entirely. Backing away slowly, her calm manner seemed to agitate the beasts further, each lowering their heads with hackles raised as though they were poised to strike.

"*Begone!*" His voice was like the turbulent waters of Altanys, roaring through her from behind. Bellamy turned to find Ffion stumbling through the brush, his commanding words utterly at odds with his disheveled appearance.

He fell to his knees in the center of the clearing, nothing shy of agony sketched across his face. "*Go!*" he shouted again, sending the wolves scattering in his wake. He took his head between his shaking hands, fingers threaded through his burnished hair.

Bellamy shivered, recognizing for the first time the jeopardy she'd voluntarily subjected herself to, for the man before her was every bit as wild as the creatures he'd just disbanded.

The animals had all but disappeared when Ffion rose to his feet, taking in an unsteady breath as he began to pace. It was then that she noticed his torn clothing, exposing the muscle spanning his broad shoulders and chest. Fists clutched at his side, an errant curse escaped his lips. "You shouldn't have followed me."

"I knew I couldn't trust you." Bellamy met the challenge in his gaze, refusing to look away even as his manic striding brought him closer. She braced herself, though her stiletto was laughably inadequate if he wished to end her here and now.

"You're right," Ffion snarled, and she didn't miss the way he trembled at her nearness. "But not for the reason you seem to think. I almost..." Towering over her, he paused, offering only a disdainful sniff before turning away. His body shuddered, rippling with pent-up need that he'd somehow managed to stave off.

Bellamy straightened where she stood, unable to control her wicked tongue. She needed him to say it. "You almost killed *me*."

"*Yes*," he hissed, exhaling in a mighty burst as he worked to compose himself. His control was slowly returning—he no longer shook or paced, but his anger was palpable. "I'm living on the bitter edge of my restraint, and you damn near pushed me over."

"Take up your complaints with the author of your grief." It was cruel to dismiss the prince's struggle for self-control and, worse, knowing how closely tied she was to the source of it all. But feelings were for the weak of mind and spirit. She had no capacity for such frivolities, especially with her despicable father so near.

She was within a hair's-breadth of completing her charge. Freedom was at hand, whether she lived or died in the undertaking.

"We'll burn the cottage en route to the village," Bellamy uttered by way of dismissal, ignoring the heat of his stare at her back.

Chapter Five

Ffion knew it would happen. He'd felt his muscles demanding the familiar burn he coveted and detested at once. So it had been and was once again.

Would that he might rediscover how he'd denied that same betrayal of his own flesh back in Neverwoode, where sift and self-indulgence reigned above all else. The fine golden dust, *pixie dust*, held no real power in and of itself.

And yet.

There, Ffion had never entirely lost himself, even when he was more misplaced and disoriented than ever before—though it was just what he'd meant to achieve by leaving his country and all that was familiar behind.

Ffion's misfortune had begun in the aftermath of one of his episodes, discovered when Queen Helena's lady had found him prone on the ground in the castle gardens, drenched in liquid gold. His family had feared for him and their kingdom's future, keeping the truth of the prince's affliction tightly guarded. He'd seen the best of Fayble's physicians, but none could cure him, and though he'd dared to hope, he hadn't believed their techniques sufficient—not when his malady was one of the soul.

No one understood the extent of Ffion's plight, but in his mind, there was no need to foster more grief with naught to be done. The king behaved as if it had changed nothing, in fact, that his position as heir apparent was firm. But in the end, the prince himself could not fathom holding all of Calaise in his palm while shouldering his shame.

In desperation, Ffion had searched the palace library for answers only to find what he feared most deeply within the text of an age-old tome, stating that a curse could not land on one undeserving. And when he'd asked his mother, she would not meet his gaze, confirming that somehow, he had earned this.

So, he'd left. The queen had tearfully aided his departure, equipping him with all the food and water a fifteen-year-old boy could manage alone. Gierson was meant to maintain appearances for his brother in Ffion's stead, but his father could never know where the prince intended to go.

To the king, Ffion was more than his birthright. He was a son. But his mother would tell His Majesty the heir was receiving treatments abroad, and there'd been no time for farewells. They would lie to safeguard the realm, said she, and the prince believed he could learn to master himself, pledging that he would not return until he'd done so.

He would never be truly good, but still, he *tried*.

For years, Ffion's spirit begged for redemption each morning and night, and he did all he could to prevent anyone else from feeling as he did.

Resigned. Filthy.

Surely, he was not blameless, but believed well enough in honor. No matter how complicated that vow became, the prince pledged he would not live a life void of virtue.

Bellamy was a complication, testing that same damnable decency Ffion had managed to preserve hours before. He grappled against the urge to return to her, slumbering where he'd left her. Yet even in such a predatory state—the one that haunted him, mind and body—he'd convinced himself to run.

The prince was still battling to reclaim authority over his wretched form when he became aware of the pixie in the distance. Despite vast woodlands separating them, her proximity was definite, and his frame quivered, limbs tingling like those of a stranger as he tested the strength of his grip against the dampened earth beneath him. Dropping to his knees, Ffion held his face in his hands, pleading for mercy that he might not give in to the need pulsing through his veins.

Why had the cursed little thing left the cottage?

Bellamy was reckless, ignorant of the creature she thoughtlessly provoked through her sheer presence alone. No doubt, she remained composed, unaffected by the notion that he'd thought to kill her.

They were similar in the worst of ways.

Yet, onward, she pressed into the heart of Calaisean territory, toward *him*, ignoring the threat he was in favor of her own designs, forcing him into painful restraint as he sought to be the deserving heir.

He had not thought much of home since he left. He'd forced himself to forget the rolling hills and endless pasturelands for four years. At first, his thoughts would often lead him back to Calaise, but when he met Petra, the memories faded altogether, and the sadness that made him pine for his kingdom waned.

Even so, Ffion was convinced that he'd only begun to remember what he'd willfully abandoned when first he recognized Marin's presence in Neverwoode months before. He hadn't dwelled on it then, unable to recall why the familiarity ate away at his consciousness until he met Bellamy, and the façade surrounding him vanished completely.

She was intrinsically linked to her father, just as the prince was following the plague Marin had levied against him.

The farther he'd gotten from Neverwoode, the more he was forced to acknowledge his scars, re-opening old wounds. While Ffion couldn't quite reconcile how the mysteries of that place had allowed him to cling to his youth and innocence, he was grateful. Somehow, he'd felt safe.

"You've given him authority over your peace." Bellamy appeared, breaking the long-standing silence between them, her bearing more tranquil than the day prior as she glanced at the prince. "I'd know the look of heart sickness left behind by my father anywhere. That was all I saw when I found you. It's happened to me before."

Ffion understood her meaning and nodded. He was not yet fully recovered from the night, still smarting from suppressing his innate needs, but the gravity of Bellamy's assessment urged him to meet the day and all it held. He'd made a promise, as much to her as to himself, and he would not let a new day dawn before seeing it through.

"It would seem we may both assume our victories then," said the prince with a wry smirk. "You have spared a rotten scoundrel from his demise, and I did not gild a cherished Calaisean bosk with... you."

It took a moment before Bellamy laughed, and the sound shook him to his core as she did, for never had he heard a sound so melodic. He dared to look at her, finding her smiling, her eyes wrinkling at the edges. Apart from when watching Bellamy scour the books Marin left for her, he had rarely seen her delight.

"If you had bested me, the woods would have been painted red, not gold. I'm only half wicked, if you care to recall." The pixie chided him with a shameless purse of her lips, meeting his gaze, and Ffion couldn't decide which half of her was looking back.

It would've been wiser for him to have fled. But if mercy existed, they would realize another triumph in short order, and their paths would diverge at last.

* * * *

Stood at the edge of town, Ffion donned his tattered cloak. It was frayed and far too short according to the current fashions, but all he had kept from home. "My hair," he offered by way of explanation. "I'm one of the celebrated flame-haired twins, am I not?" He'd bartered away the clothes on his back for the materials to craft his sling soon after his departure, fine garments only a dimwit would wear to a place like Neverwoode. But his mantle, he'd kept, and it had served him well.

"So you are," said Bellamy, draping a brilliant crimson cape over her slender frame and pulling the hood over her head as Ffion had done.

The prince had been subject to Neverwoode's wiles for four years, a little more than a quarter of which had been spent in utter solitude, but everything was just as he remembered, with Calaise bustling and full of life.

"What day is it?" Ffion inquired of his companion, the streets swarming with his fellow countrymen. Anticipation filled the air, an autumn breeze spreading the excitement like a spark igniting parched underbrush.

"No feast or holy day, to my knowledge, though I cannot say with any certainty." Bellamy remained close to the prince, her cape brushing against his knuckles with every step they took toward the capital.

The palace was set at the top of a great hill ahead of them, the roadway before it stretching to the outermost boundaries of the city and teeming with Calaisean citizens. Some of those gathered waved sticks with the kingdom's flag attached to the end while others gossiped over the festivities. Trumpets blazed in the near distance, announcing the processional.

Something in his stomach clenched — a nervous sort of expectancy growing when he realized the king was coming.

Ffion hadn't said goodbye to his father, having only sent a letter to assure the king that he was alive, but knew he'd be welcomed as a prodigal. His eyes stung with tears as people cleared the way for His Majesty's procession, the prince's heart thundering in his chest. He would be forgiven for leaving in haste, of that he was sure, and together, they would find a way past the malediction within his spirit.

All would be well at last.

The exultation grew as the king's guards approached ahead of their sovereign. A troupe of men and women whirled around a royal minstrel who sang a jubilant tune, encouraging those present to join in as they passed before Ffion and Bellamy.

It wasn't until the spectators joined in that the prince deciphered the lyrics ringing through the city, the words like a sword to his gut.

"This is no place for us." Bellamy braced Ffion's arm, attempting to haul him away, but the prince tore himself from her grip.

"On the contrary," he uttered. "For it appears I am now king."

Words he didn't realize he never wished to speak, for they meant that something devastating had occurred. The celebration continued in earnest, with each chorus shredding him to bits inside.

"All hail the king!
King Ffion, he shall be.
No greater reigns beyond the sea,
our future rests on thee."

They may as well have danced atop his father's grave. And while the people trilled Ffion's name, it was not to him they sang.

Following the minstrel and his dancers, the royal guard advanced, each member astride black Charentais mounts. Ffion recognized most of them despite his time away. Even under their helmets, he would never forget his father's watch. Row by row, they passed by, their focus never straying from the road ahead until his brother, Gierson, came into view.

"All hail the king!"

The people chanted in unison, with Gierson having assumed Ffion's position as rightful heir to perfection. He wore no crown, but a parade of this magnitude could only mean a coronation was close at hand.

His Majesty, the prince's beloved father, was gone, and Ffion had never been more rattled. He clenched his fists, fingernails digging into his palms as he tried to make sense of the scene unfolding before him. The late king could not have long since departed, or Gierson would have surely been crowned already. Yet, it was Ffion's name on his countrymen's lips.

They were waiting for him. They'd believed he would return whole, and the prince was equally sickened and moved by his family's unwavering faith in his ability to vanquish his torment.

They were only words spoken over Ffion years ago, but they ravaged his memories like an unbroken fever. The words whispered through the air like a prayer, stalking him, consuming his sanity morsel by morsel.

"*He's* here." Bellamy suddenly confirmed what the prince felt festering in his marrow.

Marin murmured Ffion's curse from wherever he lay in wait, and it reached his hearing despite the surrounding distractions. The tinkerer was there, so close to where the prince stood with Bellamy that he could discern his lurid magnetism.

It was an opportunity they couldn't afford to dismiss, no matter the public setting. The celebration was, beyond question, marked as a most pleasing diversion for the demon fairy, made into a playground upon which he might seize yet one more opportunity to slip his hunters' net unscathed.

A figure brushed past Ffion, draped in a black so void of depth that the heir's lungs were robbed of breath— a shade so dark and hollow it could be *felt*, woven to match its wearer's sinister essence.

"He doesn't think us bold enough to follow," Ffion said in a low voice, nearly smothered by the surrounding madness. But Bellamy heard, her answering stare a blaze of glowing amber.

"Then he will die a fool."

Ffion took Bellamy's hand, her pulse quickening under his palm as they moved together like shadows through the crowd in pursuit of their quarry.

With the royal procession at their backs, they tracked Marin by the gaps he'd forged amid all who were gathered. The masses kept them hidden, pressing closer to where Gierson sat proudly upon a prized Calaisean stallion. Ffion reached for his sling with one hand, firmly gripping Bellamy's with the other, both wending effortlessly between eager onlookers when the heir caught sight of Marin's hem several paces ahead.

With only a few more steps, Ffion would have the frayed cords of his sling looped around the prick's throat. They could still end him discreetly, and his disquieting cloak would serve them well should Bellamy choose to gut her father, even if the cracks between the cobbled stones pooled with golden blood.

It might have happened had Marin not veered into the formal march. His interference was too brief to be noticed — not by the patrols surrounding Ffion's twin or their mother, the dowager queen Helena, nor any observers in attendance.

Ffion meant to hasten his chase but found himself instead rooted to the earth beneath his feet, for as he sought a better course, his gaze met that of Gierson. His brother straightened in his saddle, even as his eyes exposed his shock over the revelation of the firstborn's return. Beside him, a lean knight followed his eyeline, calling more unwanted attention to him as he stood idly by.

But Bellamy did not wait for him to decide what he would do next, tearing herself from his hold. The heir barely registered her absence apart from a piercing sense of horror that he was not by her side.

And while all eyes slowly fell to Ffion, his halfling ally was becoming as good as dead.

Chapter Six

It seemed Marin would never grow tired of his games. Bellamy kept pace with her delinquent father, though she remained dozens of yards behind him. Doubtless, he knew, for the man was as wise as he was old, though he looked not a day over thirty. Handsome and brimming with counterfeit chivalry, he'd conned countless beings throughout his lifetime, using his inventions and exceptional mind for evil rather than good.

For as long as she could remember, he'd seen fit to tease and manipulate, steering every twist of fate in his favor. Whether orchestrating an ill-conceived whim or fostering discord among the naive, he sought every opportunity to amuse himself at the expense of others.

His scheming was misunderstood throughout the kingdoms upon which he inflicted himself, with the villagers readily convinced that his escapades were nothing more than random incidents, rationalizing his medaling away with convenient excuses. Never did they acknowledge the possibility of an otherworldly presence, even as his fairy brethren were well aware of his antics.

The pixie kinfolk he'd spurned were nothing if not unforgiving, prepared as they were to see Marin forfeit his life for his transgressions — the greatest of which had been perpetrated against his very own. Strictly forbidden within the fairy realm, he'd relentlessly flouted their laws in favor of his chosen designs, deceiving his kin and fathering numerous children with human lovers.

He'd left a trail of half-breeds in his wake, a legacy of the despised whose only recourse for justifying their odious presence, according to Bellamy's ethereal kin, was to rid both of their worlds of Marin's presence altogether.

A fine tasking, that.

Sending the scorned halflings to do their dirty work was the most authentically pixie ploy imaginable, but Bellamy was determined to see it through. There was more than her life at stake where Marin was concerned, with what felt like no end to his appetite for chaos.

It was enough.

Picking her way through the crowd was no easy task, and Ffion made it even less so. Indeed, it felt as though he'd fallen behind, with her sense of his presence growing dimmer with each passing step. It wasn't out of the question, given his status, his lineage, that he might leave her altogether. What he'd been doing out amongst the wilds of Neverwoode, alone, as *heir* to the *Calaisean throne*, had been strange enough to reconcile already. To lose him now would be no surprise, and going it alone with Marin had always been her plan, at any rate.

She couldn't pin her hopes on such fickle prospects.

Despite her reservations over the beastly prince, she pushed onward, only mildly concerned over what might've held him up. Showing his face here, and at a parade no less, was a risky venture, but Ffion was a grown man who could handle himself.

Just ahead, Marin ducked into an alleyway, and Bellamy's pulse picked up speed. The crowd was loud, giving her cover with their clamor, while he'd been dumb enough to isolate himself away from the main roadway. She was armed, and even had backup if Ffion saw fit to catch up and offer his aid. This was it—the moment she'd been waiting for.

Dismissing the sinister little voice shouting in the back of her mind that Marin did nothing without intent, Bellamy persisted in her pursuit, diving into the narrow passageway with her heart in her throat. She traced her fingers over the dagger hidden within her sleeve, the cold steel offering mild solace.

Bellamy crept into the shadows, well aware that her attempted stealth did little good. Marin would likely be prepared if he managed to sense her the way she did him, or even Ffion, for that matter.

The other end of the alley was closed off in a wall of stone, much like the ones to either side of her. And, unsurprisingly, her father was nowhere to be seen, which could only mean he'd ascended.

"*Blast*," Bellamy muttered, searching the space for a way up. A rickety wooden ladder appeared to be her only option, drawing a curse of annoyance as she assessed its stability. With each passing moment, her odds of success were fading. Indeed, Marin could already be gone, what with his gift of flight to carry him to the rooftops—an ability she was sorely lacking.

She climbed, ignoring the wobbling of each bar as she clung to them with shaking hands. Moving as hastily as she dared, she made quick work of the ladder, only to find a deserted rooftop.

Bellamy exhaled, willing herself to calm. For as desperately as she wished to put an end to her father, the accomplishment of such an act would not be without cost, regardless of how faithfully she guarded her emotions.

She moved toward the front of the building, peering down upon the cavalcade with no Marin in sight, not on the surrounding rooftops nor the next alley over.

Well. Another day, another failure, it seemed.

"Daughter."

Bellamy whipped around just in time to watch her father step nearer, the wicked glint in his eyes causing her anxiety to spike for one bitter, brutal moment, but she could not yield. Calming herself, she answered his sneer with an indifferent smile. "Ah. I thought you'd be long gone by now."

"You know that isn't my way. We seem to continually miss one another now, don't we?" Marin's spiteful smile matched hers as he closed in, and she fought every instinct within herself, demanding she retreat.

Somehow, she was no longer the huntress but the hunted. Pursuing Marin had ever been a test of her devotion to something higher than herself, and she was likely to die either way, whether at the hands of the pixies or through one final encounter with her father. Yet, knowing that she'd wiped him from the face of the earth would enable her to rest in peace.

"So it seems," Bellamy agreed, "though I was thoroughly enchanted by the diversions you left behind at your cottage. A shame that it met its end in flames."

Marin laughed, his dark eyes sparkling with humor. "My, but you are a vindictive little thing. Were you not merely a simple crossbreed, you'd have made for a wonderful fairy."

Bellamy pursed her lips before immediately scolding herself. Allowing his poisonous words to draw such a reaction would delight him as always. "And that's just the problem." Steeling herself, she took a step nearer. "You've broken all the rules. There are some powerful forces allied against you, including me."

Her father scoffed, an insulting sound that surged through her being, landing right where it hurt most — her pride. "All your books have made you too cunning for your own good. That, or too reckless, though you have done better than your siblings."

His soulless eyes held hers, the weight of his declaration hanging in the space between them. Eleven lives lost, each with the same futile assignment she was staring in the face. "At least," he continued, "you were wise enough to bring one who might stand a chance against me. The flame-haired prince is a formidable opponent, even if his true nature cripples him."

Bellamy dropped her arm, allowing the dagger braced against her forearm to slip into her fingers. Tightening her fist around the stiletto, she suppressed her fury over his blatant dismissal, for she required no aid. But Marin persisted, ignorant of the skills she'd developed over the years for such a moment as this. She shouldn't care about his opinion, shouldn't chafe under his scorn.

Without another thought, she made her move, lunging for the man as she swung her stiletto toward his exposed neck, just nicking the skin before he dodged her advance. Liquid gold trickled from the jagged wound, matching the shimmering remnants at the tip of her dagger.

"Why not try this again when you've a sporting chance?" Marin spat when he regained his footing. With his next breath, he held out his palm, blowing a cloud of golden dust into Bellamy's face. She struggled to see him through the veil of sift, losing her balance when she stumbled backward.

"That princeling will be your downfall," he hissed, tapping her on the shoulder with his index finger, and it was all he needed to send her plummeting over the edge of the rooftop.

Bellamy grappled for purchase, clawing the stonework walls, her fingernails grating against the coarse brick to no avail. She had little time to prepare her body for the impact upon the cobbled ground below and no way to slow her descent from her prone position. Bracing herself, she accepted her fate, twisting in a way she hoped would minimize the pain.

With eyes pinched shut, she hit hard, but it was far less painful than she'd anticipated, enveloped as she was in the steady embrace of her dawdling companion. The air in her lungs vanished in a single harsh breath as Ffion collapsed beneath her, taking the brunt of the blow as they hit the ground in a heap of limbs.

"Perhaps I can forgive your absence after all," said Bellamy, recovering herself as she rolled from atop Ffion. She sprawled on her back, reconciling the last few minutes alongside her near brush with death.

Beside her, Ffion lay in silence, his chest quickly rising and falling as if he teetered on the edge of panic. She could see it in his eyes, felt it in his rigid limbs. Placing her palm over his heart, Bellamy felt an unexpected pang of sympathy as his heartbeat scuttled beneath her fingertips.

"What's wrong?"

Ffion shook his head, pinching his temples between long fingers. "I froze. I...I'm the *king*." He exhaled, appearing distraught over an honor that would delight most. "Or in name, it seems, I am. My brother..."

Bellamy watched him gather himself, knowing the resourceful heir never let his circumstances dictate his control for long. Well-versed in restraint, he schooled his features just as swiftly as he'd lost his composure.

"So it seems," she managed, shoving herself away from him before drawing him to his feet. "And you're somehow surprised. What happened to your father?"

Ffion glanced away, offering nothing more than a shrug. "What became of yours?" He met her eyes, his words dripping with disdain.

Perhaps her question had been insensitive given his state of mind, but she'd never been tactful. "He bested me, loath as I am to admit it. That's where you come in." She gestured toward the unforgiving earth beneath them, grateful he'd been there to break her fall. "I've followed Marin from Wylewoode to kingdom come, only to lose him yet again. Soon enough, you'll be catching nothing more than my lifeless body."

"He won't run again. Your father thrives on chaos, and mine greatest of all. Where better to have his fill than right where it all began?"

"What began?"

Ffion ignored her question, instead taking her by the hand to draw her along behind him, making for the mouth of the alleyway. "I've got an idea where he'll go, and it's the last place I wish to be."

The crowds were there, thick with excitement, people far and wide as the processional continued in vain. Bellamy observed it all through new eyes, a sense of knowing invading her otherwise indifferent perspective. She pulled up short, facing the heir, his hooded gaze curious. Stretching on tiptoe, she adjusted his mantle, ensuring his face was properly veiled.

He returned the favor, carefully draping the covering over her head before moving again toward the masses. She followed, wondering if she'd lost her mind somewhere along the way as she shadowed the sovereign of Calaise, shrouded and lost amongst a sea of people.

"Prince Gierson. You've finally returned," a feminine voice purred from behind them. The surrounding din began to die down, with myriad citizens readily observing the exchange as they withdrew, giving the duo an unwelcome amount of attention.

Ffion flinched, almost as if he'd been smacked. The pair slowly turned, taking in the striking female knight sat atop her equally impressive horse. She held her helmet beneath her arm, the obsidian waves of her hair streaming in the gentle breeze. Dark almond eyes appraised them where they stood, her gaze shifting from their feet to their heads, pausing momentarily on their adjoined hands.

Bellamy shifted, easing behind Ffion as he stepped in front of her. His posture stiffened, with shoulders straight and broad like a soldier standing at attention, the only evidence of his discomfort visible in his clenched fists.

Ever controlled.

His royal heritage was showing, an air of authority suffusing his presence when he spoke. "Just in time for the celebration, it seems. And you've begun without me."

"Indeed, Your Highness, as there was no telling when you would see fit to return. You've always loved to be among your people." The woman smiled, even as her tone belied her suspicion. She held Ffion's gaze, something intangible passing between them before she eyed Bellamy once more.

While she tried to deny it, the scrutiny had the pixie ill at ease, for inasmuch as she'd struggled with Ffion, she was unprepared to part ways. Not now — not when she was so close to her quarry. And though the beast had proven to be more of a nuisance where his help was concerned, two against one were far better odds than going it alone when it came to Marin.

"Lovely to see you again, Melis," Ffion finally managed, a half-smile forming on his face. He retreated a step, grasping Bellamy's fingers in his own, pulling her nearer. "She stays with me."

His voice was low, though there was no doubt in Bellamy's mind that the woman had heard his every word. Her discontent was plain, but she could not dare to defy the prince. "Very well, sire." Melis bobbed her head, her watchful gaze trained upon the pixie assassin to his left. "You know better than most how important it is to be careful."

Chapter Seven

Her gambit was one of a woman with nothing left to lose, and sharp though the pixie was, Bellamy might as well have signed her own death warrant when she left Ffion's side.

He told himself he didn't care. She was a halfling through and through, her pixie nature flowing like a violent current. But pest or no, Ffion couldn't stomach the idea of abandoning her to Marin's wiles. The two were not the same.

Damn him.

It wasn't that Ffion wanted to kill Bellamy, but for the life of him, the prince could not determine when he'd decided he wanted her to live, or worse, that he was willing to risk himself on her behalf. There was too much at stake to forget what she was capable of—that she was an unnatural being, in part, and able to influence individuals into doing her bidding with ease should she choose to do so.

The prince had seen it happen time and again in Neverwoode, when Queen Wendolyne had used her strange gifts to manipulate a shadow kingdom and again when his beloved friend, Petra, unwittingly tamed beasts, capturing the devotion of all who encountered her without a thought. One of the sisters was bent on evil, while the other was pure as the driven snow.

But where did that leave Bellamy? Halflings were as dangerous as their wicked predecessors.

He was a fool and maybe always had been. He'd been drawn to Petra, as with every other pixie, but only once he, too, had dedicated himself to her did the beast within him truly slumber.

Petra was good. Never had Ffion doubted his friend's heart, but perhaps the freedom he'd found in Neverwoode was due more to Petra's subconscious compassion. His memories of home, of his forsaken curse, faded in her presence. If she'd accomplished such a feat unintentionally, and long before learning of her halfling origins, Bellamy could do far more. *She* could be disastrous.

"How *did* you get away?" Ffion's blood pulsed, his words triggering the monster he fought to keep hidden. He kept his voice low, the question meant for his pixie companion alone as they were ushered toward a large mahogany mount draped in Calaisean adornments of deepest midnight blue, fringed with shimmering silver tassels and cords.

Bellamy pursed her lips, biting the inside of her cheek. "It would have been too easy for him. There's no thrill in a simple kill."

There was no reason Ffion shouldn't believe her explanation apart from a nagging awareness that she could effortlessly deceive him. She seemed to hate him almost as much as she loathed Marin. And while the hostility between prince and pixie had quieted, Ffion wasn't naive enough to think they were anything more than temporary allies, if that.

He wouldn't put it past her to hand him over to her father for personal gain.

While pixies had an advantage over humans, Ffion had an advantage over both, which Bellamy had quickly sensed when they met. Whether for or against the prince, she was a direct route to her father, and from there, he would work through the rest. For his part, Marin was a grotesque creature with incomparable means of persuasion and a deep-seated antipathy for anything right or pure. Whatever the case, Ffion was ready to meet the challenge. No longer would he succumb to the tinkerer's mind games.

"Mount up, Your Highness." Melis didn't meet his gaze when she spoke but, anticipating the prince's cooperation, waited expectantly, her hands clasped at her back with eyes cast toward the ground. "They will be eager to greet you."

At one point, he'd missed her. Melis had been a confidant and an ally for as long as Ffion could remember, but four years was a long time, and he'd never said goodbye. His new title didn't ensure forgiveness either.

Or *the* title, as it were, for Ffion was king, but by all appearances, *he* was no longer Ffion. Indeed, she'd addressed him as highness and not majesty. He'd be the last to nitpick such minor decorum, averse to the proposition of reigning at all as he was, though her phrasing was telling.

Ffion obeyed Melis' directives, taking hold of the horse's leathers and hoisting himself onto its back, hoping all would be reconciled in due course. What else could he have expected upon his return? Certainly, the death of the king had never entered his thoughts, nor that he might not be welcomed with gladness by those he loved. He'd left as a hellion and had come home slightly less of one.

Astride the palace's mount, Ffion fisted its reins, extending a hand to Bellamy. Surely, she could have ulterior motives with her father so near, but if she had any intent of playing traitor, he'd deal with it then. Were Bellamy stupid enough to work with her father, he would kill her for failing to bring him the prince, and if she did wish to see Marin rot as she claimed, she needed Ffion.

He lifted the halfling into the saddle before himself when she took his hand, her delicate fingers smooth as silk. Her scent was overwhelming— not the sickly sweet smell of Marin, but something crisp and refreshing, like a pristine winter rose and just as deadly.

A part of him had wondered if she would follow through, but they both knew rejecting his company would only result in a new gravestone with her name. She hadn't hesitated. Instead, Bellamy was sat in front of him, her exquisite contours pressed firmly against the prince's torso and chest.

"Are you all right?" The roughness of Ffion's stubble brushed lightly over Bellamy's ear when he spoke. He swallowed hard when she turned to meet his gaze, caught off balance by the gleam of saffron and honey looking back at him.

"I don't trust them."

It wasn't what the prince meant when he asked, but her response resonated nonetheless.

Tresses of burgundy fell loosely over her shoulder with errant, glossy strands streaming from her hair tie as Ffion prompted their horse to move. Bellamy sank into him, her heart beating wildly enough that he could feel it pounding between them. His was no better, but he adjusted his posture, squaring his shoulders as he'd been taught during those wearisome hours spent learning the etiquette of a royal.

A king.

They trailed Melis, keeping close at her rear through the wide roads of Calaise. Ffion was grateful to be home. All was much the same when he took in the familiar structures and landscapes — it was he who was different, but naturally, they all would be. Nothing was immune to change.

Still, there was no peace when a heart warred with reason. Where one would see Ffion joyfully reunited with his family, the other demanded caution. Then again, such principles would never be wholly reunited in this life.

Onward they rode, delighting the throngs of people with their presence. Whisperings of the flame-haired twins rose above the fray, with frenetic excitement from seeing the pair simultaneously at a fevered pitch.

Ffion recognized that Gierson would've been expected to play both parts — the roles of himself and Ffion — but seeing him do so as garishly as he did through the streets of Calaise was more off-putting than he could've thought. Though he wished it weren't so, being seamlessly replaced brought forth an ache not easily remedied.

It was nonsensical, and he knew it, but that didn't seem to help the hollowness forming inside of him. And though no part of him desired to perpetuate the charade, he was to be Gierson, for now. Melis made that much clear, and Ffion could only assume someone of her station and long-standing history with her sovereigns would be aware of most palace secrets.

A small part of him felt guilty for not trusting her with his struggle before fleeing the nation, but that was a lifetime ago. She was not the sort to resent him for anything, or she hadn't been when he'd known her before. Then again, the prince had never seen her as a knight, either.

Alas, the prince's homecoming was not at all what he'd expected.

Security was never something Bellamy sought. It wasn't definite and never did it last, but somehow Ffion had challenged those convictions. Given his history with her father, he could turn on her at any moment, and she wouldn't resent him for it. In many ways, it could even be a mercy. Not that most knew her sort existed, and those who did likely wouldn't remember their own names.

The prince, or king, as it were, was the exception to nearly every rule. He was a lethal enigma, yet he'd held fast to their agreement.

Bellamy hated the way her bones betrayed her better judgment, melting into his powerful frame as he followed the unsettling dame through the palace gates. It was his castle now as king, and even as prince, it was his home — a structure as imposing and mysterious as him.

The estate's grounds were magnificent, with its gates alone a marvel of intricate detail. A manicured lawn untouched by the brisk sighs of autumn welcomed them, while at its center, the likeness of the Calaisean's true heir waited.

She had known who Gierson was since before she'd met Ffion in Neverwoode. He was unmistakably composed and indisputably commanding, exuding a level of authority Bellamy hadn't anticipated he possessed. Yet, she couldn't help but notice how Ffion's manner altered when his royal guard came upon them.

Seemingly resigned to his fate, Ffion straightened, expertly maneuvering their horse toward the awaiting company, his arms a steadying force around Bellamy as he handled their stallion's reins. Their bodies moved in tandem as he braced her at the waist with a firm hold upon their approach.

Neither brother attempted to dismount when their horses met, nor did Ffion remove his hand. The warmth of his deft fingers against her abdomen was intoxicating—both a comfort and a taunt. But somehow, it soothed the wild musings of her mind.

Nobody spoke as the gate screeched to a close at their backs, with every present being's attention trained upon the heir whose steady embrace yet sheltered Bellamy.

Gierson looked from Ffion to Bellamy, his gaze sweeping over them with apparent curiosity. His lips twitched at the edges, forming a hint of a smile, until the woman next to him cleared her throat.

The dowager queen, mother of the famed flame-haired heirs. Bellamy disliked her instantly.

Ffion dropped from the horse, his warmth deserting Bellamy, leaving her to herself with the animal's reins beside her like an offering to run, leaving freedom well at hand if only there were somewhere to go.

The prince turned his head slightly toward her, impulsively clutching the sling belted around his midsection as if he wished to do the same before returning his focus to his mother and brother, firmly seated atop their steeds.

Their captor, Melis, had made it clear that Ffion was meant to maintain whatever lies had been fed to his people, even as the events leading to the deception Bellamy witnessed were unknown to her. She'd seen enough foul play amongst her brethren to remain suspicious of the unfolding scene.

Despite their years apart, Gierson never slipped up in his roleplay, looking down upon his elder twin as if he'd been born to the elder role himself. No one was to elevate themselves above the king.

And yet.

That same realization must have resonated with Gierson a moment later when he quickly dismounted, approaching Ffion with open arms. A broad smile spread across his handsome features, by far the most welcoming face she'd witnessed amongst the scores of guards and royals.

"I confess, I didn't believe my eyes when I saw you during the procession. It's really you." Gierson beamed, clasping his brother's forearm. Ffion returned his smile and tugged him into an embrace.

When they parted, Bellamy was struck by their perfect likeness, not only in appearance and manner but in the repulsive imprint of her father etched into each brother's very core. It was unmistakable, though the effects seemed far less impactful in Gierson.

Ffion's demeanor shifted into one of careful vigilance as he retreated several steps, rejoining Bellamy where he'd left her. She quickly considered pulling him back into the saddle behind her and fleeing the grounds while they still had a chance.

Beneath her, the prince maintained his unruffled façade so it seemed there would be no attempt at running. Instead, Bellamy noted his caution through the mask of delight he wore for all those around them.

"My son." The dowager queen strode toward Ffion, a strained, upturned pout twisting her mouth into something resembling a practiced smile. "So good to have you home at last. We were not expecting you, or we would've included you in today's joyous festivities."

Ffion grunted, a modest grin his only show of acknowledgment. He couldn't ask about his ascension to the throne or what had happened to his father, and Bellamy felt herself moving to him before she could think better of her actions. Sensing her course, Ffion turned to her.

"Joyous indeed." The prince reached for Bellamy as if he sensed her dismay, his touch briefly landing upon her knee to calm her. "I would've come sooner, but alas, His Majesty, King Ffion's betrothed had much to settle before she could accompany me back to Calaise."

Bellamy's blood ran cold with Ffion's words, each ringing clearly through the crisp air. Equally aghast was his mother, whose scrutiny flicked first between the pair, then behind them at the sea of Calaisean citizens watching from beyond the barred palace walls within earshot.

"Please forgive us for the delay," Ffion continued, his features inscrutable.

It was an artful deception, to say the least, though they'd never discussed how she might be permitted to stay. Whatever the case, Bellamy would be long gone before any folly of that degree could take place. Ffion would never allow such a union for himself, but it was a show of good faith, proving his steadfast commitment to blot her father from existence.

Taking the dowager's decorated fingers in his hand, Ffion pressed a kiss of greeting to her knuckles as he fell to one knee before her. What was to onlookers an act of deference to a bereaved sovereign was to Bellamy a shrewd test of allegiance on the prince's part—one to which his mother gave him no acknowledgment as her monarchical superior, peering down her nose at him like a commoner pleading for clemency.

The woman's indifference made Bellamy's blood boil.

"Rise, brother." Gierson rushed to Ffion's side, urging him to his feet. "No need for formalities amongst family."

Ffion stood, and the one-time queen smoothed her skirts as if she had not directly insulted his succession through her lack of regard, whether others knew he was the rightful heir or not. *She* knew.

Gierson looked past his twin to Bellamy, his attention wholly focused upon her. "I didn't know the future Calaisean queen would be so beautiful."

The pixie felt her cheeks burn under his study, mentally chiding herself for the insanity of it all. Gierson, or *Ffion*, she supposed, was a breathtaking replica of his brother. Ffion didn't make her blush, so neither would she let the approaching imposter king, even if the gentle brush of his lips across the back of her hand suggested otherwise...

Bellamy inclined her head, her hand yet joined with Gierson's. His were not calloused like his brother's, who'd braved the nightmares of Wylewoode with nothing but his sling and his strength of conviction to purge Fayble of its basest evils, of which she was amongst the worst.

A wanderer king, and survivor was he. So what, then, was Gierson? He didn't seem dangerous, else not in the same way as Ffion. Marin was a being who created his own forms of entertainment, the most grotesque of which he sought through human vessels. If Gierson was another of his countless pawns, it was in Bellamy's best interests to keep him within arm's reach.

"It's a pleasure to make your acquaintance," Bellamy managed at last, swallowing her nerves and accepting what was, admittedly, an unexpected gift.

"The pleasure is mine." Gierson searched her features with interest when Ffion took to her side, causing Gierson to step away.

"Allow me to introduce you to Lady Bellamy." Ffion squared his shoulders, his tone one of duty-bound resignation.

"Our home is your home. Please, treat it as such." Gierson was most attentive, readily ignoring his surly brother. "Join me on a tour of the grounds? I should like to get to know our presumptive queen."

She could not refuse him, or it would surely be taken as a great offense, and some part of her was intrigued by him, loath as she was to admit it. Not once had Gierson shown irreverence toward Ffion despite their current circumstances. He seemed kind. Gracious. Perhaps he understood his place better than the wretched dowager.

Bellamy nodded. Her father's essence enveloped them both, swathing them in cloaks of everything wrong with the world. Whether Gierson embraced or despised the darkness bound to him remained to be seen, but she knew well enough where Ffion was concerned.

Gierson moved beside her, a reassuring smile lighting his angular face as he mounted her horse in place of Ffion, settling before her. Where Ffion was tanned and travel-worn, Gierson was clean-shaven and flawless. He looked every bit a monarch, dressed from top to bottom in what Bellamy could only assume to be traditional Calaisean fashion, ornamented with chains and pins of silver and gold.

"Tonight, we have much to celebrate." Gierson clucked his tongue, cueing the horse forward. He'd shown Ffion all the respect that could be afforded given the situation thrust upon the brothers, though Bellamy wasn't quite sure why it mattered to her. Somehow, it did.

The pixie followed, passing Ffion as she went. He cocked his head to one side and then the other, the muscles in his jaw twitching. His features were unreadable when her gaze drifted toward his, and even once she looked away, she felt him watching.

Bellamy hadn't much choice, but leaving Ffion behind left her vulnerable in a way she never wished to feel again. She didn't cling to life or fear death — for someone with nothing, there was nothing to lose. But the rising flesh on her arms suggested that the screeching metal of the palace gates might've been more than a deafening warning.

They formed a cage. Just as they kept all the outside creatures at bay, they housed monsters, of which she and her father were the worst.

Chapter Eight

Running headlong for Calaise had been a mistake. Ffion's intent was clear enough. He'd felt the burden of his duty throughout his sojourn in Wylewoode despite readily ignoring the tug of his obligations. But the necessity of his presence was, as it turned out, utterly irrelevant.

Suppressing his annoyance, he rode toward the gatehouse, pretending to be oblivious to the overt flirtation between his brother and his pixie companion mere yards away. Try as he might, he couldn't keep his gaze from straying toward the newly betrothed pair, smiling and hopelessly enamored as they bantered freely for all the world to see.

He was a *jackass*.

What on earth had possessed him to suggest Bellamy as the future queen? It was absurd. Preposterous. And worse was the eagerness with which his proposal had been accepted.

Gierson hadn't batted an eye before moving in, receiving the beautiful assassin as his intended and sweeping her up into his tender embrace, parading her before one and all as they rode for the palace courtyard. The false king hadn't missed a beat and played his role as heir apparent in flawless fashion.

Even Ffion found himself deferring to his brother's whims, and while that was nothing new, it felt far more consequential with so much at stake.

The Crown had managed to save face, suddenly able to explain away Ffion's absence and reappearance with one ill-conceived ruse, though he had no idea how they'd handled his departure on a day-to-day basis for such a time. Even so, he couldn't help but wonder what he'd lost as a result of it all.

A title. A kingdom. A captivating woman.

Ffion watched on, his stomach lurching as he observed his brother helping Bellamy from the saddle, his hands clasped securely around her slender waist. She smiled, averting her gaze as though she was practiced in the womanly art of modesty.

Well. While that couldn't be any further from the truth, her efforts had evidently been effective enough where Gierson was concerned. The man was a nitwit— a lover of finery, of women, falling prey to their many charms, yet never left to deal with the fallout of his dalliances. Such was the life of a privileged regent.

Spoiled.

Sighing, Ffion dismounted from his borrowed steed, feeling nothing shy of furious regardless of his own hand in his current plight. Why it bothered him so was another matter altogether—one that Ffion would happily banish to the deepest recesses of his mind rather than face head-on.

Perhaps he would always run.

"A little help here, Gierson. *Gierson!*"

It took Ffion a moment to realize *he* was being summoned. His mother rode to his side, tipping her chin expectantly, her features sour. He approached her horse, offering his aid, helping his mother from the saddle despite myriad servants bustling about the courtyard.

Of course, it wasn't his help that she required but his compliance, a message he promptly received.

"Join me, my son," said the queen, waiting impatiently with her hands folded before her. She was fair enough, though no great beauty — not in the traditional sense. But her cunning mind had seen her rise to her station, elevating her to the second highest position in the land, ascending from her roots as a duchess of Sundsvaile.

Never one for pleasantries, Ffion wasn't surprised to find her cold. Still, he'd hoped, perhaps, for some marginal affection after four years of absence, but it seemed it was not to be. Instead, he worked to ignore the creeping sensation that he was no longer welcome.

"Shall we?"

He offered her his arm in the customary fashion, focusing on the good that might come from his ruinous venture home, suddenly profoundly wary of setting foot inside Chateau Dufoise.

From the outside, not much had changed. It was the same grand fortress it had always been, with its imposing stone exterior and crawling vines. The grounds were flawless, with an army of gardeners working overtime for the benefit of all the arriving banquet attendees. In several hours' time, the crowds would descend, forcing Ffion's definitive return to his duties, no matter how much they might've changed.

Decorum was exact—an unequivocal expectation, no matter the circumstances.

Queen Helena took his arm, her icy touch bleeding through the thin linen of his shirt sleeve. "Please."

With her free hand, she gestured him onward. Her eagerness to escape the prying eyes of the onlooking citizenry was a notable departure from her typical enthusiasm for their attention, but he wasn't about to argue.

They fell in step behind Gierson and Bellamy, her arm daintily entwined with his as the pair exchanged pleasantries. It was the dullest display Ffion had ever seen, with the woman so thoroughly convincing in her gentility that it was difficult to see her for the murderess she was born to be.

"Are you well, then?"

Ffion returned to himself, quickly suppressing an emerging sigh. His mother was tedious on a good day and intolerable on most others. He smiled, determined to survive her skepticism despite its relevance.

"Well enough."

Helena eyed him sideways, her gaze sweeping over him from head to toe. She clucked her tongue, opting for silence at last.

His answer had been unsatisfactory, then. That was no surprise, but it was the truth. The reality was far more gray than those two simple words, filled with complications he'd never be able to voice. He owed his kingdom as much, however, even if it did mean losing his sovereignty.

The way his brother had managed it was another question altogether. Marin's imprint was evident upon

Gierson, though he appeared less affected by the pixie scourge's manipulations overall. How he'd managed to stay, and, what's more, *rule* in Ffion's stead was infuriating. Favor had always followed Gierson in many intangible ways, and never had he begrudged his brother that.

Until now.

Passing through the portcullis, they entered the great hall of Dufoise, and Ffion's heart stuttered. Larger. *Golder* than what he remembered, his steps echoed off the marble floor in a space utterly doused in Calaisean wealth.

It made for a powerful first impression. From the high gilded ceilings to the split staircase with its scrolling balusters of filigreed iron, his opulent surroundings were a breathtaking sight, flooding Ffion's mind with bewildering memories. Just beyond the stairway, deep blue velveteen draperies framed wide, stained-glass windows, the foremost of which depicted Ffion's father.

"What happened?" He turned from the portrait, swallowing the grief threatening to make itself known upon his face. "What happened to my father?"

"He left. Searching for you." Helena's countenance held no warmth, no sense of loss for her husband of so many years. "He never did accept your diagnosis."

"What diagnosis? I recall nothing of the sort."

The queen offered only a disdainful sniff, dismissing his memory as nothing more than a pitiful delusion. "You were out of your mind. How could you possibly remember? And it seems as though little has changed. A blessing, then, that your father is no longer here to see you in your denial. His favor always blinded him."

That much might've been true, and the letter Ffion had sent to his father, detailing his absence, had been a pathetic substitution for the real explanation he owed King Tolliver. It was the best he had been able to manage at the time, having chosen to run for his life rather than remain in imminent danger within the treacherous walls of Dufoise. Even so, it stung to think of it—of his father, of his desperation.

"How kind of you, seeing to it and correcting his sentiments thusly." Ffion gestured toward his brother, who was in no way at fault where his mother's preference was concerned.

"Oh, I do agree, darling." Helena smiled, brushing her fingers over his face in a faux display of affection. "A wonder it is, too, having Prince Ffion to reign in King Tolliver's stead. Now, if you'll excuse me, Gierson. I must meet his bride-to-be."

Ffion stood in awe as his mother bustled away, leaving him fuming in her haste to be as far from him as possible. She made no efforts to conceal her distaste for her eldest son, eagerly dismissing him to make a way for himself as the fraudulent spare while she praised her equally counterfeit offspring.

Each of the brothers remained afflicted, with the filth of Marin's acid-tongued plague clinging to them like a wicked stench. Both fought for peace with themselves and their curse, yet only one was seen fit to rule.

Ffion.

But which one?

He'd never wanted to govern. Ffion had wished his father would live forever—the stalwart defender of Calaise, fair and steadfast in his reign. Immortality was a wretched hope, a fanciful desire with no assurance to speak of. Children could long for such things, minds full of pretty dreams, with the whole of their lives before them.

But childhood had long since passed, wasted away in the wilds of Neverwoode while his father had succumbed to an unknown illness, searching for his long-lost son.

Madness, they'd whispered on the streets. *Hysteria*.

It made more sense now that Ffion had ventured to the other side. The citizenry had known, sharing the truth amongst themselves in hushed reverence for the dearly departed king.

He longed for privacy, eager for an opportunity to reconcile all he'd learned with the bitterness of his newfound reality. His mother's manipulative words lingered in the back of his mind—lies forging a saccharine reality in which he'd been examined, attempting to heal him of his ills.

But no such efforts had been made, with the prince innately knowing what the king also feared. His life would be forfeited in favor of his brother, seeing his mother's favored son to the throne in his stead. That she yet sought to paint such a lovely picture of the past set Ffion on edge, leaving him as wary as he'd been when he first departed Calaise.

And, worse, was the truth that her instinctive preference for Gierson as sovereign might be well-founded after all.

Ffion wandered toward his chambers, stepping into the sun-drenched quarters and closing the door behind him. Glancing around, he quickly realized something was off. It wasn't that he'd expected nothing to change, for life had continued in his absence. But his room was no longer his, tidily filled as it was with so many of Gierson's belongings.

Stacks of books, a collection of knives, wooden chess pieces sat upon a checkered mahogany board, each treasured item belonging to his brother.

The pair had been a novelty within the kingdom, the first multiples born into royalty throughout recorded history. The flame-haired twins were they, the pride and joy of the realm.

They'd reveled in their uniqueness, with one brother interchangeable for the other on more than one occasion. The duo had swapped places for banquets, for punishments and duties untold. In time, their antics had faded, making way for a more serious commitment to their roles.

And that commitment endured, no matter how unsavory it was.

Ffion stepped out of his room, making for the next door over, all the while wondering if anything of his past life remained. He turned the knob, finding Gierson's quarters much the same as they'd always been. Shaking his head, he resigned himself to a life lived as his brother.

But once again, he wasn't alone. Movement drew his attention, a rustling from the alcove just beyond the dressing partition. Perhaps he shouldn't need to feel as guarded as he did, but it had been a way of life for nearly half a decade.

Pulling his sling from his belt loop, he readied himself, amazed by how uneasy he felt in a place that was ostensibly his home. It was all for naught, however, when a familiar face emerged with an armload of clothing.

"Prince Ffion, at long last!"

Lucignolo Vachon. A welcome sight amidst a dessert of unfamiliarity. He'd been a soldier, a friend much like Melis, but he hadn't bothered to call him Gierson—both curious and refreshing.

"Luc." Ffion grinned, reaching to shake his hand as Luc dumped the clothing onto the bed beside them. "What are you doing here?"

"I'm here to help you dress for the banquet, though I understand it's being given in your brother's honor. And that he's betrothed now, too?" Luc whistled, looking Ffion dead in the eye. "Or is that you? I'll admit, I'm rather confused."

"As am I. You're the first to refer to me by my real name since I've arrived, and nobody seemed to miss me, or *Gierson*, while I was gone." The bitterness in his words was unmistakable, but it didn't seem to bother Luc, who simply shrugged.

"They didn't know you'd left, what with Gierson acting in place of both of you, but I was there, you know. Went searching for you with your father and his second, just the three of us. Watched him lose his mind." Luc crossed his heart before kissing his fingers. "We were searching for 'Gierson', as you might expect, but I'm sane enough to know the difference between the two of you, and I don't see sense in pretending."

"Well, that makes for precisely one person in the whole of Calaise, but I'll take it." Ffion felt a portion of the weight lift from his soul with Luc's words, though the worst remained. "King Tolliver... how did it happen?"

"I think he knew his time was drawing to a close— myriad afflictions for ages, had he. One might imagine he wanted the rightful heir upon his throne." Luc raised his brows, eyeing the prince. "We traversed the night in secret, seeking any vestige of the absent princeling and finding maddening clues that only seemed to lead to dead ends."

Marin. Surely, it was the wayward pixie and all his reckless games.

"The Crown's ploy has been highly successful," Luc continued. "I don't imagine more than a handful of people are even aware you were missing, but your father couldn't bear it. Fortunately, you've returned when you have. Now, the throne will be yours."

"Don't be so certain. I'm quite convinced I'm not fit to rule." Ffion paused, having finally voiced the subtle, nagging thought ever-present in his mind.

"A shame, that. Don't be too hasty in your decision."

The prince bobbed his head, hoping to change the subject. "Why are you here, anyway? Shouldn't you be out slaying dragons with your brethren?"

Luc chuckled before lifting the leg of his trousers, revealing a thin wooden rod where once his calf had been. "I'm no longer a knight, my friend. An injury sustained some months ago."

The sadness upon his face brooked no further discussion, yet Ffion couldn't help but wonder if his pixie nemesis had had a hand in Luc's impairment.

"I'm sorry."

"I'm not." Luc reached for the armload of discarded clothing, straightening the garments upon the bed. "For it enables me to grace this stodgy dwelling with my illuminating humor." He held a crisp linen shirt before himself, giving it a shake. "Now, shall we?"

Ffion smiled, grateful for a friend to ease the challenges of his return to palace life, even as he eyed the loathsome attire he'd soon be wearing. "Thank you for your help, but I've got this. It'll be—"

"Luc, you're needed in Prince Ffion's quarters. Oh —
" Melis stood in the doorway, offering a half bow.
"Prince Gierson. Pardon my interruption."

Luc merely snorted, making for the connecting
hallway with a sneer as he passed Melis by. The woman
ignored him, her eyes trained upon Ffion. "I see you've
found your way to your room. Welcome home." She
joined Ffion at his side, the pair peering through the
window, taking in the garden from below.

"It'll do for now. Until we straighten things out, at
any rate." Ffion smiled, assessing his companion's
demeanor. She didn't disappoint, her posture rigid.

"I'm loyal to the king."

"We both know that's me."

"Not right now, it's not." Melis averted her gaze,
taking a step nearer to the windowsill. Dark hair
cascaded over her shoulder, the loose ends of her braid
fanning out from her plait. She glanced his way before
again averting her eyes, with any discussion allegedly
over.

She was dancing along treasonous lines, and she
knew it. But where did her loyalty truly lie?

It was a pointless question at any rate, for Ffion
didn't know where he stood on the matter either.
Presumably, Gierson was worthy, but the stories Luc
shared about King Tolliver had him rethinking
everything. All his doubts were melting away,
knowing that his father had sought after him, eager to
see him to the throne regardless of his cursed
shortcomings.

He wasn't a boy anymore but the rightful heir. His
duty. His destiny.

"Calaisean lore holds that each bloom thrives in
tandem with a parallel soul, celebrating and grieving

alongside our people," Melis uttered, changing the subject entirely.

Ffion scoffed. "Where did you hear such a thing?"

"My mother." Melis smiled, her almond eyes sparkling with humor. "She wasn't infallible, but her knowledge surpassed most."

"Ah, your mother, the enchantress." Ffion grinned, remembering the beautiful handmaiden who'd seen his own mother through her fair share of courtly life. "She is well missed. I'm glad you've such a trove of memories to sustain you, even if the garden is lacking in splendor."

Melis laughed, brushing her fingertips over his forearm. "It's enough for me to hear you not immediately dismissing her tales as nonsense. And anyway, it's nearly winter. You would expect the garden to be in decline."

"It sounds as if you doubt her notions yourself if you see fit to simply blame the season."

Her eyes widened with the realization before she shook her head, ignoring Ffion's amusement. The exchange was comfortable and familiar, bringing about a sense of peace for the misplaced prince.

"I don't doubt her," Ffion said at last. "A wise woman, your mother. I'd be the last to deny her assertions, anyway."

Melis squeezed his arm, silently excusing herself with a bow and leaving Ffion to himself. Little did she know just how accurate so many of her mother's legends were, much as he wished they weren't true.

The prince stood alone, watching the terrace below with a newfound appreciation for all the otherworldy nonsense he'd readily ignored in childhood. It was easier when his father bore the world's weight upon his shoulders.

Perhaps he would pretend a bit longer then, forging legends of his own design.

Chapter Nine

Despite their undeniable physical similarities, the flame-haired twins of Calaise were nothing alike, and Bellamy couldn't help but note the differences in her mind. She walked arm-in-arm with Gierson, the younger of the two, masquerading as King Ffion.

It was a confusing set of circumstances, and she was firmly planted at the center of it all. Would that Ffion had conferred with her before declaring her the betrothed of Calaise. Yet his quick thinking had preserved their cover, even as it granted her access to the upper echelons at the kingdom's heart, bringing her one step closer to her cruel father.

She could sense him there, as much on Gierson as she did on Ffion, and in the very air around them. He was everywhere and nowhere — a phantom being who chose his games wisely, preserving himself no matter the cost.

The pair made their way through the great hall with a handful of courtiers at their backs, doubtless observing their every move. It made Bellamy twitchy, distracting her from her typical efforts to suss out her surroundings. It was not unlike being trapped within a beautiful gilded cage with more doors and thorough-fares than the palace in the depths of Wylewoode.

As if he felt her unease, Gierson guided Bellamy beyond the scrutiny, escorting her away from prying eyes as they entered the courtyard. The doors closed from behind, giving them the first moment of privacy they'd received since Ffion's fateful announcement.

"You're quite unexpected. It seems my brother is full of surprises." Gierson smiled, taking Bellamy's hands in his. He was gentle, composed, and very much unlike his brother.

His touch had her flushing, with his singular attention a startling departure from her solitary existence. She didn't conspire with kings or involve herself in the intrigues of palace affairs. Such inclinations would require trust, a sentiment she steadfastly avoided, not to mention her dubious background. Nobody would willingly choose to tie themselves to anyone as damned as she.

"It's an honor to make your acquaintance, Your Grace." She curtsied, low and deferential, matching his smile with one of her own as her nerves gave way to something innately feminine. "Never did I consider such a prestigious position within my grasp. It will be a privilege to serve your kingdom."

He brushed his thumb over the back of her hand, seemingly eager to soothe away any lingering reservations. "The honor is mine. Tell me, from where do you hail?"

"My people are nomadic," she replied, the words coming to her lips without hesitation. A ridiculous notion, that, but it was enough.

Gierson sighed contentedly, nodding his approval. "I admit, I wasn't privy to the plan, but neither do I disapprove." His smile widened, reaching his hazel eyes, and Bellamy didn't miss how his gaze traveled from her head to her toes and back, quickly appraising her appearance.

It wasn't vulgar, only genuine curiosity to which she couldn't object. She'd done the same, but with far deeper interest as she assessed the faux king. Indeed, she couldn't help but compare him to his brother, bringing their variance into stark relief.

"You and your brother are much the same, but also...not," said Bellamy at last. "I wonder if your nation notices."

It was a stupid observation to share. She didn't know Gierson, nor did she truly know Ffion. They were unpredictable at best, with her father as their one common thread. Internally, Bellamy scolded herself for her foolishness. She needed to be more careful.

Yet, much to her relief, Gierson merely shook his head, readily dismissing her remark. Even so, the knowing glint within his eyes told her more than any words could. He was well aware, but it didn't seem to bother him. Perhaps she'd misread them both.

"Either way, Ffion, whoever he happens to be, is a lucky man with you as queen," Gierson uttered, his countenance suddenly serious. It was an odd statement, to be sure, but befitting enough of their circumstances.

He was straightforward in a way that brought her comfort, offering a level of honesty that few were willing to. His candor almost made her trust him. *Almost.*

Silence fell between them as their eyes met, and Bellamy felt a surge of gratitude. Both brothers enabled her through different means, fueling the fantastical hope that she might yet triumph over her father. The king, whoever he was to be, would allow her to remain long enough to complete her mission, come what may.

"My son!" The queen mother hurried their way with something like anger flashing in her silver-blue eyes. She snatched his hands away from Bellamy's before remembering herself, recovering the lofty air that made all royals so insufferable. "Your betrothed and I have not been properly introduced."

Her grim smile did little to convince Bellamy that she'd be accepted into the imperial fold, but it mattered not in the long run. She dropped into a curtsy, a ridiculous spectacle in trousers, and feigned her esteem. "A pleasure, your highness. I'm Bellamy of Balthym."

"Are you indeed? It seems Gierson has outdone himself." The woman narrowed her eyes. "Have you any title to speak of?"

It was Bellamy's turn to smile. "Why, no, ma'am. My people are much like gypsies, so you can imagine what an honor it is to be this highly regarded in your kingdom. I will treasure the welcome from your people for years to come."

Her betrothed stifled a snicker while Queen Helena's hatred shone plainly upon her face. "How lovely," the queen managed before reluctantly reaching for the pixie wanderer. "Now, if you'll follow me, we've arranged for your chambers."

Bellamy nodded, folding her hands primly in a way she hoped projected some semblance of propriety. She trailed the dowager queen from the gardens, all the while ignoring the glint of amusement in the spare's eyes as he watched her pass. The wicked little smirk he wore did something funny to her insides, confirming all the more the necessity of completing her task and being on her way.

Chapter Ten

Queen Helena moved with a purpose, scarcely sparing a word for anybody in their path. Bellamy followed in her wake, taking in the beauty of Chateau Dufoise. Gold mingled with iron throughout the cavernous manor, forming a network of veins underpinning the domed framework of the grand hall. Jewel-toned accents punctuated the interior, blending myriad elements into a dazzling display of wealth.

Their footsteps echoed through the foyer as they made for one of the two main stairways, and Bellamy picked up speed, earnestly keeping pace with the woman who seemed eager to rid herself of the pest at her heels. Part of her couldn't blame Helena, thrust into circumstances beyond her control. Ffion had inflicted the two determined women upon one another for better or worse, and that in front of the whole kingdom.

It was little wonder that the queen had no use for her.

"Ma'am," said a servant with a bow, finally having caught the queen's attention. "Is there anything I may do for you?"

"Fix *this*," she hissed, gesturing behind herself toward Bellamy before passing the young man by as quickly as she'd approached.

The poor fellow watched on helplessly, briefly meeting Bellamy's gaze. She smiled, nodding her reassurance for whatever it was worth, only to nearly collide with the queen mother, who'd abruptly stopped. "Oh—"

"Forgive us if your accommodations are lacking," said Helena, ignoring her charge. "We had no notice of your arrival. Selah will see to your needs."

Bellamy entered the room, finding many of the furnishings draped in dust cloths. The fading rays of sunset filtered through one of many arched windows, casting the chamber in hews of honeyed warmth at odds with her crude surroundings. She turned, finding Helena observing her from where she stood in the doorway.

"Selah is nearly as new to us as you are, only she doesn't speak. I wouldn't bother trying, if I were you." Her face was a mask of scarcely contained fury. "Perhaps you can learn the ways of Calaise together."

The subtle dig within her words did not go unnoticed by Bellamy. She was foreign. Other. Apparently, just like her attendant.

"You'll be prepared for the banquet, and you will not disgrace our family. Surely you understand. Welcome to Calaise," she spat before slamming the door.

Blazes.

Bellamy was at the mercy of her host's whims and fancies until she completed her mission. And despite the favor afforded to royalty, she wanted no part in that future.

Her attendant approached then with a subtle smile, and Bellamy's breath caught, for the woman was stunning. She was slight in build, with hair of silver-white pouring over her shoulders and down her back. While such coloring often suggested advanced age, Selah was anything but old — perhaps closer to the age of Bellamy herself.

Even in the plain shift worn by the female staff, Selah stood out, with aquamarine eyes reminiscent of a storm-tossed sea framed by thick, dark lashes. Her ears were lined from lobe to helix with slender, pin-like piercings neatly spaced, while a small ring adorned her nose, set above full, pink lips, and it seemed nothing about her was purely ordinary.

Selah appraised her curiously in return, as if she would have much to say were she able, and somehow, that was comforting to Bellamy. "Pleased to make your acquaintance," said the halfling after a moment. "Apparently, I'm to make a debut of sorts before long, and I'm utterly inept where the womanly arts are concerned. Will you help me?"

Selah's smile grew as she reached for Bellamy's hand, guiding her toward a sizable copper tub obscured by a privacy screen. Steam rose from the water within, while a table beside the vessel held the promise of freshness in the form of various soaps, oils and scrubs.

How long had it been?

Bellamy couldn't readily remember the last time she'd bathed, but after all was said and done, she'd buffed herself into cleanliness, grateful to be free of the grime and stench of her travels. As she washed, Selah made quick work of her chambers, turning it over and making it livable.

She'd unearthed a beautiful marble-posted bed from beneath the coverings, bedecked in silken linens and more pillows than Bellamy could count. In the far end of her quarters, a smoldering fire crackled in the hearth, warming the stone interior that looked to be untouched for some time, the firelight illuminating a nearby armoire.

The wardrobe was ornate and taller than Selah, who busily inspected the contents within. A surprising number of garments filled the chest as if it had been prepared for her arrival, but Bellamy knew that couldn't be so. It was just as likely to be full of the palace excess, though anything was bound to be more becoming than the clothes she'd arrived in.

Or, perhaps not.

Selah presented Bellamy with a dress that could only be described as a sheer wisp of fabric, a satisfied smile pinned to her face.

"No way," the halfling uttered, suppressing a giggle, for her counterpart's enthusiasm was contagious. "I'd rather dance in trousers."

Dance...

Panic streaked through Bellamy, realizing that she'd not only be dressed for the occasion but would also be expected to participate. What had Ffion gotten them into?

As if she sensed her trepidation, Selah moved for Bellamy, placing her hand on her forearm and reassuring her with her gentle touch. She pointed toward herself before performing a flawless pirouette and topping it off with an elegant curtsy. Lifting her head, she nodded in encouragement.

"Oh, I can't do that," Bellamy muttered. "But I'll try."

Repeating Selah's steps, she failed miserably, toppling into the woman and sending them both into fits of laughter as they recovered, with Selah reaching for Bellamy to pull her to her feet.

She steadied her charge, communicating through a series of gestures that there were more etiquette lessons in store before directing her to the vanity, where she performed a miracle upon her hair and face. With swift fingers, she tucked and curled, pinning the lengths of Bellamy's tresses into a voluminous bun at the nape of her neck, with a handful of strands falling loosely about her shoulders.

Her skin glowed, cheeks rosy and lips rouged, and her eyelids were dusted in shimmering gold, matching the flecks in her wide eyes. Selah lined her eyelids in kohl with a steady hand, completing the look and leaving Bellamy awed by the beauty staring back at her in the mirror. Indeed, she hardly recognized herself.

"Thank you," said Bellamy. "Perhaps it will be to the queen's liking, though my courtly conduct will leave something to be desired."

Selah pressed her lips together, shaking her head. She held up a single finger as if to order Bellamy's racing thoughts, only to point toward the infernal dress.

If one could even refer to it as such...

* * * *

Selah had somehow accomplished the impossible, coaxing Bellamy into the sheer fabric that clung to every curve while falling in breathy layers from her hips to the floor. Much as she hated to admit it, it suited her.

The mist blue tone complimented her tanned skin, and her hair was woven with blooms in shades of cream and rose gold, matching the floral accents sprinkling the length of the skirt. And while her gown was airy in nature, she'd been able to conceal her stiletto with a blush-colored ribbon strapped to her inner thigh.

It was a necessity in her mind, for she'd sensed the enemy lurking amongst the opulence of Dufoise. There was no telling when another opportunity for justice might present itself, and she could not come up short like last time. Not again.

For the moment, Bellamy felt a bit more concealed, draped in a lightweight cape for the chill of the evening. Selah had led her to the terrace at the rear of the palace—a captivating space filled with soft light and flowers as far as the eye could see. Brambled hedges of green formed a maze-like pathway from the garden and onward to the remainder of the grounds, with every turn neatly kept.

The flora was another story altogether, almost wild in its splendor. Petals in shades of amethyst mingled with blood-red and some blossoms she'd never before laid eyes on. It was a sight to behold at eventide in the lambent starlight, and she wondered how vast and tangled the grounds beyond the shrubberies were.

It afforded her some form of privacy, at any rate, away from the prying eyes of all the castle attendants and courtiers who wished to spy on the future of Calaise. It was a proposition she was nowhere near prepared for, what with the expectations, the decorum demanded of royalty in all their pompous tradition.

Bellamy paused, adjusting her feet in the over-small shoes pinching her toes. No complaints would be uttered — not after the incredible efforts of Selah, who'd seen her appearance from ragged to resplendent in only an hour's time through her gifted handmaidenry.

Her attendant was an invaluable gift, supporting her through the chaos of her transition from woodland life into palace luxury. It was an uncomfortable proposition, removing her freedom of choice in one fell swoop as she became the most visible woman in the whole of the kingdom.

That had never been Ffion's intent, of course. It was a necessary inconvenience she knew well was temporary. There could be no alternative.

Selah bowed before her, taking on the male role as she moved Bellamy through the ins and outs of courtly etiquette. In a matter of a few tries, she had mastered a respectable curtsy and the proper way to receive a kiss on the hand — a greeting Bellamy had no use for that had the pair of women giggling over the silliness of it all. Still, introductions were the easiest part.

Reaching for Bellamy's hands, Selah set one upon her own shoulder while taking the other hand in hers. She took a step nearer, placing her palm on Bellamy's waist and pulling her nearer. With a reassuring smile, Selah began to lead, moving from side to side and throwing her counterpart off balance.

"Sorry," Bellamy groaned, flustered by her ineptitude. "Again."

Selah nodded, happily obliging, only to wince as Bellamy stepped on her foot.

"*Blazes*. My apologies." Heat rose in Bellamy's cheeks as she stepped away. She lacked every grace, every innate feminine sensibility, with an upbringing outside of society. And while she'd made it on her own in life, she couldn't help the distinct feeling of loss. It didn't bother her often, but reality got the better of her every now and then, bringing her complicated childhood into stark relief.

She shook her head, dismissing any hope of improvement. "You're so kind to help me, but I'm afraid this is beyond my abilities." In her mind's eye she could see it—the utter spectacle she'd make of herself in short order, shaming the kingdom and damaging her chances to remain within the palace walls.

Her father would win again, free to roam amongst the courtiers unscathed, while she'd be cast out with another opportunity lost.

"It's really no use," Bellamy continued. She sighed, making peace with her impending humiliation. "I shall make an absolute fool of myself."

"Undoubtedly," came a voice from behind her. Bellamy turned to find Ffion, dressed in a royal blue doublet and crisp linen shirt. Whorling gold threads caught the moonlight, drawing her eyes toward his broad shoulders and chest. He was a force for the reckoning, smiling fiendishly right at her.

Bellamy scoffed, feigning annoyance even as she felt a surge of excitement at the sight of him. He was arrogant. Rude. Yet some wild, broken part of her relished his beastly spirit as if feral blood called to its equal deep within her. "Quite the help you are, as ever," she managed, recovering her senses at last.

"I may be. Perhaps I can be of some assistance. Truce?"

"Truce." She suppressed her amusement, knowing that any pact with a brute like him would be short lived at best. He moved toward her then, his eyes never leaving hers, and she reached for his shoulder without a thought, her other hand finding his as he fit his palm to the flare of her hip.

Selah retreated, stepping toward the edge of the terrace where she watched on, her lips quirked in amusement. But Bellamy's focus lay solely upon the man before her. His fingers were warm, their touch melting through the thin layers of her skirt, and her pulse raced as he pulled her closer, their breath mingling in the scant space separating them.

A bewitching melody rose from the silence, flowing in time with their motions—a beautiful voice that had as yet remained hidden. Selah hummed a lyrical refrain, filling the air around them as they began to move, and it wasn't long before Bellamy found a rhythm alongside Ffion.

Their steps fell in tandem, and it seemed the scoundrel was not only attractive but an expert teacher as well, damn him. Try as she might, the enchanted halfling could not bring herself to look away, and before long, her steps came effortlessly as if she'd been dancing her entire life, even when the movements became more complex.

Bellamy lost track of time, with the warmth of Ffion's body pressed against her own, bringing unexpected comfort amid all her turmoil. Their arrival at the palace had been fraught with untold peril. Indeed, gaining access to the inner workings of the kingdom's hub had been the easiest part of a plan with no discernible origins. One moment, she'd been a filthy hybrid on an ill-conceived journey, only to find herself in the next moment to be betrothed.

The judgment she'd faced was understandable given the ridiculous circumstances, but that didn't excuse Queen Helena's heinous treatment of her or her attendant, Selah. Thinking of the callous old woman only stoked the fire burning within Bellamy's soul.

She was determined to impress.

And if Ffion's steadfast guidance were any indication, he'd be there to see her to success. Taking her in his arms, he turned her outward, twirling her away from himself before drawing her near again, and the smile on his face disappeared when they met, his nose brushing hers. He paused, seemingly contemplating his plight as his gaze flicked briefly toward her lips. "You'll do," he breathed as the impish little smirk he liked to wear returned. "My mother will be pleasantly surprised, I imagine, for I do believe she thinks you unfit for your new station."

"She's right," Bellamy agreed. "But I never give up so easily."

Ffion chuckled, taking her by the hand as Selah's ballad softly faded into the twilight, leaving Bellamy in companionable silence alongside her accidental partner in crime. She was surprised by how familiar it had become, their easy banter and mutual disdain for an otherwordly empire uniting them in their efforts.

"Growing up here must've been lovely in some ways." Bellamy gestured toward a rambling vine sprinkled with tiny pink flowers, marveling over how its simplicity could paint such an arresting portrait. "The palace is a wonder, and this terrace is a masterpiece all its own."

"It wasn't all bad. But this is far from the full splendor these gardens can achieve." Ffion sighed, leading Bellamy down one of the many cobblestone pathways. "Much has changed in my absence."

He was rather lost in thought, and for the first time, Bellamy saw his humanity on full display — the loss of innocence, the struggle for survival. He masked his burdened heart with a callous pursuit, keeping the self-pity mere mortals would be inclined toward buried deeply within his divided spirit.

"Do you regret it?"

"I can't." Ffion shook his head, meeting her gaze. "I was out of my mind. Still am. Leaving it all behind suited me well, but that won't stop me from doing what's right. Whatever it is."

The pressures of a kingdom weighed heavily upon his shoulders, even as he spurned the obligations of his birthright while masquerading as Gierson. She could see the strain in his face, the uncertainty of his fate as heir or spare or nothing at all hovering over him like a guillotine seconds away from severing his future irrevocably.

Bellamy looked away, admiring an unusual flower of cerulean amongst a sea of vibrant crimson. Larger than the others, its edges were tipped in rich golden hues, with a network of iridescent veins spanning each delicate petal, shimmering subtly beneath the starlight.

"Well, now. If that isn't a flower fit for a king." She smiled, tipping her head toward the bloom before her gaze strayed toward Ffion's once again, and though she scolded herself for her infernal intrigue with the rogue royal, she couldn't help but wish to see him happy.

Ffion didn't disappoint, his smile matching hers. "Perhaps. But even more befitting of a queen." He winked, drawing a laugh from the halfling as their eyes leveled. His insinuation was clear, taking Bellamy aback. That he would readily champion her for such a role was beyond any reason, much as she wished to be worthy of the honor. Yet, with Ffion, so many traditional conventions had been turned on their heads.

What was one more?

Something distinctly intimate passed between them as if they could sense the longings of one another's hearts—each desired freedom, even as they wrestled daily with their endless demons.

Bellamy made to reach for the opaline blossom without a thought, overcome by its beauty and something more she couldn't quite describe. It reminded her of—

"*Please*," said Ffion, taking her free hand in his own. "Let's see how it fairs with the coming winter. Flowers like these thrive in the cold." He stroked his thumb across her knuckles, one by one, eliciting a shiver born of more than the brisk evenfall.

Bellamy nodded, suddenly eager to move indoors, for the ruffian had just saved her life.

And something told her that he knew just that.

Chapter Eleven

No expense had been spared when it came to outfitting the interior of Dufoise, and it showed from the decor to the fabrics and even in the food. The ballroom shimmered as flickering flames danced atop tall ivory candlesticks, making for an elegant scene with its subtle, golden glow, and tables laid with all manner of delicacies ensured an extravagant evening would be had by one and all.

The preparation had to have taken hours, days even, all for a supposed celebration that never should have been.

For Ffion, it all brought back memories of his father — a man who should still be king. The baroque walls plated in gold and silver, the deep blue draperies framing the windows. All of it formed the backdrop to every major Calaisean event, where the king relished presenting his sons to everyone in attendance.

Echoes of His Majesty filled the hall, but it was not in the prince to grieve him just yet. King Tolliver was forever lost to his kingdom, to his sons, but Ffion wouldn't disgrace his memory by yielding to broken-heartedness until he'd atoned for his death.

Too much rested on his shoulders for him to crumble now. Marin would answer for all of it, for the twins' mutual afflictions, and for their father's untimely passing. That hour could not come soon enough.

It was painful to make pleasantries with strangers when his skin itched for the twilight-shadowed greenwoods beyond the grounds of his home, and the party had not even quite begun. He would run once the sky blackened and his mother's guests had numbed their scrutiny with drink.

"From where does the lady hail?" a paunchy nobleman inquired of Ffion, who had long since stopped listening to the gentleman as he carried on about this and that and something about the Duke of Le Trouleux's regrettable case of gout.

Ffion snatched a stemmed flute of champagne from one of a dozen palace servants weaving through the growing swarm of bystanders. "I beg your pardon?"

"The king's intended." Adjusting the lapels of his tailcoat, the lord leaned in closer to Ffion, dropping his voice when he spoke. "She is rumored to be a true Venus."

The prince offered a small smile in response. Rare indeed, with eyes he could live a thousand lifetimes and never forget.

Bellamy was far more than she seemed when they first met, and it was troubling to think it might all be a ruse. He would be a dunce to believe one so utterly breathtaking couldn't be as equally cruel, but for a moment, Ffion made himself forget.

He couldn't be sure how or why something had shifted between them. But when the doors opened to welcome a new king alongside its future queen, the prince couldn't look away.

"Forgive me." Ffion politely excused himself, finding a place amongst the crowd as the music swelled, with the string quartet performing the same haunting melody hummed by the chambermaid earlier that very evening.

A circle formed around Gierson and Bellamy within the heart of the ballroom, and it was strange to pretend that all was well when Ffion should have been the one standing beside her. He'd grown accustomed to being watched over the years, even if he never particularly cared for the attention. It was a relief in many ways to see Gierson take his place, but tonight, it made his stomach turn.

The prince observed unnoticed from the edge of the dance floor, watching his twin sweep Bellamy across freshly polished oak floors in her gown of sheer, billowing gossamer.

Sheets of fine liquid silk floated around the pixie like she was dancing on air, her dress the color of a dense morning sea mist. Flesh-toned mesh fit closely to her gentle curves while cascading layers flowed over it, accentuating her form in a near-scandalous manner for a gown with an otherwise modest silhouette.

Leaves and florals of the same translucent material, with lifelike satin butterflies in varying sizes and shades, embellished her skirt, torso and bust, the material so delicate the outline of long, slender legs could be seen from underneath. The mesh rambled up Bellamy's lithe figure, covering the contours of her chest and shoulders, traveling down her arms to her fingertips in one seamless piece into whisper-thin gloves.

Ffion was rapt soul, mind and body at the sight of her.

His pixie moved with an otherworldly elegance, whirling across the floor by Gierson's lead, who seemed as much a spectator as their gathered citizenry. He watched delightedly, spinning the bewitching fairy around the hall with fluid grace.

The prince committed to memory the feeling of Bellamy in his arms. He couldn't help it. She'd been perfection against him in the fleeting moments they'd spent together in the gardens, and Ffion knew he'd observed their lesson with the same intrigue he saw in Gierson's eyes.

Selah's rendition of the ancient ballad replaced the version played by the harpist and her stringed quartet within the prince's mind as he tried vainly to cling to his afternoon reverie, ignoring the bitterness clenching his chest.

Gierson dipped Bellamy's petite frame, her back arched elegantly over his hand before straightening herself in his steady hold as the music faded. They were nearly nose to nose, Gierson smiling down at his perceived intended, captivating onlookers with their performance.

Ffion had never doubted the halfling's ability to beguile her audience. But it was unnerving how quickly he'd fallen prey to her charm and how, with one dance, she'd won the aristocracy. He was losing in a battle of wills against himself, fighting to remember how perilous she might be should he lose sight of what mattered most.

She was the very embodiment of temptation, this Bellamy, and he a willing victim of her allure.

Bellamy met Gierson's gaze as he offered her his arm escorting her to the front of the hall, where they would receive the people together. Ffion, acting as Gierson, would be expected to join them, along with the dowager.

But Bellamy watched Ffion, her intense regard trained upon him as he made his way toward her and his brother while his mother stood adjacent to Gierson as their widowed matriarch.

The air around them became a heady, noxious veil suffusing Ffion's consciousness, and while fully bright with candlelight, the room seemed to darken. It was a bold statement of Marin's arrogance to taunt his quarry so openly. Though the prince had not yet seen him, he was alert to the man's presence and, given the look of revulsion in Bellamy's eyes, so was she.

Ffion nodded in acknowledgment to his twin, bending at the waist in a stilted bow before taking his place at Bellamy's side opposite Gierson, all in deference for the celebrated King Ffion and his intended.

A sham if ever there were one.

Gierson stared back at him, plainly discomfited by the gesture, however necessary, and Ffion was grateful for a brother who was ever an unswerving advocate. Doubtless, it was as strange to him as it was to Ffion, but they'd do what was required for the sake of the monarchy.

Tensions ran thick between Ffion and Bellamy as well, even as he found something resembling peace standing beside her. He remembered Petra and her calming manner. The two weren't so different, save for Bellamy's aversion to him.

They were adversaries by nature, though it was Petra who had instilled in him the only sliver of empathy he'd had for the half-breeds. Neither had definitively fallen from grace, nor had he, despite the lies breathed to him at night when his skin felt foreign and vile in the way it trapped his bones.

"He will not leave Dufoise," Ffion uttered to Bellamy, whose expression remained impassive. He'd pledged Marin's death to her that morning and was determined to see his vow through. Their chaos would end that night.

And should it demand a ransom, he'd let his life be given freely as a settlement.

Surveilling produced no proof of the demon fairy's attendance, his presence evident only in a lurking sense of foreboding humming through the revelry. Guest after guest passed through the receiving line, offering flatteries to the point of nausea, completely oblivious to the hidden danger.

The tedious duty persisted for what felt like an eternity, with Ffion exchanging greetings and pleasantries when, at long last, he spied the purveyor of his damnable shame.

From beside him, Bellamy remained poised in spite of her father's nearness while Ffion fought the urge to rush the bastard then and there. He flexed his hands to quell the fury rumbling through his core, but it was nearly beyond his control.

He'd killed more of them than he could count, yet the sight of pure-blooded pixies would always send a shiver through him. To the naked eye, they were exceptional in nearly every way, but anyone who was aware of their ways understood the deceptions concealed beneath their façade.

Ffion hadn't seen the truth until he'd been forced to impale one of the wretched things on the night following Marin's devilry. That was when his view of Fayble and the world had changed irrevocably. The pixie had toyed with him, goading and mocking the prince until he'd forgotten himself entirely.

So Ffion had attacked the creature as it grinned back at him with its razor-edged teeth until it realized he was faster. It still sickened him to recall the first time he'd witnessed the color in another being's face pale by his hand, but the feeling was always replaced with deep satisfaction when he remembered the wings that were revealed once life abandoned the fairy.

They were anything but beautiful.

Marin smiled, bearing his gleaming white teeth with obvious amusement as he positioned himself to receive his welcome. Surely, he had to have known how destructive his timing was, with the prince already so near the edge of his restraint as night beckoned.

Calaise would be left in good hands with Gierson, and perhaps that was how it was always meant to be. Ffion was ready and willing to sacrifice his birthright to save his realm. Never would he so much as hesitate.

Only two people stood between them.

There would be shrieks of horror when the present company watched him crush Marin's windpipe, and he wouldn't relent until he felt the warmth leave his body. No dilemma over honor tormented Ffion when he thought of Marin writhing in his grip. He'd squeeze the demon's airways until no breath reached his lungs, stilling his heart. There was nothing more right or noble than to let a soul descend into everlasting turmoil. Hell would lap him up with tongues of fire, enveloping him in molten anguish until time itself ceased to be.

Eagerness coursed through Ffion as the gathering's final attendant offered a curt bow, leaving Marin to stand before him next. A ripple of adrenaline flashed through his nerves like bolts of lightning ricocheting within his blood. He would never be king, but somehow, this meant more.

There was no question Marin knew the bedlam that would ensue should the prince lose himself in the presence of his people. Either he believed himself clever enough to elude any encounter he might provoke, or he wrongfully assumed Ffion capable of sound judgment in early eventide, merely intending to remind the trio before of him of his boldness.

Beside Ffion, Bellamy was the picture of unrivaled composure, and for a moment, the room around them melted away when her hand found his. She didn't dare to glance his way when a single, gloved finger brushed lightly over his knuckles, awakening reason and violent longing at once.

With one gesture, his blessed halfling had prevented a devastating turn in the evening's celebration.

Calaise meant nothing to Bellamy, and it would've suited her well enough to watch Ffion kill her father without dirtying her own hands. Maybe it was as simple as a greater opportunity presenting itself in the form of a potential union with the king of a great nation, though she didn't seem the type to care for such things. She was unrestrained by the limitations of courtly obligation, and something told the prince nothing in her desired anything but freedom.

Ffion inhaled deeply, with his self-control no longer on the bitter edge of imploding. Still, he'd meant what he told Bellamy that very day. Her father would not leave the grounds alive.

From before him, Marin chuckled, his fist resting over his heart as he inclined his head toward Ffion. "You're every bit the man I knew you'd be." Marin's mouth arched into a cruel smirk as he spoke. "Humans think themselves above beasts when, really, they are one and the same. Eventually, the monster within will be all that's left. Isn't that so, my beauty?" He turned his attention to Bellamy, who watched her father, mirroring his sneer, her lips upturned at the corners in a pretty half-smile.

"People lead miserable existences, feigning and chasing virtue when there's little to spare. Rather like sheep, don't you think?" Bellamy's brows knit together thoughtfully, her smile fading as she continued. "It's easy to miss the wolves wandering amongst them."

Marin scoffed, stepping nearer to his daughter and the prince, drawing Gierson's partial attention. Until that moment, Ffion's brother had given no indication he recognized him, but the subtle shift in his demeanor when Marin ventured closer suggested otherwise.

"Wolves are not so different from sheep. Neither is likely to survive a venomous strike from a serpent," Marin quipped.

"How fortunate for both wolves and sheep that snakes aren't known for their intellect," said Ffion, his tone utterly indifferent.

Marin laughed then, a mocking, mirthful burst that struck Bellamy in a way Ffion couldn't bear to watch. He moved, instinctively forming a barrier between the pixie and her father.

"My congratulations to the happy couple," Marin offered by way of departure, addressing Gierson at last, even as his words were directed toward Ffion and Bellamy.

It was no secret to him that Ffion was the king in wait, and his visit an unmistakable reminder that he could raze their family's reign to the ground. Each time the prince failed to control his impulses resulted in another opportunity for Marin to expose the lies held tightly within the palace walls, and every forsaken deception was a desperate ploy to secure his future rule — deceptions that could splinter, leaving Calaise at Fayble's mercy.

Ffion had been a young boy when he'd left his home behind. He'd hoped to return whole one day but had rested nonetheless in the assurance that Gierson would assume his title should he fail to succeed.

He'd hated his brother for it, for convincing Calaise of his false identity. But most of all, Ffion despised himself for being the lesser of them both. A curse was uttered over him, but so had it been with Gierson, and Calaise would thrive under the spare.

Not so under the firstborn heir, whose compulsions overpowered his sanity, throwing him over the edge into delusion.

But pixies never played games that could not also be lost. There was always a risk buried within the heart of their diversions, no matter how slight it may be.

And Marin had placed the wager against himself.

Chapter Twelve

The bloodlust in Ffion's eyes was both thrilling and terrifying.

He trembled beside Bellamy, his body thrumming with energy that likely went unnoticed given the alcohol-induced merriment all around them. She wondered how long he could resist the chaos gripping his spirit when daytime soon expired.

She forced herself to relax, feeling her stiletto cold upon her thigh, grateful for its wicked fidelity. She wasn't a born killer but would willingly become one to avenge every unlucky soul that crossed paths with her father.

He was near. She couldn't see him, but the halfling could feel his presence nipping at her consciousness. The double doors leading to an outer balcony had been left open, and it would be just as easy for her father to leap from its heights as it would be for him to depart through the foyer. Full-blooded fairies were fleet-footed, with the most profound advantage being flight. But, unlike

Marin, they avoided direct confrontation before large gatherings, preferring to remain anonymous.

Nothing about her father was typical, least of all his games.

She would follow, then, when Ffion inevitably slipped away, accepting her own demise if that's what destiny ordered.

He'd fled the night before to spare her from the thing that dominated him, and Bellamy saw how it ravaged his spirit. Yet the prince *was* in control, even as he claimed to fight the urge to rip her apart. She knew he was capable, but Ffion was sound of mind. She couldn't bring herself to believe that it would ever come to that.

It was obvious that her father knew of Ffion's profound discipline, or he would not lavish him with provocations. Pixies bored quickly of their prey, and this game began years ago. Marin had assumed the worst of both in proclaiming whatever ill fate he had over the flame-haired brothers. If baiting the princes publicly were any indication, he was growing impatient, eager to win whatever diabolical wager he'd gambled — and that against nobody but himself.

She watched Ffion question his own decency as a result, and it broke her heart.

Across the ballroom, the elder prince watched as Gierson accompanied her back onto the dance floor. It was strange to be with him, the younger twin, who so effortlessly bore the weight of both names to preserve his brother's birthright. They'd spent only a handful of minutes together since she and Ffion had arrived, but he'd made a solid impression.

Her father may have cursed horrors over the brothers, but both had proven themselves superior to his machinations in their own right.

"My brother is a blessed man," Gierson uttered to Bellamy, his hazel eyes searching her features with covetous appraisal before averting his gaze. His assessment caught her off guard, and it pleased her more than she cared to admit.

"Do not make me blush in front of all these people," she lilted, smiling shyly. "You don't know me quite well enough to make such an observation in any case."

Gierson chuckled, and if his compliment had not heated her cheeks, his laugh surely did. "I suppose we all have our secrets, but I think you and I understand each other better than most others might."

His words suggested something Bellamy had suspected — that he, too, sensed a difference within her. He'd hidden it well when they'd met that afternoon, a small proof of his discernment. *What* set her apart was another matter altogether, and she wondered how well acquainted the spare was with Fayble's untold evils.

"Would His Majesty care to divulge what he believes my great secret to be?" Bellamy accepted Gierson's lead as the stringed ensemble opened a new number. It was a bold line of questioning, but she had to know.

Music again filled the air, their bodies brushing against one another, hands joined at Bellamy's waist and back. She was unfamiliar with the steps as with their first dance, but Gierson guided her smoothly through every one. His breath tickled the curve of her neck as they moved together like they had earlier, and just like before, Ffion was all she could see.

Pacing the outer edge of the ballroom, the heir did not look their way. He didn't mingle, keeping to himself where he quietly observed his surroundings, presumably awaiting the best moment to leave.

A gentle twirl brought Bellamy back to Gierson, who expertly drew her to him. "I would be envious if I didn't think him deserving," the spare said, his words refreshingly honest. She felt his smirk dissolve, his cheek skimming hers as he grew serious. "My brother and I have met darkness. We know its nature and ilk, and so do you. But you aren't like them. Not quite."

It was unnerving to be truly seen by someone so unknown to her, but freeing just the same. She'd felt similarly with Ffion, though their meeting had been less than friendly. Even so, the eldest prince never betrayed Bellamy's roots. Neither, it seemed, would Gierson. Their small circle of trust made for a shaky alliance, but if Ffion delivered on his promise, none of it would matter, and she'd be gone before sunrise.

Either that, else dead.

"I assure you, I'm unlike anyone you've ever known." Bellamy sighed, her tone light even as she began to feel panic, for Ffion was no longer where she'd last seen him.

Gierson turned Bellamy to face him, his study revealing everything his words would not. "I know."

One song melded into another, and the spare's touch lingered, his thumb running over her knuckles absentmindedly as the festivities persisted around them. The moment lasted just a breath, long enough to inspire whispers amongst those nearby before they parted.

"Adoration is a remarkable thing to watch, is it not?" Helena said above the hushed murmurs, and Bellamy searched for Ffion in earnest. The last thing she needed was for the dreadful woman to make a scene when she only wanted to leave.

"I would agree if it didn't mean I must watch my dear brother salivate over His Majesty's intended,"

Ffion teased from behind Bellamy, his voice echoing through her awareness like the rumbling of a perilous midnight storm. "But, I daresay I cannot fault him for it."

Bellamy didn't turn to acknowledge him, even as his words made her heart scuttle. Indeed, she began to understand the continent's fascination with the Calaisean heir and his spare.

Several guests laughed at the brotherly jeering, including Gierson, who appeared equally amused with a broad, good-humored grin. Yet to Bellamy, it was rather more like a warning when she could sense Ffion's restraint dangling by a thread, much as it reminded the spare that he was not, in fact, heir apparent.

Her muscles tensed, tingling with anticipation when Ffion moved nearer, though her back was still turned to him. He was every bit the wolf she imagined him to be, slowly, carefully advancing on his mark. The prince skirted around Bellamy, and as he brushed past, he stroked his fingers across hers, skimming the outer edge of her palm. It was a hidden gesture, stirring something long dormant within.

Ffion strode a few paces beyond where Bellamy and his family stood, the eyes of his citizenry trained upon him. He paused before a large arrangement of vibrant florals, plucking a single, flawless winter rose stripped neatly of its vicious thorns.

"My father was brilliant with flowers," said he, a faint smile lighting his face. "When I was young, he taught me the differences between all those grown here at Dufoise. Most are used to soothe ailments or adorn extravagant platters, but one in particular always fascinated me. King Tolliver told me a folktale about the origin of winter roses." He moved toward Bellamy, extending the flower he'd chosen for her, and she couldn't help but note the subtle tremors coursing through his limbs. She accepted it without hesitation, grateful for even the pathetically thin barrier of mesh covering her hands despite the bloom's bare stem.

"It's said that a winter rose will only take root in soil infused with liquid gold," he continued, "causing unique gilded veins to splay through its leaves and a luminescent shimmer framing its petals. They are also said to attract the very thing they kill."

The heir seemed to waken from his trance, shaking his head as if to dismiss the lore as simply that, brushing it away with a sweep of his palm before meeting Bellamy's gaze. "There is no other bloom so rare, but here they thrive, and so shall it be for you. Welcome to Calaise, Lady Bellamy."

She was not noble, and only a king had the authority to declare her such. Twice, Ffion had announced her name with the title before it, so by the word of His Majesty the King, she was Lady Bellamy. And even if the people knew nothing different, *she* was acutely aware of the gift he'd bestowed.

Bellamy dipped into a shallow curtsy, careful to maintain the same elegance Selah had displayed when she'd demonstrated how to properly recognize royalty. "Thank you," she breathed, rising to face the heir once more. His gaze was dark, resigned to what lay ahead.

They would meet in the palace gardens, where Ffion had shown her the steps of the ball's first dance, his anecdotal monologue pointedly revealing where Marin would be waiting. She hadn't been aware of the history surrounding the deadly rose she held, nor did she know whose pixie blood had been shed in those gardens to cause it to bloom in such lustrous fashion.

Perhaps that was for the best.

The prince backed away from Bellamy and Gierson, bowing garishly as he donned a wry smirk, his hands held together as if in prayer before he addressed his engrossed spectators. "I thank you all for being here tonight to celebrate His Majesty's forthcoming coronation and his future bride. Calaise is greatly favored."

Helena observed Ffion carefully, her brows creased with evident unease. The dowager's disdain for her firstborn was palpable, reminding Bellamy of her own father and his contempt for anything beyond himself.

Untainted by Marin's perversion as she might be, Ffion's mother was equally guilty of duplicity as far as Bellamy was concerned, and utterly irresponsible in her apathy for Ffion's well-being. Even now she looked at him as if it would be his fault, were the lies she'd choreographed to catch up to her.

The dowager made to move toward Ffion, when he directed his attention to her instead, stopping her cold. "Forgive me, Mother, but I must take my leave." He took Helena's hands in his, squeezing them affectionately despite the vague air of irritation between them.

"Of course, my love. Your travels have surely exhausted you. Be well and rest, Gierson." Helena's actions and speech were treasonous, but Ffion didn't blink. Instead, the heir set his jaw, the muscles tensing when he inclined his head toward her by way of departure.

Bellamy wondered just how far he was willing to be pushed. Her gaze followed him as he approached the large doors through which they'd arrived, imposing and powerful in his composure — every bit a king.

"Since we have your attention," Helena began, causing Ffion to halt when she raised her hands, governing the room. "Tonight, we celebrate our future, our king. My beloved son." Helena took to Gierson's side, standing opposite Bellamy, her skirts swooshing like a disquieting midnight wind when they swept over the floors underfoot. "Today, all of Calaise took part in the age-old tradition recognizing His Majesty's impending ascension to the throne. It is a joyous day, as it shall be in two short weeks when your king and his bride are joined as one in holy matrimony before God and country!"

Bellamy's eyes found Ffion's, where he remained chillingly still. He clenched his fists at his sides as applause filled the room, undoubtedly shocked by his mother's blatant disregard for his presence.

Helena beamed, patting Gierson's face before she continued. "As if this weren't all excitement enough, the coronation will follow, solidifying our sovereignty as we grow our influence throughout the whole of Fayble." She raised her flute of champagne. "To Calaise!"

"To Calaise!" came the jovial reply, with every gathered courtier oblivious to the treachery perpetrated by the cruel matriarch, who stood triumphantly above the fray, her lips puckered with satisfaction.

Bellamy observed the entire display with scarcely contained disgust, frustrated that such a farce could so easily stand. The oblivious citizenry would continue blindly onward, lapping up the lies of their queen as she usurped the throne through her son of choice.

It was enough to make Bellamy want to stay on, if for no other reason than to defeat the nasty dowager, though it was not her war to wage.

The struggle and all its myriad battles belonged to Ffion alone, but when she looked his way, he was already gone.

Bellamy excused herself a few moments later, to nobody's disappointment, with Queen Helena readily dismissing her for the evening. She'd fulfilled her role as the king's intended well enough and would not be missed amongst the seas of alcohol and impenitent boozing.

Gierson bid her goodnight with a pleasant smile, though his gaze trailed her as she left, and she prayed he wouldn't follow. If Ffion had sensed Marin's nearness, so had he.

Though unfamiliar with the layout of Dufoise, Bellamy found her way to the gardens with little difficulty. Her father's stench was everywhere, an overwhelming sweetness, calling anyone crazy enough to answer. The halfling stalked his path, fully aware of the nightmare-given flesh awaiting her at its end.

She was ready, and even if it meant her future died alongside him, it would be worth it.

It would be a relief.

But instead of finding her father, whose essence spread like inky tendrils through the late king's garden, Ffion was alone. The heir shouted into the night, and Bellamy waited, concealed by brambles and shrubberies, as she observed his madness.

"Are you such a coward that you'll not face me?" Ffion's words cut through the canvas of stars, searing themselves into Bellamy's mind. "What is it all about if not this? Do you wish only to provoke me until my end of days? Or do you remain in hiding because you know you're about to die? Come out!"

Derisive laughter was the only response, dancing through the garden in a mirthless display that sent shivers down Bellamy's spine. She reached for her stiletto, prepared to answer his mockery with a vengeance made of spilled gold.

Chapter Thirteen

The beast within wanted to be let free, but Ffion's resolve didn't waver as his body ached with the insistent demand to become what he hated.

Marin would expect him to become a monster, for he'd seen the merciless nature the heir embodied when his affliction overcame him. And so, the fairy bided his time, awaiting the abomination's emergence.

Yet, Ffion endured, refusing to submit to such primal instincts, no matter how tempting. In truth, the ferine version living deep inside his soul would make quick work of the pixie scourge, and that would be a shame all its own, for the man deserved worse. The prince had determined long ago that when, at long last, he met with Marin face to face, he would be unbroken.

Ffion's accusation of cowardice had proven ineffective, having only incited the tinkerer to more antics, which was no surprise. Doubtless, he believed he could contend with the heir in his human form far too easily, thus accounting for his preposterous game of hide and seek. Surely, it was too dull for him to prevail over a common mortal, but he wouldn't resist for long.

Marin would underestimate him.

"If you were hoping to clash with the despised outcome of your devilish tongue, you'll be disappointed. You wouldn't survive anyway," Ffion called into the night, though he was wholly alone by all appearances. "I suppose you might consider it a great challenge after watching so many of your sort fall by my hand. But, surely, *you* would believe yourself more clever than they." Scoffing, he shook his head. "I confess, I did expect you to be bolder than this."

Though he never said a word, the demon's nearness was felt, turning Ffion's stomach, his proximity enough to make him physically ill. Swallowing hard, the prince squared his shoulders, determined to usher Marin through to his end without giving him the satisfaction of seeing the effect he had.

Behind a pixie's preternatural beauty flowed the lifeblood of darkness itself. Not the simple absence of light but a vacuous, unholy husk of something reminiscent of the mortal form. Like any other camouflage used by wild creatures, sift fooled many, but once that veil was lifted, there was no going back.

He couldn't see Marin but he sensed him. It was in the nearly imperceptible shift of the breeze or the way the garden mice were drawn to his bearing in the same way moths drew near flames.

A pixie's aura hypnotized their quarry, luring their prey before rendering it senseless with the fine golden dust discarded from their wings and skin. Watching and learning from the innocent beings of Wylewoode had helped Ffion early on. He'd observed, waited, and then struck.

Hunting, for the prince, was an act of ruinous calm. He knew what he became was wrong, but the twisted, fractured part of him longed for it. Yet, there was no guilt when a demon was felled, and that was all full-blooded pixies were. In that way, he'd managed to justify himself, reasoning that he was doing the world a favor even if it did, in the end, result in another being's demise.

Remembering how he'd come to be the predator that he was, however, always left him questioning himself, whether he was ridding the kingdom of evil or no. Indeed, he feared the day when his true nature would consume him entirely, just as Marin had promised it would.

But this was not that day.

To his left, he heard muted movement, paired with the heady sweetness of his adversary. "I do hate winter roses," said Marin, his voice echoing through the garden.

It was all around Ffion, awakening the hibernating flora with his words, sending luminescent particles of sift into the air, winking like stars in the eventide moonlight as the fairy advanced.

Every sensation was heightened when the prince was at the edge of his sanity, and Ffion didn't have to see Marin to know just where he was. So close was he to giving in, he could hear the rhythmic pounding of his enemy's heart inches from his own, warmth radiating from the fiend's hidden figure.

But they were not alone.

A streak of auburn shifted from behind Marin's invisible form, and his pulse fluttered, alerting Ffion with his awareness of something or, rather, some*one's* company.

The prince acted without a thought, wrapping his hands around the air before him and, through sheer, blind luck gripping Marin by the gullet.

The pixie cried out as his airway was cut off, grappling against Ffion as he slammed his elbow into the heir's forearm, like a chisel driving deeply in to his bones.

But Ffion's hold didn't falter. Gilded veins pulsed beneath his fingers, shining in the darkness as he tore Marin's cloak from his shoulders, tossing it aside, and only then was the devil's face revealed.

Ffion glanced where his mantle had fallen into a heap of woven gold, amazed by its effectiveness as a weapon of war. Marin had departed from Neverwoode with several such items — all his inventions — and they were probably just as powerful.

A streak of movement in Ffion's periphery saw Bellamy reach for her father's cloak, unnoticed by the fairy who clenched his teeth as he wheezed under Ffion's command, his neck straining under the stress of the prince's strength.

"Who is the coward now?" Marin rasped. Saliva sputtered from his mouth, his face turning a sickly yellow pallor only a pixie could have. He was daring Ffion to kill him swiftly, for mercy, but Marin didn't deserve that kindness.

Death was a certainty, but not so easy, and not for the prince alone.

Ffion smiled, shoving the demon away as he released him from his grip. The heir caught sight of his pixie as her slight frame rippled out of sight, shrouded in her father's ghastly creation of weaponized sift with a thin, shining blade clutched within her palm.

Behind Marin, Bellamy faded into nothing.

"You're not his kill," said she. Her father searched, flailing about before focusing on the stone underfoot where his mantle had lain. He chuckled, his thumb sliding over his lower lip as if suddenly realizing he'd fallen into his own trap.

"Oh, darling, don't make me hurt you," Marin said, his voice lost to the chill of the night. he was, evidently, as blinded by his design as Ffion had been. He grinned, an evil twist of his mouth that ensured her was up to no good. "You always were my favorite amongst the twelve of you — the one in whom I took root."

"Or just the last one standing." Bellamy's response was so flippant that Ffion imagined her brow furrowed in annoyance, full lips pursed as she considered her next move, when Marin hissed in sudden pain.

Shimmering liquid soaked his thigh, causing him to falter a step. He ignored his daughter's clean cut, sniffing the air as if he might smell her in the silent winds. Marin's eyes widened as Bellamy slid the razored edge of her stiletto across the width of his abdomen. They were black as pitch when Ffion met his stare until she struck again, leaving a slash of thick, wet gold that stretched the length of his arm.

All at once, Marin's façade evaporated, along with his composure. Fury took over as he bared the fangs Ffion had always known were there. Concealed by an illusory mask of unearthly allure was a devil who'd been hiding in plain sight. He lunged in vain for Bellamy, grappling at the air, only to catch her by the cape. She shrugged the sift-laden shroud from her shoulders before slipping out of reach, her gown trailing her in a billowing cloud of gossamer.

Marin was quick as a viper, his fingers tipped with pitch-dark claws. His wings spread at his back, propelling him forward after his daughter, though he remained grounded. Ffion made for Marin then, just as his talons sank deep into the sun-kissed flesh of Bellamy's shoulder, wrenching her to the garden floor and shredding her finery into strips of fine, tattered gauze.

Evading the heir, Marin skirted around the late King Tolliver's deadly roses, soaking them with his blood. "How fitting," he chided. "This was where I learned that your father would one day rule. And here again, I saw the same derangement in him as I now see in you." Cursing in pain, he clutched his belly, continuing his manic diatribe. "You may be one of two sons, but it's within you that I see Tolliver reflected most absolutely! His nature devoured him in the end, a frenzied, tortured man. I believe his queen even called him feral. This is where he tried to kill me, too."

He could have been lying, but Ffion didn't think so. His confessions reeked of desperation, sharpened to sting and wielded for maximum damage, but to no avail.

If his father was feral, then Ffion was a ruthless beast, though he'd never let Marin see what he'd made him. Not fully. "Now it will serve as a monument adorned in petals and thorns."

The prince rushed him. He was faster, more powerful, with a kingdom ready to answer to him should he find himself worthy. He didn't expect Marin's death to break his curse, but it would bring him some semblance of *conciliation*.

Ducking Ffion's blow, the fairy spread his nearly translucent wings. They were massive and hideous, a tapestry of thin onyx seams throbbing under their weight. Marin was everything sinister in the world, and

Ffion was more than willing to risk his life for his foe's to cease.

Ffion dropped to his knees, skidding over the earth as Bellamy rose to her feet, challenging her father's menacing presence. They had only a moment, a blink, to make him answer for his sins against them and all of humankind, or he would take flight, and they might never be given this chance again.

Marin's wings agitated the sky with languid beats, the ground shuddering from the effort, but whether by chance or by fate, it made no difference. Ffion whipped his sling from his waist, its cords a balm to his calloused hands as he stood in one quick motion.

If the demon could have flown, he would've, but he'd remembered too late what the hysterics of King Tolliver had done when he'd caged Dufoise in iron. Ffion had never tested the theory posed within the legends — there'd been no need. But it seemed his father had saved him from the agony of a chase.

Marin would have to have realized he was crippling himself by entering through the palace gates, and his arrogance would damn him for a thousand lifetimes.

A knowing glance passed between Ffion and Bellamy as he braced his weapon, clenching one end in each fist before positioning himself behind Marin's quieting wings. He made his move with unmatched haste, and the fairy stiffened when Ffion looped his sling over his head, securing it beneath his jaw. He wheezed against the pressure crushing his windpipe, and in less than a breath, Bellamy yanked a long iron spike from the garden bed beside her. The heir clamped down on his sling, tightening the cord around Marin's neck as Bellamy plunged her stake into the hollow of her father's throat.

Her aim was true, sending Marin's darkness seeping from his pores like a poisonous vapor. The color was fading from his features when Bellamy jerked his head back by his silken hair. Infinite black stared back at her, his body slumping against Ffion's chest.

He was dead, and Ffion noticed a change instantaneously when Marin collapsed in his arms. The earth seemed to exhale, but the blight he'd seeded was enduring, groaning in some unknown, forsaken place. Still, the ground shuddered.

"I am nothing like you," Bellamy spat, loosening her grip. Marin's chin fell to his collar, and she jerked the spike from his neck before letting it clatter against the cobbled stone.

She wasn't like him. If there was anything Ffion knew with any certainty after that night, it was that he had grievously misjudged her. He wondered if the torment in her gaze was as fathomless as the scope of his own trauma, all the while considering how desperately he would regret it if she left and he never saw her again.

Bellamy retreated several steps, a small, errant sob escaping from somewhere deep within her. She covered her mouth with a gloved hand, staring at her father as Ffion hoisted Marin's lifeless body over his shoulder.

He wanted to go to her, but time was not on their side, nor presence of mind for the heir. Eventide cast a thick indigo shadow over Calaise, and hours remained before it would surrender to a soft sunrise glow. Ffion's affliction had not yet claimed him, but if his tenuous authority over himself slipped with Bellamy so near, there would be no saving her.

At his pixie's back, a paver cracked where she'd dropped her stiletto. Marin's blood colored the once-silver blade and suffused the brick beneath it where a winter rose sprouted. One and then another — everywhere his essence splattered upon the earth. Bellamy retrieved her blade, turning it over the sheer mesh covering her arms. She wiped it clean before sliding it back into its sheath at her thigh.

Her hands were trembling. Ffion would see to her every injury if she let him when he returned. If she remained.

"The palace halls will be empty with my mother's ball coming to a close. Return to your chambers and request a fire for your hearth."

Bellamy didn't balk at his directives, nodding as they watched more gilded roses bloom at Ffion's feet, where Marin's vitality drained from his wounds.

"Burn the dress."

The prince instantly regretted his words, absently studying her statuesque silhouette and how the gown flawlessly accentuated her curves, now gold-stained. Ffion had refused to marvel at her beauty before, but now, he would hate himself if he denied himself such a gift. She would likely be gone when he returned.

"It isn't safe for you to come with me," he continued. His voice was rough, even to his own ears. He was tempting fate with every heartbeat but couldn't bring himself to leave, with Bellamy meeting his gaze as she was. She looked away, her eyes glistening under a sliver of beaming crescent moon.

The pixie opened her mouth, a sentence forming on her tongue before she stopped. She straightened as she caught a petal-pink lip between her teeth. "Feed him to the wolves," she breathed.

So that's what he did.

Chapter Fourteen

Gierson spied Melis from where he stood upon a secluded balcony just outside his mother's celebration, grateful for the reprieve. The festivities were excessive as ever, but this one, mercifully, was coming to an early close.

Blessed decorum. While propriety was often an odious chore, it served everyone well tonight.

Once Ffion had made his grand exit, many guests accepted his departure as a polite suggestion to follow his example. Palace courtiers remained, but otherwise, the hall was clearing quite nicely.

It didn't surprise the spare when Bellamy excused herself. She was not his, no matter how diverting her presence was. Gierson had been immediately enamored with the woman. She was different than his typical conquests, making her more desirable than most, and watching her depart, undoubtedly to track his brother, frustrated him more than it ought. The creature was off-limits and arresting beyond compare.

There was no harm in allowing his mind to wander after her if he himself could not.

But then there was Melis.

The spare made his farewells, as was expected of His Majesty, making quick work of the protocol. He would go to the lady knight, knowing well that she would never understand. She didn't need to.

There had always been a chance Ffion would return to Calaise, though Gierson had thought him dead or thoroughly mad. If anyone had seen him in those early days of their so-called curse, they would've feared him, as they should. And when the fairy, Marin, had dared to show his face earlier, the tension had been palpable, elevating long-forgotten memories to the fore.

But Gierson couldn't bring himself to care. He remembered what Marin had done, the fates he'd wished upon them both, and was nothing if not better for it. He was, in a word, unphased. Indeed, he'd pitied Ffion for the ways in which the malediction affected him, even as he was equally grateful to have avoided the same fortune. In time, however, his sympathy had turned to ire.

It was largely their mother's doing, no doubt. She had her favorite son, as had the late king, and it had driven a wedge between the brothers. Gierson didn't exactly fault Ffion for his susceptibility to Marin's ill-wish, but it did give him cause to doubt the heir's ability to lead Calaise successfully — an apprehension ardently nurtured by his mother.

He couldn't help it, really — not after watching His Majesty spiral into hysteria before his eyes. The spare understood why Ffion had run away all those years ago but had not found it within himself to forgive him.

Besides, their father surely would have seen his eldest son unfit for the throne if he'd stayed.

So, Gierson played heir in his brother's stead, and the world was the better for it, though the whole charade had been nothing shy of tedious. Certainly, then, the perks he'd enjoyed as a result of his title, real or otherwise, were well deserved. But in the end, he didn't care if anybody else agreed with his reasoning.

Gierson knew he would find Melis under the beech trees near the western wall. She didn't look his way, her porcelain skin glowing under a silvery-blue moon.

"You're angry." The spare advanced toward her, she the striking dame of His Majesty's royal guard, though tonight she was without her armor. He studied her silhouette, appreciating the thin linen of her crisp white blouse and the way her trousers clung to her curves.

"I'm not."

Concise as ever, and full of lies. Melis watched Gierson, tipping her chin toward him. Glossy onyx tresses fell over her shoulders, and the prince closed the distance between them, coiling a lock of her hair around his index finger. She retreated a step, and Gierson's hand dropped to his side.

He didn't hide his smile when she moved away, chuckling to himself even if no part of him found her antics amusing. "You are. Did you think this day would never come?" he demanded, and she turned to meet his gaze. There was no humor in his words, only irritation when Melis clenched her teeth.

A sniff of disdain escaped from the woman in response, her mouth opening and closing without a word.

"There are expectations, Mel — "

"*Ffion* is king," Melis snapped, moving for him as if she might dare to strike him. Instead, Gierson took her hand in his.

"He is." He leaned toward her, tracing the length of her neck with his nose before pressing his lips to the hollow beneath her ear. "That is why *I* am *here*."

Melis' breath caught, and she rolled her head to one side, allowing him better access, which he took without hesitation. "I came here to talk," she uttered. "Nothing more."

Lies.

Gierson knew the beautiful dame well, and if there was anything he believed with certainty, it was that she wanted him. Nothing serious, nothing real. But she always needed more.

The arrangement suited them well, as they'd both readily acknowledged the truth. There *were* expectations. And until now, Melis had never seemed bothered by any of them.

"Do you want me to stop?" The spare paused, his hungry, impatient gaze finding hers once more.

Melis ran her fingertips down his torso over the buttons of his shirt. He'd abandoned most of the finery he wore for the night's affair, but every stitch that remained was too much.

"*No.*"

Gierson chuckled again, this time because he'd been sure she wouldn't refuse him. She studied him in that way of hers — half desirous, half aggravated by her own weakness for their encounters. He was sure she felt no shame, not when she sought his company more often even than he, though she declared her indifference toward him in every other regard.

He didn't mind in the least. It was much easier that way, where both were free to explore whatever they wished without jealousy overshadowing their time together. He loved to look at her but did not love her, and she would never love him. Each had their secrets, which neither cared enough to learn, and neither did they make any fuss about their dalliances.

It was simple and would not last.

Melis loosed Gierson's shirt from his pants with eager hands when the earth beneath them seemed to gasp. The knight staggered backward, and Gierson caught her by the wrist before she lost her balance entirely.

Then he felt it, deep in his bones — in the same innate manner blood found its course through veins, in the way lungs filled themselves instinctively with air. It was subtle but unmistakable after the initial swell surged underfoot.

When Gierson had observed Marin's presence within the mighty walls of Dufoise, there was not a moment that he'd believed Ffion could resist the hunt. Such endeavors never interested him. He'd resolved to leave them to themselves, knowing the spectacle would cease one way or another.

This was it, he supposed.

In Calaise, rain nourished the lands in plenty, and in the cold winter months, snow, but the dormant roots that made Gierson's home so lovely and vibrant with color were being roused by something they seemingly craved.

Ffion had told his people the legend of winter roses less than an hour before Gierson had abandoned his feast. His twin's ramblings had plainly been intended to distract and inform, and his words were true.

For his part, Marin had remained on the premises. Gierson had sensed him every bit as well as his brother would have.

And so did Bellamy.

Melis steadied herself, gaping at the anomaly occurring at the western perimeter. "What is this?"

Beyond the copse of beeches standing high above them, vines of green tore through the earth along the palace wall. Like a deafening crack of thunder, brambles shot from the ground, wild and violent in their ascent. Blooms of rich cerulean tipped in gold sprouted from the stems, climbing up and around late King Tolliver's iron fortification.

Moonlight glinted off gilded petals and leaves, and Melis inhaled sharply. "Winter roses," she whispered, touching her fingers to her lips as if she didn't believe her own words.

It was no coincidence that the roses were flowering on the night Marin ventured through the gates of Dufoise. His blood would have fed them, and so long as they remained, through them, so would he.

"You waited too long." Melis turned her back on Gierson, who watched with utter fascination as the flora spread like wicked tentacles.

She wasn't wrong. But the crown belonged to his brother and always had, no matter how Gierson felt about it. She'd pushed and schemed alongside Helena for the last couple of years, angling for his ascension in Ffion's absence, but to what end? There was always a chance his brother would return, and what would the people say when there were again two of them?

The spare was glad to have Ffion home in any case, despite his misgivings. Let him see what the weight of his birthright demanded. He was weary of assuming both roles.

As for Melis, she would return to the palace, and there, she would seek him again. It never took her long to recover from their disagreements.

Such was their cycle.

* * * *

Rivulets of gold fell from the tips of Marin's wings as Ffion carried his corpse deep into a thicket of oak trees. He realized belatedly that they would leave a path—one of rare blooms—but it was of no consequence. Nothing identifiable would remain of the demon by the time anyone noticed.

Ffion listened intently to the haunting night song of a pack of gray wolves as he trekked further from Dufoise. With Bellamy at the palace, the farther, the better. He followed their cries, tracking them through the forest until their yellow eyes stared back at him like glowing embers under a cloak of eventide.

Wolves never hid from the heir. They were kindred somehow, a fortunate consequence of the beastly thing he became those years ago. One by one, the wolves emerged from behind lush woodland vegetation, advancing upon Ffion.

Maybe they understood that he could shred them apart. That, or the creatures did not feel threatened at all. Either way, they'd never made a move against him, and tonight, he came bearing a hearty offering.

His pixie had wanted her father fed to the wolves, so he would be. The heir hadn't thought much about how life would look once Marin was dead, but never had he considered that it might happen so effortlessly. The fairy was ancient and had grown stronger with age.

And yet...

Ffion felt no change within himself but hadn't exactly expected to, even if he had hoped. It was no small feat that he'd endured the night without his affliction taking hold, though the urge had never left him. The harsh Calaisean terrain did him no favors where control was concerned, with the pressure of Marin's weight heavy on his shoulders as the heir navigated banks and slopes without relying on one of few perks offered of his curse.

The wolves greeted him, circling around him with predatory grace and Ffion treasured these moments with them, regardless of their oddity. They helped maintain the delicate balance demanded by nature and didn't hide what they were. Neither did they acknowledge others' fears, existing intuitively in a pack that protected one another as family. Many would see them as villains, but the prince was awestruck by their sovereignty.

Marin fell with a thud into the dirt at their feet. It was strange to see the perpetrator of Ffion's dreadful purgatory laid prostrate before the most beautiful of beasts. The irony was not lost on him, remembering how Marin had mocked the creatures only a short while earlier. He fancied himself a serpent, so he was trampled like any venomous, slithering thing deserved to be.

There were times when Ffion didn't quite recognize what he'd become, despite the years that had passed since Marin's revelation of himself to the Calaisean princes. He should've looked away as the wolves gathered. Instead, the prince watched them rip the fairy apart without mercy. It was everything he'd earned, and still not enough.

Hours passed, and the prince had not torn his gaze from that place. Some part of him couldn't reconcile how someone so powerful and wretched could be wiped from the earth that swiftly, even when all that remained were stripped bones and bits of wing that even vultures could not stomach.

Ffion was still himself, though night had not withdrawn. No longer did his heart pulse within his skull, and he did not feel the unrelenting groans of his beast demanding to roam under a waning moon. Sunrise would arrive in due measure with a pristine new day primed to spread over Calaise, and his absence from Dufoise would be noted when it did.

Ffion assumed it was more of the vile birds that had scavenged what remained of Marin's carcass only to realize, instead, that what he sensed was more pixies. He recoiled at the rhythmic beat of their approach, his body responding instinctually.

More than one, the prince noted, their flight unhindered by iron as Marin's was. They wanted to be heard, else they would've come on foot, avoiding the sound of pre-dawn winds lashing their wings as they fought against nature's will. A small mercy, that.

One shadowed form landed in the branches overhead, while two more hovered above where Ffion stood, resting casually against the tree at his back.

"I was expecting more," said the first pixie, her voice melodic.

"Already, we have something in common," Ffion called to the trio. "Join me here where we can better acquaint ourselves. I'm in want of new companions, as this one seems to have expired." Gesturing to the heap of bones before him, he prowled toward where the devil that once was Marin lay.

A path of winter roses had burgeoned, and soon, there would be more, for doubtless Ffion would see the pixies into an earthen grave alongside Marin. Ffion nudged the dead fairy's remains with the toe of his boot, bringing forth a sickening rattle of bone met with bone. "I hope he wasn't a friend of yours," the prince remarked, chewing his lip with mock sincerity. All the while, his muscles yearned to greet the threats suspended beneath the clouds.

"No, no," the second pixie trilled, another female by the sound of her voice, joined by a male, who was the one perched within the towering oak. It wasn't entirely rare to spot a grouping of this sort, but their partnerships never lasted, which came as no surprise when fairies thrived on deception and savagery.

"By now, you understand that our kind are solitary beings. This one will not be missed after the chaos he fostered," spat the male. "However, I believe you're familiar with the half-breed we sent after him. It grieves us to disappoint her, as you might expect, but as it turns out, we cannot let her live." He leaped from his perch without warning, gliding with the breeze rather than against it. The females followed suit, flanking him as they made toward the palace.

Blissful agony tore through Ffion's limbs and chest. His frame shuddered as he gave into the bloodlust that seared his core, wrenching his body and altering it into a deadly weapon. The pain only refined him, purifying his irrepressible strength. It was everything he feared and craved at once and an impossible force that no one should ever own.

Ffion would not beat the pixies to Bellamy with the winds flowing in their favor as they were, but their wings would be of no benefit within the iron walls of Dufoise. He would not be far behind.

Nothing would prevent him from reaching Bellamy. He pushed his muscles to their limits, hurtling through the woodlands with an urgency he'd never known. Ffion's thoughts were murderous, despite his garments already soaked with one demon's essence. Soon, the palace grounds would be painted gold, regardless of the tainted flora that would bud once he showed the fairies their grievous error.

Few knew that the lore surrounding pixies was true, and for Bellamy's sake, as a half-blood, he would take that secret to his grave. Centuries came and went, but musings of her pixie brethren's depravity ever endured.

No longer.

An ocean of starlight cast a dim glow over the manicured lawn just outside the mighty walls of Dufoise, where Ffion's senses were overwhelmed by a familiar fetor. What most would consider lovely was, to the prince, more foul than the nauseating rot of a long abandoned carcass.

Before him, his father's towering fortification was alive, covered with gilded roses. Despite watching Marin's corpse be consumed by the wilds, Ffion could hear his laughter echoing straight from the depths of Hades. Each of his kind deserved that same fate, and this was the night the prince came to accept his damnable instincts as a blessing.

Ffion approached King Tolliver's iron gates, enveloped in luminescent blooms the color of deadly, fathomless waters. Thorned vines snaked around its bars, filling the vacant spaces so only winking fragments of light shone through from the palace lamps yet lighted from hours earlier. The pixies were effectively trapped once they'd ventured over the walls.

So was Bellamy.

They were not far ahead, though they had breached the fence before his arrival. Opposite the wall, they would not waste a moment, sure to find Bellamy by her unique scent alone. Ffion was out of his mind, blind with fury in his desperation to get to her first, yet his head had never been so clear. His body was rigid, prepared for the latticework of brambles to slice his flesh when he tore them down.

But the stems recoiled as the prince reached out, and Marin's laughter ceased.

Chapter Fifteen

Any attempt to sleep would've been a fool's errand. Bellamy was unsettled despite the small fire Selah had kindled in her chambers. She was safe. She was whole — mostly, at least. And, at long last, she'd won what felt like a never-ending war, stood alongside her flame-haired prince as they'd tag-teamed Marin into his hell-bound eternity.

Yet, her attendant's strange eyes betrayed her concern as she cleaned the flesh wounds branding Bellamy's shoulder, and the halfling worked to ignore Selah's unease, though she felt it, too.

It was all too easy.

Marin was the villain in Bellamy's every nightmare, and suddenly, he was gone. It should've been a victory, but his presence seemed only to multiply.

She'd not thought of the prince as anything more than a temporary ally until these last few days, but Bellamy could scarcely think of much else. It sickened her to think of him alone in the woods, bearing the burden of her father. Nothing would harm him, but it was the torment in his darkened gaze that pained her to leave him to himself. Private thoughts were often darker and more perilous than any tangible threats seeking to lay waste to a person's soul.

Her father was dead, and the future was hers, but Bellamy couldn't bring herself to trust any of it. Leaving before Ffion could crumble her resolve any further was surely the wisest course. She was free, after all. She'd never wanted anything more than to live out her days in solitude.

Selah hummed softly as she carefully plucked the pins from Bellamy's hair. Her gentle melody calmed the pixie's nerves, but her mind could not shake the sight of Ffion disappearing into the night with Marin slung over his broad frame.

With all the hairpins pulled, Selah continued her ministrations, brushing Bellamy's long tresses, the boar bristles massaging her scalp as she did. Without a word uttered, so much was said in that quiet place they shared. There was no judgment in Selah's study, only a ghost of what Bellamy believed to be the woman's private sorrow.

She placed a hand atop Bellamy's, conveying her understanding, and all the pixie could do was wonder what had driven her new friend to seek employment at the royal estate.

A friend, she realized.

Bellamy had not had many in her life. There were the boys she'd come to love during the years she'd spent in the sift mines, the first and only souls who had ever returned her affection, and then there had been none until Ffion and now Selah.

The maid scrunched her nose, gently squeezing Bellamy's fingers before rising from the cushioned stool beside her. She'd dreaded the moment when Selah would leave her with her wretched thoughts. Even in the silence, her companionship was a godsend.

With the pixie's gown slung heavily over her arm, Selah moved toward the hearth, tossing the garment into the flames and watching for a moment as it sizzled away. Bellamy hadn't had to explain a thing, watching with gratitude as the woman had managed all of her needs without an ounce of direction given. She smiled warmly, as if to assure her halfling charge that everything would be all right, shutting the door behind her as she left.

Neither her garish accommodations nor the plush, cloud-like duvet atop Bellamy's bed were enough to tempt her into slumber when eventide meant only distress for the prince. She understood why he'd told her to return to the palace, but never should she have obliged. He was protecting her from his curse, though she would never think of it as such.

A gift or an asset, perhaps, but never a curse. One so guiltless, honorable, and attentive could never embody something that vile. Ffion was all those things and had assumed her quandary without a second thought.

Deep down, she knew that had her pursuits not aligned with his, she'd have been subject to a fate worse than death, but he'd helped her nonetheless. Once, the prince had despised Bellamy, and still, he could not watch her meet the destruction Marin would have perpetrated upon her. She owed him the same kindness even as her idleness was driving her to distraction.

They'd arrived in Calaise with little more than the clothes on their backs, and those had probably been burned the moment Bellamy had peeled them from her body. Robed in embroidered silk overtop an equally elegant nightshift, she considered sneaking off to Ffion's chambers to abscond with a pair of breeches when a shadow obscured the soft glow cast over the floor from outside. It was gone just as quickly, but the hairs on her arms had already risen.

Stupidly, Bellamy assumed the iron walls surrounding the premises would prevent further encounters with more of her immoral brethren. She'd never trusted their word declaring they'd no longer pursue her following Marin's death, but part of her had hoped they'd grant her a slight reprieve once she'd followed through on her part of the bargain.

But pixies delighted in their manipulations. Bellamy was grateful to have tasted freedom during those months the fairies had given her to hunt her father, brief as they were.

Bellamy had not stopped trembling since plunging that iron stake into her father's throat, the horrid sound of him choking fresh in her mind. She'd killed him. *They'd* killed him, rather, and she didn't feel the slightest bit of remorse. She wondered how Ffion could think himself a beast, but perhaps her lack of regret made her one, too.

Retrieving her stiletto from the hand mirror on her vanity, she moved silently toward the window. The stone was cold under her bare feet, much like the silver blade in her palm.

Thin, talon-like nails raked over the glass pane, and the halfling's blood turned to ice. It wasn't fear exactly, even if she was acutely aware of how unlikely she was to see a new dawn. Moonlight filtered through a veined wing, giving it a yellow tint that made it somehow more disturbing. Those wings were far more menacing than what was seen by the naked eye for any unfortunate enough to see them.

It was a female, judging by the silhouette of the dark form opposite her. The fairy hissed something through the pane, hovering high above the ground as it watched her. She could run or plead for her life, but that was not her way. Bellamy would sooner die than pander to any pixie's intimidation, and there'd be no peace unless she faced the threat.

The creature would find her regardless, so where better to accept its challenge than precisely where she was? With any luck, Ffion would return to finish the demon off before it could flee. Until then, Bellamy would throw every bit of wrath she felt into defeating it.

She cursed the tremors coursing through her limbs as she reached for the window, willing herself to breathe before inviting the embodiment of hell into her quarters. Steeling herself, she clutched her stiletto – the only thing Marin had ever given her. Once, she'd cherished it, but that was all far behind her, and she'd not forgotten the lifetime of disappointment that followed.

Had he considered that she might use it against him one day? Or that it would stir within her a ruthlessness nearly as inhuman as him? She would raise Marin's deadly gift against any pixie she lived to challenge and become as merciless as her father. In the name of retribution for his evils and the atrocities sewn by every other pixie to walk these lands, the halfling would give all she had to see them fall.

Bellamy opened the window, the invisible breeze filling her lungs with a vow that it would all be over soon. Soft winds rustled her hair as she squared her shoulders.

Outside, the fairy hovered, watching. Its eyes reflected the candlelight illuminating Bellamy's chambers, the most profound depiction of depravity she'd seen, perhaps the last.

Every muscle in her body tensed, awaiting the pixie's attack. Instead, it remained there, outside the palace in wait—just another game meant to disorient her. The creature hissed something her way when, behind Bellamy, the door to her room burst open with a jarring thud. She glanced over her shoulder to see a male pixie standing in the archway, the oak door swinging uselessly on its hinges with a pitiful creak.

The halfling spared one more look toward the window, where she saw the first fairy nimbly climbing over the sill, her wings tucked neatly away as she gained entry. A third shadow lingered behind her, another female whose wings beat quietly, undulating where the first had been just outside. She narrowed her gaze on Bellamy with a raised brow, calmly observing the other pixies, male and female, closing in on the halfling from both sides.

"What will you do?" asked the third fairy. Her voice trilled through Bellamy's consciousness, a song of death and malice, camouflaged by the bewitching lure only a being so foul could wield. It was a contemptible gift, a weapon the halfling kept locked away—one of the many things she loathed about herself and her heritage.

Bellamy didn't dignify the female with a response, only a tilt of her head as she bit her lip, considering her options. She would not show fear, but they knew they had her.

The first pixie moved slowly closer, step by step, prowling like a jackal. "You did us a favor when you killed your father, but his sins remain in you." Her words dripped with disdain even as they were cloaked in the honeyed sweetness tainting every utterance from their mouths.

"I assumed as much." Bellamy sighed, her display of resignation only partially for show. She would act only when no other choice was given. They would fatigue her with their manipulations and then wear her down physically before allowing her to die. It wouldn't be quick, but dreadfully tedious and prolonged for their enjoyment.

It would have also been so for Bellamy's eleven siblings, of whom she was the last, to her knowledge.

The male fairy's lips twisted into a cruel taunt, but his sneer quickly faded into shock as his accomplice cried out into the night.

"He's here," the female circling Bellamy said, tearing her attention from their unified pursuit.

Ffion.

Chapter Sixteen

Bellamy felt his presence, and all at once, it gave her hope.

The pixie before her blanched as she witnessed the third plummet from the sky when a stone, smooth as granite, landed at her feet.

Bellamy utilized the distraction, throwing herself toward the first fairy and burying her stiletto into its abdomen. The demon gasped, attempting to regain purchase while grappling to remove the blade from her stomach. Bellamy forced her toward the open window at her back, the pixie's fangs now covered in gilded blood, before spitting more at the floor.

As the fairy stumbled backward, Bellamy pressed on, gripping the steel she'd used against her father in those dark hours, her knuckles coated in gold for the second time that night. Despite the male advancing upon her from behind, Bellamy didn't ease her assault, instead twisting her stiletto as she plunged it deeper.

The pixie howled in agony, clawing at the air around her when she realized what Bellamy had done. Apparent disgust contorted her opponent's unearthly features, her face crumpling as she inhaled sharply, wheezing when Bellamy withdrew her blade. She followed up with a heel to the belly, sending the fairy's small frame toppling over the sill behind her.

Bellamy couldn't afford to watch the monster fall, but she heard a nauseating crack that confirmed her demise. And Ffion was there, somewhere below her window. Bellamy felt his presence, a merciless storm of ferocity and composure ever at war.

She already owed him her life after his assistance with her father, and now again after he'd knocked the third fairy from the air, where she'd awaited her turn at Bellamy. Once, she'd thought his sling pointless in light of his incomparable strength, but he knew his enemies well.

"Now, this will be fun," the remaining pixie crooned. His warm, inviting voice unnerved Bellamy as Marin's had. He was no more than a step away, toying with his prey, and her heart thundered, beating so wildly that her head spun.

Bellamy felt his nearness, his sinewy form rigid as he reached for her. Not fingers but claws would close around her neck if she didn't move, and this one would want to savor her last moments.

"He'll kill you, you know." Bellamy's words were even despite her vision darkening around the edges.

"Unless I leave now," the fairy concluded, sending a chill through Bellamy. "It's kind of you to warn me, but I doubt it."

A single talon brushed her cheek from behind, the man closing the distance between them. He could slice her throat with little effort, and she feared she'd waited too long. Bellamy leaned into him, her back to his chest, and carefully raised her hand to her face. Her fingers gently touched the claw resting upon her cheek, demanding her muscles to relax. She was only half wicked, but it proved helpful from time to time.

Like her infernal kin, Bellamy relished a game.

"We both know that beast outside will end me the first chance he gets now that my father is dead," the halfing purred, her hand covering the fairy's. One wrong move, and it would tear her throat open. "I could help you."

He laughed. "*No*."

He grabbed the elbow of her opposite arm and wrenched it toward himself. Bellamy yelped in pain from the pressure of his claws digging into her bare flesh. Her stiletto clattered to the floor, drawing another laugh from the pixie. Tightening her grip on his hand at her face, she sank her teeth into his leathery flesh until he shoved her away. But Bellamy clenched her jaw, teeth tearing the muscle in his hand as she stumbled forward. His claw scraped the hollow of her cheek before she moved out of reach, running for the stool tucked beneath her vanity.

Bellamy took the chair by one of its four legs and shattered it against the towering column of her bedpost. The leg splintered free, but the male was already on her. He groaned with a stream of gold pouring from the hand she'd bitten. It had allowed her to escape, but he was much too quick.

The pixie threw Bellamy to the ground, her spine slamming into the stone. Her vision went utterly black for a breath, only to remain blurry, flickering in and out like the flames dancing atop the sconces on her walls.

His body was heavy over hers, his wings draped to either side of where she lay pinned beneath him. Bellamy clutched the broken stool leg in her palm, though it would do her no good. He was far stronger than she, and the halfling could hardly see anything but depthless black eyes. She turned her face from his, the stone under her temple rough and cold when she saw her blade inches away.

The fairy followed her gaze, striking her face with his knuckles before batting Bellamy's stiletto across the room. Her cheekbone stung, but she'd endured far worse when she worked the sift mines, each time she dared to shelter the seven who'd become her lifeline and brothers.

But her opponent's hold slipped from her forearm when he swiped the blade away, affording her the only chance she'd likely get. In one quick motion, she sliced the splintered end of her makeshift weapon through one of his wings, and he bellowed — a horrific cry of agony. His other wing slammed into her as he struggled to remove himself from Bellamy's strike, and the halfling rolled out from under him, crawling on her hands and knees, desperate to put space between them.

Bellamy pulled herself off the floor as the fairy yanked the wood from his shredded wing. His stare was murderous, even as shimmering blood pooled around him. He lunged, shoving her into the wall with his hand tightly gripped around her throat. She could barely breathe, the pain radiating through her lithe frame only motivating her more.

Light glinted in her periphery, and Bellamy grasped the flickering candle, searing the pixie's hand with the flame, before bringing her knee to his groin. He cursed, his hold on the halfling failing enough for her to free herself, though she'd nearly fainted from the crushing pressure upon her windpipe.

Bellamy slid to where her stiletto lay several paces away, snatching it from the stone. The fairy recovered just as quickly, his steps featherlight, but she sensed his approach and waited. He was near enough that she could hear his breath, and just when it caught, Bellamy turned as he prepared to thrust himself toward her. The halfling sank her blade into his thigh, removing it swiftly before he fell. He gasped, reaching for her with blind fury, his claws positioned directly in front of her heart.

Footsteps approached, drawing the pixie's attention toward the window, and Bellamy stabbed with all her might, slashing his neck. With a taloned hand, he clawed at his wound, the truth of his condition registering on his face.

Ffion appeared as Bellamy crawled backward, attempting in vain to avoid the fairy's unsteady mass as it fell on top of her. Ffion hurled the demon from her and dropped to his knees before her.

"I'm so sorry," he said, reaching for Bellamy. The prince carefully touched her, a guttural growl rumbling somewhere deep within him as his knuckle traced the tender bruise that had already formed where she'd been hit. His words were fierce despite the softness of his study as he looked her over.

Ffion's gentleness soothed every aching part of her.

Bellamy had not seen him in this state. He'd not yet recovered from his heightened form, but no part of her feared who he was. The heir was undoubtedly more defined. His muscles were larger, straining the linen tunic he wore, every bit of his powerful physique taut with pent-up energy. The halfling understood why her brethren dreaded him.

But to her, he was Ffion.

Together, they wrapped the remaining bodies, escaping by the same window through which the fairies had arrived and dragging them to the edge of the palace grounds. Never before had Bellamy seen anything like what awaited them there, with the iron fortifications of Dufoise entirely covered in winter roses.

She was weakened by their proximity but couldn't allow Ffion to dispose of the three pixies alone. "Let me help you."

"I won't be long," the heir assured her. The lifeless bodies lay on the grass, nourishing it all the more with their thick, gleaming blood. "I can't let you risk it."

Stood at the least conspicuous palace gate, the brambles shrank away from Ffion as he approached, and Bellamy's breath caught. Would that they might offer her the same decency…

She knew better.

Yet, risking the same scene she'd only just survived was the last thing she wished to do, and keeping near to the beast was certainly the best way to avoid a repeat. But Bellamy's stomach twirled as she eyed the poisonous wall, swallowing hard. "If I move quickly, perhaps…" Bellamy's words trailed. "There must be somewhere I can make it through the walls."

"We'll find a way, but for now, keep hidden until I return."

For once, she did what he asked of her, too affected by the loathsome vines to push him further. It felt like hours, with the prince coming and going through the roiling gate, disposing of the bodies one by one.

Then, at last, Ffion emerged from the trees outside the gate, having hidden away the evidence of their crimes. The pixie could barely make him out through the tangle of flora, but she felt him as she had before when they'd journeyed near to one another in search of Marin.

He'd abandoned his soiled tunic somewhere along the way, though his trousers gave his exploits away. They were stained gold, as was the lawn where he entered, but next to the rose laden walls, one would be hard-pressed to notice.

Ffion had returned to himself, too, with no remaining vestiges of his beast in his body, in his manner, though each fractured piece of him was beautiful.

"They're gone," said he, and Bellamy nodded, distracted by the tempest brewing behind his eyes.

They found her quarters in blessed silence, grateful that the manor had long since retired. Together, they would wipe away the evidence of all that had happened, even if the minor wounds on Bellamy's cheek betrayed the chaos they'd both endured.

Ffion opened the door, entering first to ensure their safety, and when Bellamy followed, she stifled a gasp.

Someone had come and gone, removing nearly every remnant of the eventide disturbance. But, despite the efforts, winter roses had begun to sprout through the fine cracks where their blood had spilled.

"*Selah*," Bellamy whispered. It had to have been she who'd quietly scrubbed away the horrors that had taken place. They were both strangers in that palace, Selah having only recently arrived herself. She couldn't know the depths of what set the maid apart, but whatever it was in Selah that made her so unique was beyond anything familiar to Bellamy.

Ffion thoroughly inspected her quarters, striding toward the closed window before turning to meet the halfling's stare. "You let them in. Why didn't you wait for me?" His voice was rough, brimming with resentment when he spoke after a deafening pause. "I would have helped you."

"They will come for me either way, whether here or later, when I'm on my own." Bellamy averted her eyes as she said the words, only to find herself searching for Ffion's once they'd fallen from her lips. She didn't want to be alone.

His gaze never strayed from her, and she saw the same desperation she felt looking back at her. The heir was as much a stranger inside those castle walls as Bellamy or Selah. And though she couldn't possibly know his mind, Bellamy hoped the intensity of his study mirrored the need she felt for him at that moment.

"Stay," she said. "Please, stay with me."

He nodded, silently agreeing to lie beside her, banishing the haunting images from her mind. The heir held her close, and dawn painted the sky as she finally drifted off to sleep.

Because with Ffion, every part of her was safe.

Chapter Seventeen

Ffion wandered the halls of Dufoise, rehashing the memories of Bellamy scrambling away from the trio of fairies the night before. His musings were masochistic and not the least bit helpful, for she'd not truly needed his aid, but he continued in his brooding nonetheless, with what-ifs plaguing his mind.

In the time he'd known her, his pixie had seemed untouchable. Like all otherworldly monsters, she was extraordinary, far from the sinful villain the prince once thought she might be. And though she was anything but frail, for a passing moment, she'd become so vulnerable that Ffion prepared to shred anyone who so much as looked at her sideways.

Whether unwittingly or not, the pixie within her drew him in, and Ffion was losing the fight. Waking with Bellamy in his arms had changed everything, making him painfully aware of the pieces of his soul he'd cordoned off for years. He was being reckless, and he couldn't bring himself to care.

Sleep hadn't pulled Ffion under until the sun began to rise and the beauty beside him had finally settled.

Nightmares.

Bellamy thrashed and whimpered through the lingering twilight, her body shuddering against him for hours. Once, he'd thought himself damaged beyond repair, but what would it mean to be so thoroughly despised? While Ffion understood loneliness and self-loathing, he'd not been rejected by his people as she had been.

The temper he'd seen as a cancer before seemed more justifiable each day as he became aware of all the atrocities committed by Bellamy's cruel relations. She deserved better than to live a life of fear. The same was true for all of Fayble, yet few knew of the dangers that stalked ignorant prey day and night for their own callous amusement. Humans were the fodder fueling fairies' mirth, and the cycle had persisted for long enough.

Brisk air rustled the burnished strands of his hair as he exited the palace, stepping onto the wall walk connecting the outer rooms of Chateau Dufoise. Sizable stone archways lined either side, trimming the bridge overlooking a quiet hamlet that lay between Calaise proper and Loch Apsarus.

He could almost pretend the palace grounds were not a veritable cage from where he stood.

Judging by the sun's high post in the sky above, it was nearly midday. Ffion had half expected to be met with cries of horror when their predicament was realized, making the silence that greeted him confounding.

Quiet footsteps drew Ffion's attention as Selah approached, clearing her throat. She curtsied before joining him, offering him a much-needed cup of coffee after his turbulent night, and Ffion inclined his head, grateful for her thoughtfulness. He savored the bitter brew, gazing out over the lands sprawling from the castle at their center toward the walls lining the perimeter in the distance, each crawling with the infernal winter roses.

It went without saying that Calaise was worth every drop of shimmering blood he had spilled, though he'd never envisioned being locked within the confines of Dufoise as an outcome of his crimes.

"Thank you." Ffion turned to meet the maid's eyes. She was lovely, if not a bit terrifying, due to her preternatural presence. But most of all, Selah was kind. "Whatever you wish, I will see that it's done."

Selah's lips parted as if she were about to speak before spreading into a modest smile as she waved him off. Still, he'd meant every word. Ffion wasn't sure how she'd done it or how she'd known, but the evidence of Bellamy's struggle in her chambers had vanished. Nothing he could do would be enough to repay the maid for preventing prying eyes from discovering realities best left unknown.

As if she'd read his thoughts, Selah squeezed Ffion's arm. Her aquamarine eyes were evidence enough of her unique origins, even as her pointed gaze conveyed the words her tongue could not. She didn't trust her surroundings — that much was clear. He saw a familiar sadness in her, not unlike the sort that haunted Bellamy and himself.

Selah bobbed her head before excusing herself as quickly as she'd arrived, her stride one of refined elegance that Ffion had seen before in those same beings of lore that seemed to find him no matter which corner of the continent he dwelled within.

He huffed, dismissing his absurdity. She was a simple maid and, God willing, nothing more.

Steel shrieked beyond a thicket not far from the woven vines left behind by Marin, followed by cheers that drew Ffion's immediate attention, his first thoughts of Gierson. Perhaps he'd misjudged his brother's apathy over the situation. And, if the spare was, indeed, already taking action against the threat coiled around the chateau's mighty gates, maybe their priorities weren't so different after all.

Ffion's body thrummed with energy despite the sleepless night as more cheers erupted opposite the copse of trees ahead of his arrival there. He moved through them, his steps growing more urgent with every clash and rasp of metal, and he reminded himself not to be foolish. It was easy to forget, to move like one who wasn't something *other*. It had not been an issue while he was away, but in Calaise, vigilance was essential.

It wasn't long before he came upon a handful of his father's guards taking part in various training exercises before a group of courtiers lazing upon the grass atop a mishmash of blankets. Their enthusiasm for the spectacle caught Ffion out, for not one seemed the least bit distracted by the jungle of winter rose vines at their backs.

Among those practicing was none other than Gierson, who displayed his mastery of the sword against Melis, much to the spectators' delight. Sunlight glinted off the dame's saber as she lunged toward the spare, his chainmail preventing the tip of Melis' blade from puncturing his sternum.

Their audience gasped as their perceived monarch was bested, but Gierson only laughed, batting her sword away. Stepping toward her, he tipped the knight's chin upward, gazing down at her with a wolfish grin. He behaved as though he hadn't noticed Ffion's arrival, his eyes trained on Melis as if no one else existed.

He chuckled, stepping away from her, and she gulped, her cheeks flushed from the encounter. Once, she'd been a close companion, but the friend Ffion had known wasn't one to fawn over anyone, much less either of the flame-haired heirs. It seemed that, too, had changed.

Ffion fumed. To anyone who didn't know better, Gierson was the incumbent king, betrothed to another, even as he shamelessly made advances toward a woman who was not meant for him. Never would Ffion see Bellamy married off to his brother, but neither would he have her publicly disregarded.

He clapped his hands slowly, drawing the attention of those present as he moved nearer. Whatever this idiocy was, it was nothing Ffion wanted his reign to be associated with now or ever. He couldn't stomach these deceptions much longer. His people were being lied to left and right, from the true identity of the rightful heir to the duplicity regarding their recent entrapment at Dufoise. Gierson's conduct with Melis also implicated the king as a philanderer—something Ffion was decidedly not.

Yet, it was *his* name under which every action, every lie occurred, and his twin appeared well at ease doing so. Try as he might to ignore it, his limbs twitched with a need to release the growing tension in his body. Would that his brother might not pay the price.

"A shame our Melis has already worn you out." Ffion sauntered across the turf with a cocky grin. "I had hoped to learn if your skills had improved, but alas."

Gierson quirked a brow. "I cannot recall the last time you joined us for training, brother," he teased, and the grass crunched beneath his boots as he moved to welcome him to the field. "I'd be fascinated to see what techniques you've adopted during your travels, though I'm aware the sword is not your favored weapon. Or is that simply an excuse?"

A challenge then, and more. He considered the knowledge Gierson had betrayed. Ffion's hands were dirty enough without severing limbs or flaying flesh unnecessarily, but his twin could not have known his distaste for swordplay without observation.

"I assure you, it is no excuse." Ffion's smile widened as he strode past a cluster of courtiers, nodding acknowledgments to several before finding himself before Gierson. "One does not need swords if he's quick. I wonder if you'd dare to find out what I mean."

"Are you proposing hand-to-hand?" A glint of intrigue brightened Gierson's eyes, and Ffion knew he had him. Neither would back down now.

"All's fair," Ffion clarified, and his brother grinned.

"All's fair," Gierson agreed.

Excitement rose amongst the gathered attendants, many of whom Ffion had watched in their foolery the night before, tripping over themselves to win favor with their king.

Only Gierson was not their king, and Ffion couldn't care less about etiquette or station. Still, it pleased him to be presented with the opportunity to show them a bit of himself.

Much to Ffion's amusement, Gierson took the first swing, drawing a collective gasp from the gathering. He was nothing if not predictable, which only served to build the true king's confidence. He feinted left, easily avoiding the spare's wild slash, his amusement growing when his twin scowled, groaning as he recovered from his missed attempt.

"You're more formidable than I might've expected," said Gierson, reclaiming his air of superiority in short order. "I can only imagine how much effort has gone into your training. You always did require more practice than I."

Ffion ignored his jab, circling him like a lion, determined not to rise to the bait. "My travels have been a bleak but constructive mentor, yes."

Gierson scoffed, lifting his chin. He matched his brother step for step, with neither willing to risk an embarrassing mistake. He was more disciplined than usual, but Ffion was well acquainted with pushing boundaries, and provoking the faux king was one of his greatest joys.

Maneuvering around his twin, Ffion forced him into position, ensuring he'd also battle the blinding sun suspended in the bright, cloudless sky.

Gierson quickly realized his disadvantage, eyes squinted against an invasive glare. "Who needs a mentor when you'd so readily cheat?"

Silence had served Ffion well. He watched, evaluating his impulsive counterpart, who quietly seethed as he did the same. Everything surrounding Gierson was darkness, and Ffion had always assumed the same to be true of himself. It required daily effort to suffocate the shadows—something it appeared for which his brother made no attempt.

Since they were young boys, their father had taught them to heed their instincts, and everything within Ffion had promptly recoiled from his brother. Suspicion had always prevailed, even as he'd hoped to keep him close and establish a friendship. But trust was far, with a spare who was brash — ever hasty in his daily life.

And while resentment doubtless colored Ffion's unannounced return to Calaise, Gierson was blatantly goading his brother, and he was in no mood for more games. He lunged forward, startling his brother with his speed.

Despite Gierson's agility, he was unprepared when Ffion caught him by the arm, twisting from before him as he hoisted the imposter king across his back. With his free hand, he braced his brother's shoulder, heaving Gierson's large body heels over head, flipping him to the ground in a tangle of limbs.

Fury sparked within his eyes when he landed with a thud, knocking the wind from him in one powerful burst. "I see you're as wild as ever," he wheezed, but Ffion wasn't through, his temper flaring anew. He took to the ground, pinning Gierson beneath his sprawling frame.

"I'm only giving Calaise the show they desire. Was it not your intent to distract them from their captivity here at Dufoise?"

"You're a savage fool!" Gierson spat, his face red with exertion. He fought back, bucking as he strained against his twin's hold.

At times, Ffion wondered if Gierson wasn't the better man. More capable. Wiser. *Fair.* But hearing an insult wielded to wound had him thinking otherwise.

Wild.
Feral.
Savage.

The list was long. Ffion had heard them all but never spoken by an ally.

They were like a pair of naughty children.

Bellamy arrived just in time to watch the lookalikes clash, each as eager to best the other with words as they were with their acts of combat.

If only she'd arrived sooner. She'd lain beside Ffion in the night, feeling his pulse hammering through to the morning hours, knowing he was at risk of becoming the version of himself he didn't trust. He'd stayed with her anyway, maintaining authority over his body, demanding compliance for her sake, and again, she'd done nothing for him in return.

Others who'd come to watch their sovereigns were utterly rapt, unable to look away as the men grappled with one another on the field. Despite their cordiality when first she'd arrived with Ffion in Calaise, what unfolded before the enthralled onlookers now was undeniably tense.

Even the royal guard could not peel their gazes from the glorified pissing match, and they were meant to *protect* both idiots.

The dame, Melis, also stood idly by from several yards away, her features a mask of bewilderment. Not one among them was prepared to act, and when Bellamy turned to the twins, she understood why. Doubtless, it was easy to confuse one for the other, but for her, the contrasts were like those of a waning moon competing against the vibrant, burning rays of a new dawn.

Ffion had taken control of their struggle for a second time, his knees on either side of Gierson, rooting his arms to the earth beneath them. He glanced toward

Bellamy as she prepared to pare him from his brother before someone realized he was so much more than what they knew him to be.

She issued a silent plea, jerking her head to the side in the hopes that he might yield, only to draw Gierson's attention as well. He flashed his teeth at her in a broad smile, only to be rewarded by Ffion's fist meeting his jaw.

The crowd cried out, but Bellamy couldn't hear a word of what they said. Whether concerned or thrilled by the unfolding drama, someone had struck the perceived king.

Bellamy ran to them as Ffion picked himself up, glowering at his brother as he rose to his feet. Gierson tested his jaw before propping himself onto his elbows, nostrils flaring with each intake of breath.

"How humiliating for you to see me this way, Lady Bellamy." Gierson shook his head, wincing as he massaged his injured jawbone. It was already discolored, and she could only imagine the impact of a punch from someone like Ffion.

"Think nothing of it," Bellamy replied, unsure of what to do next. But when she looked at Ffion, she knew she needed to do something, for he appeared on the brink of havoc.

"A hand, Gierson?" the true Gierson asked of his brother, who stared back at him as if he might hit him again.

Ffion obliged without a word, and though she couldn't explain it, some part of her wished he hadn't. She hadn't been certain what to make of his twin. He was charismatic and kind, but she did not care for Gierson's antics.

And even that was unfair, for Ffion had only just returned. Yet someone like him, who eagerly risked himself for everyone else, surely deserved what was rightfully his.

"Thank you, brother," Gierson said. Letting go of Ffion's hand, the spare picked bits of grass from the links of his chain mail. "Forgive me, milady, for I am in a state." He smiled shyly as his eyes met hers, and again, Bellamy understood why every woman who encountered the brothers could not help but to flush.

Remembering herself, she dipped low before him and then to Ffion beside him. "Who am I that you would ask my forgiveness for anything?"

Gierson took her fingers in his, drawing her closer. "You're my future bride. All deference is yours." He moved nearer, cupping her face with his free hand before gently kissing her lips. His mouth was soft against hers, and there was no one present who was not witnessing the presumptive heir stake his claim.

Including Ffion.

He said nothing as Bellamy pulled away from Gierson, with something murderous flashing through his gaze as he turned to leave the field.

She didn't wait to follow him, promptly excusing herself, though few seemed to care once the king's guard returned to the field, joining Gierson.

Bellamy felt his presence in the air around her when she searched for him in a copse of trees so high they might one day reach the stars. At the very least, they made for a breathtaking hideaway with a fragrant earthen aroma she wished to bottle all for herself.

It made sense that this was where Ffion sought solace. The woods would be more like home to him than gilded walls and mighty portraits of men and women who had long since given up their spirits. It was much the same for Bellamy. She'd been nomadic most of her life, always in search of her father.

Purpose. Family. The woodlands embraced her like she belonged, and in many ways, she did.

"Will you not speak with me?" Bellamy called out to Ffion. He was near. She could smell the salt on his flesh, along with those scars the heir wore as permanent memories of his kills. They were very much like perfume — an essence of savory traces left by the fairies he'd ended without mercy.

Even after she'd realized who he was when they met, she hadn't been able to resist his scent, though she wondered often if the prince had thought of killing her then.

"I need not justify anything to you," said Ffion, his sculpted features coming into view from before her. He stood with his arms crossed, leaning against a tree as if it may be the only thing he'd be willing to say.

"Of course not," Bellamy agreed, her ire growing. She stepped toward him, unafraid of a challenge "It's already bruising, and you think your people won't talk? You struck the king — "

"*He* is not their king!"

"Neither are you if you don't do something to change the present course! Whether by your awful mother's hand or Gierson's, now there is a wedding and a coronation to think of, *Ffion*. You cannot wait to take action if you desire the throne!"

The prince pushed off the trunk, prowling toward Bellamy. "*You* will need to choose, ma fée. You cannot fall for my brother while supporting me as the Calaisean king when he fancies *my* life for himself."

Bellamy slapped him, her palm stinging from where it landed upon his cheek, and Ffion captured her hand, his featherlight touch standing in stark contrast with the utter mania brewing behind his eyes.

Ffion watched Bellamy, his dark gaze finding hers as their breaths mingled in the small space separating them. Her legs felt foreign beneath her, betraying her body and will when the heir explored the swell of her hips with his fingertips, unraveling her sensibilities as unadulterated longing pumped through her veins.

"*Ffion.*"

He stilled, and Bellamy couldn't breathe. Never had she felt anything so pure, so intoxicating.

"You deserve to be free," Ffion's gruffed as the rise and fall of his chest moved in tandem with her own.

And then he was gone.

But Bellamy remained, fascinated by the surly beast who was leaving his own mark upon her heart. She couldn't make sense of any of it, could think of nothing else for the remainder of the day, which came and went in unremarkable fashion with no further word from the true king of Calaise.

Yet in the dusky, early morning hours, Ffion slipped into bed beside her, his scent ever changed from a night met with terrors she would never comprehend. There, he clung to her, and Bellamy settled into him as his heart found a steady rhythm against her.

He was bliss and agony at once, and for better or for worse, Bellamy had found her sense of freedom amid the chaos of her captivity within the gates of Dufoise.

And never could she have chosen better.

Chapter Eighteen

There was nothing truly unfamiliar about Ffion's predicament. The whole venture was somewhat expected, save for the size and fury of his prey and the outcome, but he had little worry about such things. A handful of pixies had left their marks over the years, leaving him scratched and maimed more than a few times, yet never had he succumbed to their wiles.

Until now, at any rate.

Bellamy was a different sort, or so he told himself. In her, he sensed goodness not unlike what he'd recognized at first in Petra. Each was blessed by their humanity, lending them a level of grace and decency to offset what he knew they viewed as a cursed piece of their souls.

Such notions broke his heart, for he understood the pain in despising fragments of his own being, and he didn't wish that upon anyone. That Bellamy could believe such things of herself made him crave retribution all the more. The woman was every bit as fierce as she was vulnerable, making her worthy, in his mind, of becoming queen.

He hadn't hesitated when he said as much for the first time, set upon by a kingdom's worth of people in the streets of Calaise when first they'd arrived, and he was just as sure now.

More, even.

And in his mind, in his heart, he believed his methods to be the only way forward — to shield her from the blight that was every pixie being. He'd been caught off guard before, finding her cornered and at the mercy of the vile creatures.

To know that her brethren were now actively hunting her in spite of her success against her father, and worse, had her trapped within the confines of Chateau Dufoise was utterly alarming.

Surely, they never intended to let her live a life of peace, whether she'd held up her side of the bargain or not. Their word meant little, with deception as familiar to them as breathing. Ffion could not allow such trickery to stand.

He'd made it without difficulty through an unguarded gate at the far end of the grounds, exiting through the twisted thorns and vines encasing the ramparts hemming in the estate. There was no sense in patrolling the wrought-iron railings, it seemed, for the winter roses were a sentry all their own, enveloping any brave souls who'd attempted to breach their walls.

Ffion had watched more than once as the shambling vines had entangled stalwart soldiers, brandishing axes, wielding fire, only to be overwhelmed by the creepers that were more serpentine and alive than they should've been.

Likewise, his brother was no help, eager as he was to entertain those who were trapped rather than find a solution. Socking him in the jaw had been equally useless, but it had made Ffion feel a bit better. All within Dufoise were well and truly captive, held at the whim of a departed madman who somehow yet managed to inflict his selfish games upon the residents, save for one.

The heir had no such restrictions, whether due to his birthright, his curse, or some unknown con from Marin that lingered on in his absence. He passed through the opening that emerged when the winter roses moved aside, easing away as if they feared him.

Rightfully so, for he was out for blood.

A pixie's scent was distinct, an odor that made his stomach turn with its sickly sweetness. It was the smell that had permeated the forests of Wylewoode, like a faint mix of apple and birch made more pervasive by the manic lawlessness of its former ruler, Queen Wendolyne.

He'd picked it up not far from the outskirts of Dufoise, following the path into the treeline and beyond to the edges of the surrounding kingdom. There was no telling how many remained in Calaise, nor how many he tracked, but any surviving population was too many.

Pulling the hood of his cloak over his russet hair, he attempted to blend in as he entered the dim, overcrowded tavern. Music thrummed from one corner, so dark he could not readily see the troubadour, while countless men drank their mead, shouting stories and lies to one another over the din. But mutterings of strange happenings dominated the conversation as the citizenry struggled to understand the isolation occurring within the kingdom's heart, seeing their beloved flame-haired twins into confinement when they'd only just begun their journey.

With any luck, he'd remain unrecognized, free to hunt the pixies he sensed amongst the fray. He moved toward the bar, keeping his head held low, avoiding the eyes of all his countrymen. He was tall and broad, noticeable under the most favorable of circumstances.

"Ale, please," he shouted to the bartender, who gave a curt nod as he reached for a tankard, filling it to the brim. Ffion dropped a handful of coins on the counter, taking a deep draft of the brew, though it did nothing to quell his agitation.

His quarry was near. Ffion inched his way down the line, slowly weaving through the gathering. There wasn't much that gave a pixie away — just an otherworldly allure accompanying their foul scent. A mop of blond hair stood a half-head above the others, and the heir prepared himself for confrontation, confident that the creature was his target.

He ditched his mug, reaching for the slender dagger hanging at his waist. Would that he had more privacy, but a tavern full of half-drunk laggards was better than failure. The beast dwelling within him was like a coiled spring, eager to strike as the prince drew closer to his mark.

Ffion slipped the dagger from its loop, fisting it within his hand from beneath his mantle. Never did he relish this obligation. It was a blight upon his soul, even as he knew without question its necessity for the sake of his kingdom, his people.

His queen.

A hand closed around his forearm, and Ffion rounded on his assailant, only to find himself face to face with Luc. He huffed, his heart pulsing a furious beat in his ears. "What are you doing here?"

"What are *you*?" Luc never minced words, nor did he readily act with the deference due to his sovereigns. That was something Ffion had always respected about the man. It's what had made them friends.

Ffion ignored his question, glancing over his shoulder to find that his quarry remained, decidedly unaware of the pixie hunter's presence. "I'm tending to some unfortunate duties. And yourself?"

Luc shrugged, adopting the same indifferent air he always seemed to wear. "I've been locked beyond the palace walls since the evening of the banquet. Felt pretty useless ever since. How'd you manage to escape?"

The truth was almost as fantastical as his otherworldly farce of a life, picking off creatures of lore before they could wreak any further havoc on the people of Calaise. But to say as much would see him branded a lunatic. "I can't remember," said Ffion at last, offering a shrug of his own.

"Ah." Luc smiled. "Probably for the best. Maybe you can show me the way back in, then. I'd love to get back to my duties."

Ffion scoffed, knowing fully well the game he was playing. He didn't blame him, for Luc had to be as curious as any of the townspeople over the enchanted state of Chateau Dufoise. Not one villager had entered the inner recesses from beyond the outer walls. There was no easy answer.

"If I find a way back, you'll be the first I welcome home alongside me." Ffion clapped him on the shoulder, doing his best to avoid notice. "I must be on my way now. Enjoy an ale on me in the meantime." He offered a handful of coins by way of departure, feeling like a brute for being so dismissive.

Luc merely grinned, accepting the gift with a nod. "I'll hold you to it, my friend."

Doubtless, he would.

They parted, and Ffion breathed a sigh of relief as his comrade sauntered away. Luc had let him off more easily than usual, ever eager to hold his feet to the flames when he knew he was onto something. Shaking off the encounter, the heir returned to the task at hand, only to find that the blond man had disappeared.

He was close, of that Ffion was certain, scenting the stench easily even amongst the body odor and filth trapped within the tavern. Following his nose, he wasn't surprised when he found that the pixie had made for the exit. The prince slipped through the door, grateful to leave the chaotic alehouse behind.

Tailing the creature was a relatively simple task made more challenging only by the distance he was forced to keep. The element of surprise was paramount if only to give Ffion a slight edge.

Slivers of moonlight cut through the trees, illuminating his path in fractured light that made keeping his footing a struggle as they moved farther through the woods. Felled trees interspersed with holes deceptively masked by brush nearly took him out when his boot moved beyond the earthen floor into a ditch.

"*Dammit.*" He hissed as he caught himself, nearly crushing his face against a moss-covered tree trunk. Communing with wolves, it seemed, did not grant him all the same innate abilities to conquer the wilds in the dark of night.

"I know what you are," said a thin voice not far ahead. Ffion paused, taking to the trees in the hopes of finding a better vantage point. From below, a boy not more than twelve squared off with a pair of pixies, one of which was the blond fellow Ffion had been tracking.

The child was bold, fearlessly facing the two creatures even as he was armed with nothing more than a sizable stick. They prowled around him, appraising him as a lion does its prey, a manic glint in each of their eyes.

"You're an abomination. Unnatural," said the blond one.

"Look who's talking," spat the boy. He feinted left before springing toward the larger of the two, a brawny sort with dark features who hovered just out of reach.

The pair of pixies laughed, swirling around the boy above his head, stirring up leaves and dust in a whirlwind that sent him into a coughing fit. Regardless, he pushed through it, swinging wildly at the duo as they took turns diving toward him, taunting him to the bitter edge as tears of frustration formed in his eyes.

Ffion had seen enough, launching himself from the trees in a furious rage. He crashed into the blond one, hurtling toward the ground with the bastard bound in his sturdy grip. They hit the dirt, and Ffion landed atop the pixie, knocking the wind from the man before quickly snapping his neck. In the next moment, he was on his feet, yanking his sling from his belt loop and lunging for the other one.

"*The beast.*" Backing away, the remaining pixie bolted, streaking in the opposite direction only to heave himself into the starlit sky.

"You are the beast!" The young boy was plainly alarmed, his wide eyes full of panic. "Please don't…"

Ffion paused, caught off guard by his urgency. "Why were you all the way out here?"

"I knew they were coming for me, and I wasn't going down without a fight. I followed them into the woods, for I know that's where they live." Defiance filled his features, even in the face of uncertainty.

"You're a halfling," Ffion said, mostly to himself. He'd been puzzled over the pixies' interest in the child, but their intent to finish him had been clear.

"I've heard of you," the boy continued, slurring his words. "And I know that I have pixie origins, but they do not rule me. *Please*. Let me go." He swayed on his feet, his eyes rolling back in his head.

The prince jumped to his aid, catching the child before he hit the earth. His body was limp and heavy, with something wet covering Ffion's hand. It only took a moment to identify it as blood.

Helping the boy onto his back, Ffion laid him out, examining him for injuries. Turning him up on his side, he could see the wound as his blood continued spreading, blooming across his tunic in a dark, crimson stain. A jagged gash ran the length of his lowest rib, the flayed skin shining in the spare light.

"Let me help." Luc emerged from the shadows, running toward Ffion and kneeling next to the boy. He ripped a length of fabric from his own tunic, balling it up over top of the wound. "Here. Belt it on."

Ffion came to his senses then, removing his belt as instructed, wrapping it around the young boy's abdomen to secure the cloth, and only now was his mind catching up to him. Luc had come from nowhere, finding Ffion entirely off his guard and at the mercy of anyone or anything.

He'd be no good to anybody if he were dead.

"Where'd you come from?" Ffion demanded. He cinched the belt, taking great care to secure it properly.

The boy was pale, his color rapidly draining, but he was breathing.

"I followed you. We've only just gotten you back." Luc felt for the boy's pulse, his army prowess coming in handy, and Ffion was at once grateful and overwhelmed. He had only a cursory clue as to how to help the child, and Luc displayed no hesitation.

"Look," Luc gasped, pointing at the damp cloth. Amber-tinged moisture suffused the rag, turning to gold as his wound continued hemorrhaging.

All Ffion could manage was a strained, guilt-riddled silence. How could he explain what had occurred? Otherworldly phenomenon was not quickly accepted. Hell, he didn't readily admit it to himself.

"I watched your father lose it, you know." Luc's words were not malicious — only matter of fact. "I know there was more to his madness than what he let on. I know there was more to your absence. There was more."

Ffion understood all too well what had occurred, and there was no good way to explain it. Ignoring Luc's assertions was for the best, impolite as it was. "I know someone who can help him. Help me bring him home."

It was a risk, but taking the child to Bellamy was about the best solution he could manage. As a halfling targeted by pixies, it might also be safest for him within palace walls where there would be more eyes on him, more protection. Ffion would have some explaining to do, no doubt, but given his hybrid nature and his unkempt appearance, the child was likely on his own enough already.

Still, they'd have to find a way back in, and that was the trickiest part of all.

They lifted the boy from the ground, placing him in Ffion's arms. The journey felt like it took an eternity, with the two men taking care to protect his wound during their jarring trek through the twilight woods.

The palace grounds came into view, with winter roses spanning the length and breadth of the wrought-iron fencing. The pair made for the same section through which Ffion had first escaped, finding it overrun again with the same thorny vines and blooms.

Luc cringed. "How do we breach the walls? They're too...*alive*."

"There's a gate." Ffion nodded in the general direction, prepared to leave Luc behind. "I hope to see you soon, but we can't risk you traversing the overgrowth."

"*No.* I'll not do this again." Luc shook his head, his frustration evident upon his face. "He didn't let anyone in to help him in his struggles either. I won't have the same thing happen to you."

"*He* who?"

"Your father. He couldn't do without you, and I see it happening again." Luc took a step nearer, as emphatic as Ffion had ever seen him. "Only his sole focus was the loss of you. And you. Yours is worse—an entire kingdom."

Ffion sighed, amazed by the insights of one he hadn't seen for more than a handful of minutes in years. "It's not a good idea. There's no telling what might happen, and I'm unsure how I've made it through there myself. Those *things* could devour you, and I can do nothing for you. I've repeatedly watched the same happen since they first assailed Dufoise."

"Lead the way," said Luc, evidently unshaken by his warning. He pointed toward the boy in Ffion's arms. "For his sake."

He was wasting time. With no further hesitation, Ffion moved toward the gate, and just as before, the winter roses receded, shrinking away from the beastly presence that had invaded their space.

From behind, Ffion heard Luc's breath catch, apparently as incredulous over the slithering vines as he, yet there was no backing away. The heir made his way through first, tucking the boy in his arms closer to protect him from the poisonous flora. He squeezed through the gate, taking care to avoid brushing against the retreating creepers, and the child didn't stir, lying lifeless in his hold.

With his attention diverted as it was, Ffion had paid no mind to Luc, who'd quickly followed in his wake. His friend was nearly through when he became entangled, with one of the vines enveloping his calf and drawing him backward toward its awaiting brethren.

Luc flailed, kicking the greenery with his free leg, hacking at it with the heel of his foot, yet the creeper never ceased, drawing him headlong toward trouble.

Ffion stood helplessly by, with the too still boy weighing heavily in his arms. He looked about, searching for some way to help his friend — an ax, a hammer — but it wasn't necessary.

With a swift tug, Luc was free, having left the lower portion of his leg behind before scrambling away. He hopped up, balancing himself on a nearby tree. "We should go."

"Are you all right?" Ffion nodded toward his missing limb, remembering only days ago when he'd seen Luc's prosthetic for the first time.

"Fine. Let the viney little bastards enjoy that chunk of wood." Luc grinned, bringing a smile to Ffion's face despite the never-ending turmoil.

Time was wasting. Hobbled but never broken, the pair of men made their way toward the palace, eager to help the young boy. Ffion could only pray that his instincts had been solid where Bellamy was concerned, with yet another halfling to protect.

Chapter Nineteen

Nothing in Bellamy's life had been consistent, and dwelling in the palace was no different. Monotony had seemed to be the norm when first she'd arrived. There were dresses to fit, baths to be had, small talk to be made. On its face, the life of a queen in wait had appeared largely dull, but, as usual, she couldn't have been more misinformed.

Her life had been flipped upside down the evening she'd been attacked, setting her on edge in a way that had her continually on guard. That was doubly so in Ffion's absence. As crazy as it was, being without her beastly counterpart made her feel like she was lost in the wilderness. Navigating the ins and outs of royalty had been easier with him leading the way, calming her, guiding her.

When had he become so important?

Ffion's nightly roaming had been taking its toll on him in a variety of ways as well. His desire to protect the kingdom had consumed him, with nightly journeys beyond the palace walls to purge the pixie populace leaving him visibly weary. And even as she understood the driving force to be his people, she couldn't help but suspect that her welfare played a role in his venture, too.

Bellamy's nights were long, waiting as she did for Ffion's return. Occupying herself while he roamed the night was futile as her mind wandered his way with the slightest hints of his presence, and having Gierson around only further complicated her struggles. Ffion's face was everywhere, with his flame-haired twin an ever-present reminder of his absence.

She waited, lying awake in her bed with nothing but intrusive thoughts to keep her company until he returned each evening. Her one consolation came when he joined her, slipping into bed beside her under the cover of darkness.

It was a scandal waiting to happen, but she didn't care. Neither did he, exhausted as he was and unwilling to leave her alone through the night. His warmth was a comfort, sustaining her until Selah came, shooing Ffion from her room before dawn, doing her level best to keep the pair from rumors that were all too true.

As it turned out, Ffion wasn't the fiend she'd imagined him to be. For her, he quietly endured the frustrations of his palace duties, lightening her spirit when they shared a moment of solitude or amusement. It made her heart skip a beat when, before he'd leave her bedside, he'd run his fingers through her hair, almost as if he couldn't help but to touch it.

Blazes, what had happened to her?

Bellamy hustled along, keeping pace with yet another one of Ffion's charitable pursuits. Several days before, he'd returned with an injured young boy for her to tend, and he'd healed in no time. Day and night, Bellamy had nurtured him, dressing his wound and ministering to him in his loneliness and confusion.

It wasn't long before he was on his feet, with the jagged gash upon his back becoming an aurous scar, yet visible but far less painful to the lad. Kit was a curious sort, his energy a welcome reprieve from the routine of royal expectation, even as he spent much of his time roving about the hallways seeking untold mischief.

"Slow down!" Bellamy called, earning a devious smirk from the boy as he dodged around the corner, ducking into the library.

There were worse places to be. She followed Kit in, closing the double doors behind them, certain she was about to be a less-than-willing participant in a game of hide and seek.

"All right, Kit. Try as you might, I *will* find you!" Bellamy smiled to herself, picturing the precocious boy hiding beneath a table or behind a drapery.

She wandered through the library, taking her sweet time as she swept from one end to the other. It was a cavernous space, with ceilings that stretched three stories high, housing a vast collection of books — more than she could ever hope to read in her lifetime.

Beautiful editions of some of her favorite books lined the shelves, bound with leather covers and adorned around the edges in gold leafing. She pulled *The Mutinous Doubles* from the shelf, one of her favorites, tucking it under her arm. It would be a dream come true, if only she had time to read, but there were too many places for a rowdy lad to hide.

A cozy fire crackled at the library's rear, set before a pair of wingback chairs, and Bellamy wondered over the purpose, for the space seemed little used. Indeed, she'd never come across another soul within save for a random attendant or two.

Pale moonlight poured through the windows, and she refused to think of Ffion. She would not picture him in the cold of night, alone and at the mercy of her cruel, scavenging brethren. She would not imagine him facing off against them, outnumbered and fighting for the sake of his kingdom against creatures with no virtue — self-serving liars who would stop at nothing to see him ended.

She was half pixie, half wicked, but never would she surrender to that callous side of her soul. Bellamy shivered, closing her eyes as she offered a silent prayer for his safety before doubling back toward the center, making her way toward the spiral staircases leading to the second tier of the library. When a nearby shelf giggled, she knew she was near her mark.

Shuffling closer, she poked her head around the corner. "I've got you!"

"So you have," came an unexpected voice, for kneeling beside Kit was Gierson.

"It took you long enough," said Kit with a broad smile that reached his piercing blue eyes. He was a handsome fellow, who would have many a girl pining one day.

"That's because you're very clever." Gierson mussed Kit's hair, drawing another laugh before rising to his feet. "Now, let's get something to eat."

It was a friendly gesture from the prince, not to mention his presence there at all. Rambling about with the halfling urchin boy, though Gierson had no idea of the child's origins, was a truly un-royal undertaking — a kindness that Bellamy appreciated.

Gierson was unpredictable, bearing the imprint of her father with none of his despicable attributes. The cursed brothers bore the weight of their affliction in utterly different ways, but then again, nothing much about them was alike beyond their appearances.

Kit bounded ahead of them with unrelenting enthusiasm while Bellamy and Gierson fell in step behind him. The prince offered his arm, and Bellamy obliged, wrapping light fingers over his forearm. He looked her way, smiling. "The brother I've always known will be good to you."

That caught her out, for never had she seriously considered the prospect. But with her inability to leave, perhaps she should've.

"I know he will," she finally managed, averting her gaze. It shouldn't have had her so flustered, yet it became impossible for her to think about anything else. They made their way out of the library, where Gierson paused, facing her.

He took her hand in his, his expression earnest. "My brother has only just returned, and even now, he's never here."

She avoided his gaze, knowing she was the reason for Ffion's constant absence. His brother couldn't understand, given as he was to doing his mother's bidding and seeing to the daily needs of the manor.

"I think, perhaps, he has no interest in being king. All this time gone, while I've never known anything else. Where does it leave me?" He sighed. "You should have a say, you know."

"What?"

"You'll be the queen." He brought her fingers to his lips, kissing the back of her hand. "You should have a choice." Raising a single eyebrow, he stepped backward before bowing, a heartbreaking smile pinned to his face. He followed after Kit, leaving Bellamy to her own devices and very much alone with thoughts she wished not to address.

She had a choice, and so did Ffion. In truth, she couldn't begin to guess what he wanted. He could be king or choose a life beyond the walls. He could choose someone else.

* * * *

Bellamy strode through the halls with a gift for Luc in her hands. She'd been working on it for days, tinkering as she did from time to time, and she'd been grateful for the distraction that her pastime provided as her conversation with Gierson, her uncertainty, had her out of her mind.

She found him in Ffion's quarters, noting with disappointment that Ffion was still absent. It was well after two in the morning, and most nights he didn't run much beyond midnight. It was improper for her to be there, decidedly unladylike, but she happily justified it all in her mind.

"Milady." Luc bowed. "What brings you by?"

"I've something for you. Something I've been working on." She moved toward him, unwrapping a remodeled version of the prosthetic she'd been altering. She'd had to guess with some of the measurements, but hoped that it would be an improvement over what he'd previously worn.

Luc was incredulous, taking the gift in hand. "Why?"

"Why not?" Bellamy smiled, quickly showing him the way around the various belts and buckles. "I hope I didn't overstep."

"Not at all." Luc strapped it onto his lower leg, testing it out with a couple of steps. He hopped in place, a grin spreading across his face. "This is more than I knew to wish for. Thank you."

"It's nothing. I've missed my tinkering."

Luc shook his head, seemingly overwhelmed. "Where did you learn such things? It's as if it's a piece of me."

"I worked with a talented blacksmith in Llundyn," said Bellamy. "I needed a way to get by, and he and his father taught me much. I helped fashion a hook for a hand for another friend of mine."

"Indeed?" Luc chuckled, making his way once again toward the work he'd been after. "I do believe your talents will be wasted when you're queen."

Bellamy laughed in return, for surely he was right. She turned to dismiss herself before Luc spoke again.

"I'll send him your way when he returns, but he doesn't often come here first. Never, in fact."

Bellamy nodded, blushing fiercely under his study. To his credit, he said nothing more, allowing her to return to her quarters with the prince firmly in the forefront of her mind once more.

Being in her own space did nothing to quell her nerves. Each time she glanced at her clock, it refused to move, even as it felt like hours had passed. She prepared for bed, climbing under the covers where she watched the candlelight dancing upon the walls. Selah had finally retired, and Bellamy missed her company, having grown accustomed to the comfort of her humming lulling her off to sleep.

At long last, the door opened and closed. Bellamy lay still as Ffion's presence filled the air, with relief and frustration warring inside her. He moved about slowly, casting long shadows across the room before easing into bed beside her. He burrowed deeper, his frosty body sending a shiver through Bellamy's, and try as she might, she couldn't suppress her annoyance. "Where were you?"

"*Belles.*"

His voice was breathless, and she quickly turned toward him, finding his face streaked in gold. "Oh—"

"It was bad," he admitted. "I was out of my mind, more than I've ever been, and worst of all, I can't remember anything."

She reached for him, stroking her knuckles over his cheek. "Nothing?"

"No." Ffion swallowed hard, his eyes heavy with fatigue. "But then I heard her—your handmaiden. The very song she hummed when first we danced. It reminded me why I fight, and then it led me home." He met her gaze, taking a loose tendril of her hair between his fingers, twirling the silky strands absently.

Bellamy wriggled nearer, wrapping herself around him to warm his chills away, bringing them closer still. "No more," she whispered. "You should never have been in this alone. If they want a fight, they can bring it here to us. Let them come."

A low growl rumbled through his chest, and she felt it deep within her core. The sound set her heart to racing, thrumming through her veins and heightening everything she felt. Ffion was strong, full of courage that set him apart, though she could see he was on the edge of breaking.

"What if I lose myself?" he uttered, his breath tickling her face. "What if I harm you?"

"I fear nothing." She brushed her fingertips over the length of his spine, willing him to calm. "You're exterminating evil, and you're not the beast you seem to think. Strange as it is to say it, I trust you."

That brought a smile to his lips, and she couldn't help but respond in kind. And so, the pixie killer and the pixie queen lay side-by-side, slipping into the most peaceful sleep either had had in weeks, with souls lighter than they'd ever had in the whole of their lives.

Chapter Twenty

If ever there had been a question regarding which of her sons Helena favored, the answer was made clear each time she was forced to endure her elder boy's company, and the bruises left behind on Gierson from his brawl with Ffion only worsened the matter. When the palace staff closed the doors, her demeanor shifted, her countenance sour when she eyed her reckless son.

Gierson was with her, his hand placed affectionately at the small of her back — an ever-present shadow at his mother's side. Ffion had requested a meeting with both of them earlier that day, and while the invitation was to neither's delight, given his position as rightful heir, they could not refuse.

His twin had readily accepted, but Helena had replied with a list of obligations demanding her attention. In a note served to Ffion by one of the manor's numerous grooms, she'd suggested their appointment might be more convenient if it took place after the wedding, to which the heir had politely declined.

Ffion was tiring of taking orders as much as he was done pretending. The past several days had exhausted him, but they'd only made him more confident of the path forward. He would protect Calaise from the throne and meet its threats without hesitation, whether political or physical. He would rule with the devout authority of his father.

He'd taken King Tolliver's motto to heart. *Courageaux est le sacrifice,* said he. *Brave is the sacrifice.*

So, Ffion had run, weathering the storm of his feral emotions — the beastly mania consuming his body and spirit within the enclave of Neverwoode. At the time, it seemed the sacrificial thing, allowing his brother, who appeared of sounder mind, to assume his role as heir apparent. Ffion readily believed Gierson and others to be more deserving of such a life. He'd felt lesser, expendable, prepared to surrender himself where necessary for the sake of others with more purpose than he. For Rory and Artyrus. For Petra and James.

But hiding within the kingdom of Wylewoode had been the easy way despite its ills and dangers. He hadn't viewed it as such then, but the truth was what it was, leaving him prepared to make up for lost time.

Indeed, he was determined to approach them with gratitude for the years they'd preserved his place and wished to help them understand that he was ready to re-assume his role. He only hoped it would not be contentious.

Footsteps faded down the hall from beyond the closed doors. Apart from His Majesty's second man and the dowager's lady posted just outside, the sovereigns were blessedly alone — a rarity in a palace bursting with staff and nosy courtiers.

Gierson bent at the waist in a formal greeting while their mother barely inclined her head to the rightful king, though she would not otherwise acknowledge him thusly. The relations were not what Ffion would have hoped after so long apart, but time would either mend or rot what lay between them.

"I thank you both for all you've done in my absence. It would not have been easy to keep the truth of our circumstances veiled for all this time, particularly in light of the late king's passing." The heir bowed his head in deference to his father's memory, ignoring the ache that accompanied his every thought of King Tolliver.

"May he rest in peace," said Helena and Gierson in unison.

"You need not recognize the efforts, brother," the spare continued, his tone crisp. "It's been my honor to act in your stead and one I should be grateful to relinquish when the time is right." He left his mother's side, crossing the room to clasp Ffion's arm. His twin smiled, an expression they shared with all their features matching from head to toe, though the forced nature of Gierson's bearing struck him.

C'est la vie. They would reconcile in due course, then.

Their mother remained paces away, her features pinched with impatience. She sighed, haughty and indignant, though the structured bodice of her dress did not move. "Is that all?" The dowager narrowed her gaze upon Ffion, and it seemed more a challenge than a question, like he was yet a boy in her eyes. She did not hold the same opinion of Gierson, who had, without question, matured into a man of worth, at least in her infallible opinion.

Yet, never had Ffion thought himself better. He'd simply been assigned a duty by birthright to his country, and his father had never hesitated to affirm as much, even in the face of the heir's malediction. King Tolliver had known of his son's affliction and had not altered his decision. Instead, he'd spent his final days searching for his lost son, believing *Ffion* worthy of his crown.

Once, Ffion had wondered if his father understood the full scope of Marin's actions against him, but he was coming to believe that Tolliver's depth of understanding was very real. And knowing that he remained his father's man in spite of it all left him with no further doubts.

Regardless, Helena's scrutiny was the height of impertinence — no less than Ffion had come to expect from her in the days since his return. He'd avoided most interactions with her, given his continued pursuit of the demons lurking beyond Chateau Dufoise, but it was intrusive nonetheless.

The prince couldn't suppress the smirk that formed as he addressed his mother. "Not quite. I'm resolved to accept my role." Ffion paused, allowing the dowager and his brother a moment to digest his words.

Helena's severe mien eased into a ghost of a smile. "Well. We've only done what is best for Calaise. You missed so much while you were away. It certainly makes sense for Gierson to continue —"

"As *king*, Mother. I will assume the crown, as it is my birthright, and I, *Ffion*, will stand before my bride at the altar."

He watched as the dowager carefully considered her words. She was already guilty of treason, but then again, so was Gierson. Helena maintained a regal air, befitting the queen she once was, and strolled gracefully toward her sons.

"You are not ready and will not fool your people into believing you are." She took his hand in hers, feigning a warmth he knew she did not possess for him.

"I intend to meet with my father's council regularly until my coronation and thereafter," Ffion went on, undeterred by his mother's condescension. "They, and Gierson, will ensure I do not misstep. It is their duty to Calaise and to me to do so. I recall His Majesty's advisors well enough to know they can be trusted with my...peculiarities."

The dowager dropped his hand and retreated a step, her mouth pressed into a thin, petulant line.

Gierson bowed to his brother once more. "You'll not fail."

His words were truly accommodating, but Ffion struggled to look past the nagging resentment he harbored toward his younger twin, however unjustified it was. He should be grateful, but the spare's wandering eyes had not escaped his notice.

It was absurd, of course, for Bellamy was a vision even at her worst. He couldn't expect others not to notice. This was Gierson's greatest offense as far as Ffion was concerned, though there were doubtless others bred of grief and a deep-seated resentment for his living a life that did not belong to him.

But then again, Ffion's life had become Gierson's in so many ways that he wondered if his twin would harbor similar feelings when he found himself as the spare once again after so many years learning what it meant to be first in line. He wouldn't blame his brother, for he understood all too well.

"Do not think you will be pushed aside." Ffion clapped his twin on the shoulder. "I wish you to act as my private secretary, if you're willing. I hope you will see the offer as a token of my gratitude and a role that will allow us to labor side-by-side for the good of Calaise."

Helena huffed, moving closer to them. She turned to Gierson, her brow raised and the thin lines framing her lips more defined with her bitter glower. "So then, you expect him to continue ruling on your behalf while you play pretend. Selfish boy," she spat.

"The crown is not mine, Mother," said Gierson. "It will be a relief to give up this charade, and I'm honored by my brother's suggestion."

"He is unfit —" she pleaded, her eyes softening when she looked up at her second-born.

Gierson placed his hand on her arm, averting his gaze to meet Ffion's. "Are you?"

"I am well," Ffion said, believing it only as the words left his mouth. "I am fit but aware of my shortcomings, and I'll rely greatly on my council until I'm certain I'm well-versed in the demands upon me as ruler of these lands."

"His Majesty says he is fit." Gierson held the dowager's gaze as he spoke, though more appeared to be left unsaid.

Ffion did not know them, and he reminded himself of this daily. The once-queen's callousness was readily evident, but Gierson's natural charisma, alongside his bond with their mother, left him as a lingering question. The tightrope between familial loyalty and subversion was threadbare, and the heir was committed to proceeding with care. It was his fervent hope that His Majesty's council might grant him clarity.

"Very well then," Helena agreed. Her manner suggested otherwise, but Ffion nodded in thanks, even if he did not require her approval to do everything he desired.

He was king, regardless of any preference on her part.

"As for the wedding," the dowager continued, her features twisting into something spiteful and scheming. "You understand that you cannot possibly be the one standing before the archbishop."

Ffion was not in a mood to argue. "Please explain how it differs from what my brother has done in my absence. Was the reasoning then not due to our likeness?"

Helena took a fortifying breath. "You were still a child when you left Calaise." It was a pathetic attempt at justification, but deceit was all the heir could see. His mother was no better than the pixies he'd laid to rest.

"The eyes of your people were not on you then," she continued, "not as they are now. Calaise knows only Gierson. Your citizenry will recognize your differences, unlike when you traded places as boys. Your brother has been both you and himself for so long, they will surely identify you as the wanderer you are. Your complexion suggests that you spend your days in the fields with the herds rather than overseeing the welfare of your countrymen, not to mention the scars and bruises all over your body. You are gravely mistaken if you think the palace staff doesn't talk. It has been no small undertaking to maintain your secrets, I assure you." She folded her hand before herself, making no effort to disguise her unwillingness to concede.

Gierson remained silent, revealing no evidence of his feelings on the matter. And while Ffion had the final say and the authority to trounce the dowager's argument then and there, he would never know all of the pieces or people at play, nor on whose side they resided if he did so.

"I suppose you're right," Ffion conceded after a drawn pause, not wholly for show. He'd considered his options and weighed their merits. None were good. Submission, however, afforded him time to observe. "We can't risk Calaise questioning its crown for any reason."

"Well then, are we finished?" Helena smiled, pacified enough for the moment.

"For now," Ffion nodded. "Thank you."

Helena thinned her lips, ignoring the prospect of further discussions. She'd won her victory, and that was enough, though her haste was shortsighted. Giving Gierson's hand an adoring squeeze reserved for him only, she didn't look Ffion's way before exiting the drawing room, leaving her sons to themselves.

King Tolliver was said to have given into madness, and Helena had never permitted Ffion to view himself as anything more than an echo of the late king. They were one and the same in her sight, which was why she would sooner commit treason than see him take his father's place.

The heir couldn't recall the last time he was alone with his twin. He strode across the immaculate wood floors, polished and gleaming, much like his brother. Gierson was dressed and flawlessly arranged for another day in Ffion's shoes, while the eldest prince wore a pauper's finery of filth and scars from a night spent defending his homeland.

"I cannot imagine how frustrating it must be," Gierson said at last, seating himself on a plush settee opposite his brother, who gazed out of the window in contemplation.

Ffion was drowning in uncertainty, with so many new angles to consider in Helena's absence. The dowager had been transparent with her intent as clear as the pane of glass before him. Gierson, however, was an enigma — dutiful and loyal, but to whom?

It felt traitorous to assess his brother's intentions, but Ffion would be irresponsible if he neglected to determine his character. So he let him speak, for in another man's silence, the guilty would often convict themselves.

"We both know my presence is a formality on that day. Sheerly for the courtiers to witness, nothing else," Gierson continued, unbothered by the enduring quiet. "There will be no religious ceremony to speak of — only the appearance that one has privately taken place. She is yours."

The notion that Bellamy did not belong to herself set Ffion on edge. She was no one's, nor would she be, unless she gave herself over, heart and soul.

"Is there anything you would have me give her during the ceremony?"

So.

Ffion turned, taking in the earnest countenance of his brother. With one simple question, Gierson had thrown in his lot, siding with the dowager in his agreement to not only attend the ceremony but also stand at the altar to receive Bellamy as his bride, though he was under no obligation to honor Helena's wishes.

It was answer enough.

"No," said Ffion, forcing a smile of his own. "A blessed day it will be for our kingdom."

Gierson grinned, rising to his feet. He reached for Ffion, squeezing his shoulder as if he were a dear old friend, though they scarcely knew one another anymore. "Yes, brother. The nation will rejoice."

With that, he left Ffion alone, offering a bow in parting. His actions did little to mollify the heir, however, knowing that Gierson would likely stab him in the back at the first opportunity. Their proximity alone worked in Ffion's favor, for he knew he would not die within Dufoise by his brother's hand.

That would've been too easy for Marin and his games.

For now, Ffion would keep the details of his future plans close to his chest, with the exception of Bellamy and Luc, whom he trusted unequivocally.

Luc was loyal to Calaise, if not for his sake, then for his late father, Tolliver. To Ffion, it made no difference. Besides all of that, Lucignolo was no fan of Gierson, nor had he ever been.

And Bellamy.

She had saved him. Without her, Ffion would've continued to weary himself each night, seeking their enemies and falling deeper into a pattern that would only lead to his destruction.

Calaise would be blessed with her as its queen, but she deserved more than what would ultimately confine her. She hadn't complained, hostage though she'd been since the infernal winter roses had bloomed, but he wouldn't prolong her imprisonment through marriage bonds. He would find a way to give Bellamy all she desired, even if it meant her leaving him behind.

He'd been alone once, and was prepared to sacrifice his peace for hers.

Little time remained before the wedding, and if his pixie wasn't gone before then, she would not escape the marriage that followed. Gierson would not refuse her before God and country as Ffion was prepared to, much as it pained him, and she would be trapped for good.

Even if the thought of letting her go felt like losing a piece of his soul.

Chapter Twenty-One

Bellamy had never been so pampered. It did come with its risks— if she breathed a little too deeply, or when Kit made her laugh unexpectedly. She'd become more of a pin cushion than a bride being fitted for her wedding gown.

There were two dresses. One would be worn for the first of two ceremonies—the civil declaration for all palace courtiers to witness—and the other for a private service conducted by the archbishop and the feast that followed. Or so Bellamy was told. She knew not a single thing about weddings. The halfling had never been to one, nor would she have imagined promising herself to another.

She couldn't seem to reconcile her feelings at any rate. Bellamy had never intended to go to the palace in the first place, but Ffion had changed everything. Somewhere along their broken, vengeful exploits, he'd become vital to her, and she was terrified about where her heart might lead her.

He'd contrived His Majesty's betrothal to *Lady Bellamy of Nowhere* out of necessity, and, whether by fate or consequence, there was no easy way out of any of it for either party.

Dufoise was, itself, in turmoil, clinging to a monarchy that had maintained its authority for over a century even as it was trapped by a poisonous reminder that nothing on that side of eternity was unbreakable. Yet, according to the old crone Helena, her impending nuptials would, by some miracle, soothe away the citizenry's worries.

She couldn't think of a more ridiculous scenario.

Bellamy would've preferred to relive every horrid part of her past than wear the shoes Helena's seamstress had put her in but she tried to hold still, her toes pinched to the point of numbness.

"Almost done, milady. Please be patient," said the buxom woman seated on the platform before her. She'd introduced herself as Mathilde along with her apprentice, Colette, and each seemed less than pleased to be tasked with Bellamy's bridalwear. Mathilde spoke through a needle held between her teeth, and the pixie clenched her jaw, anticipating the moment it would stab her in the ribs. *Again.*

It happened so many times that Bellamy would've sworn the seamstress was doing it on purpose.

"Hold still," the woman's peevish assistant barked, plucking another straight pin from the small box in her hand. Mathilde tacked another spot on Bellamy's waist before retrieving another. On it went, every few marks causing the pixie to flinch. She didn't dare look over at Selah, who was stifling her amusement by fussing with anything she could find nearby.

Bellamy was trying, she really was, but the women were insufferable.

"Are you all right, Belles?" Kit asked after she failed to conceal her discomfort yet again. He winced as he watched the seamstress and her aid, making no effort to hide his distaste for either.

"Quiet, boy," Mathilde huffed, casting a scathing look over her shoulder at him, to which Kit responded with a smirk.

"I'll do as *my queen* orders," he jeered, and Colette muttered something under her breath, drawing Bellamy's attention.

"I didn't quite catch that." She wasn't their queen yet and likely never would be, but she was not one to tolerate insults. "Speak up so we all might hear what you have to say."

Colette and Mathilde glanced at each other before the aid cast her gaze to the floor. "I beg your pardon, milady."

"No, please. Repeat yourself." Bellamy waited.

Kit bit his lip, his gaze darting between the women before landing on Selah. The maid smiled at him, their features colored with mischief.

Colette straightened, her chin tipped in defiance when she said, "You'll never be the queen Her Majesty, Queen Helena is."

"I see." The pixie halfling waved her off, giving the aid time to recover herself, her face blotchy red from her moment of bravado, before their eyes leveled. "I assume your words were meant to wound, but you could not be more right," Bellamy began, pulling her skirts up to step toward the insolent woman.

Colette blanched, perhaps awaiting the sting of her palm against her cheek. Instead, Bellamy took the aid's hand in hers. "I will be nothing like your former queen. I will never treat anyone, whether noble, merchant, or beggar, with contempt. You will not see me act as though

I am in some way more worthy or superior than they, for I know what it means to feel the pangs of hunger in my belly and mourn a life I never believed I would have. I should hope this nation longs for more than a queen who does not concern herself with its people."

Mathilde exhaled sharply behind Bellamy while Colette's ocean-blue gaze pooled with tears.

"Forgive me," she said, her lip trembling. Bellamy squeezed her hand before resuming her place at the small podium, standing before the clothier.

Selah subtly nodded in approval to the pixie as she continued idling close by. She was the friend Bellamy never knew she required. She had her boys in the mines, of whom Kit was a precious reminder, and then, there was Ffion. But the silver-haired siren was the female bond she'd been missing. Their connection was instantaneous, transcending what could be said aloud, and Bellamy was beyond grateful for her.

The pixie was learning to receive blessings without reservation. Not always had she done so, and in her fear and anger, she had failed to snatch the bits of joy even a life such as hers could gather.

Mercifully, each day was new.

Mathilde and Colette proceeded with their alterations, remarking about the gown and what remained to be done. It was beautiful and would fit Bellamy to perfection once finished, with a structured bodice and voluminous skirt.

The dress was simple in the best of ways, made of pristine white satin, smooth as glass. A band of matching satin draped loosely around Bellamy's upper arms, from which sheer billowing sleeves covered her down to her wrists, ending in delicate cuffs drawn together with buttons of pearl. Her shoulders were bare, but she was becoming used to such things in

Calaise, having worn more than one dress that exposed her in ways she was less than accustomed to. Even so, with a train that would flow behind her as she walked down the aisle, she looked and felt lovely, even if nothing about the design reflected who Bellamy was.

A knock sounded at the door, coercing her from another ill-conceived reverie. She'd been unable to avoid them lately, wondering when exactly the apathy that had preserved her throughout her days had abandoned her.

It was appalling to consider what sadness could shadow the meditations of a human heart, even if just half of her own was so weak.

Selah glided across the room to the door, and Kit readily followed after her, though she didn't seem to mind. He was much like having a puppy, or Bellamy assumed so, with the way the lad kept close. And it had not taken him long to make himself at home within the walls built for kings.

"Wait 'til you see her," Kit chirped to whoever waited outside. "Come in!"

Bellamy tensed, her body reacting instinctively, causing another pinprick to her rib. She watched in the mirror as Selah dipped into a deep curtsy while Kit moved aside, allowing their visitor entry.

Ffion appeared in the doorway, with Lucignolo close behind. The heir's bearing was unlike that of the man Bellamy had come to know. He entered the room without greeting, his smile fading as if night somehow beckoned while the sun soaked the lands with its brilliant, golden light.

Bellamy could scarcely breathe under the intensity of his fathomless gaze, Ffion's eyes drinking her in like a pool of placid water in scorching desert heat.

"This was a mistake," said Luc, breaking the silence, though it seemed the prince did not hear him at all. A distinct sense of urgency rang through his words, but Ffion slowly approached Bellamy, heedless of how it may be received by his mother's seamstresses.

"I recall," Lucignolo began again, "that a bride isn't meant to be seen in her dress ahead of the wedding."

The heir didn't react or turn aside. Rather, he stood behind Bellamy, his hazel gaze blazing against her bare shoulders and back. She watched their reflections in the tall baroque glass, damning her traitorous need to sink into his enveloping strength.

"The *groom* cannot see her," Mathilde corrected Luc, her focus never leaving her work. But while she hadn't noticed anything amiss with the heir, who was still Gierson in the minds of the realm, Colette tried in vain to look away.

"If you'll excuse us." Bellamy's voice was foreign to her, but she could think of no other way to proceed. "I require a moment with the prince."

Luc hesitated but soon took Kit's arm, guiding the boy out of the room, which suddenly felt far too crowded. Ffion's attention flicked toward the clothiers, his countenance remained unchanged despite retreating a step from Bellamy.

Mathilde made no effort to adhere to the pixie's directive, but Ffion's notice of Helena's designers seemed to unnerve Colette, who promptly abandoned her station, nodding by way of her hasty departure.

"Alone. *Now*," the heir commanded, his stare meeting Bellamy's through the mirror before them. His words rumbled through her core like a violent thunder, and she could not look away.

Mathilde scoffed but obeyed, and Selah tailed her into the hall, where Bellamy knew she would be waiting.

It was a horrific breach of decorum to be left to themselves as they were, so it was of great benefit that neither she nor Ffion cared.

He lifted his fingers to Bellamy's hair, coiling her silken tresses around his fingertips in a way that made her pulse quicken. Her flesh rose as the back of his hand grazed her neck, and when she turned to him, his gaze only darkened.

"This isn't—"

"I don't care." Ffion closed the distance between them, breathing her in. He leaned down, his mouth skimming the curve of her shoulder.

Bellamy wanted to give in to the only thing that had ever felt right and good in her life, savoring the warmth of him so near. It was different from those quiet hours when he held her to himself as sleep gently overcame them. This was desire, ardent and desperate.

The halfling's thoughts were a blur. Ffion's presence stirred something so powerful within her that it should've been forbidden. In many ways, it was, but she couldn't will herself to conceive of a world where the prince didn't reduce her to her most primal instincts.

He groaned, his hands hovering at Bellamy's waist as if indulging himself would irrevocably unravel him, just as it would her. Closing his eyes, Ffion paused, flexing his hand before his gaze found hers. The chaos had not left them, but his breathing steadied as he stole one final look at her from head to toe, his study lingering.

"You…" Ffion's voice was rough and low when he finally spoke. "I cannot allow you to become shackled to a kingdom that is not yours." His words were not at all what Bellamy expected to hear as she watched him search for the explanation he knew she would insist upon.

"You shouldn't be here, trapped in this ill-fated palace, waiting to fulfill a promise you didn't make." He laced his fingers with hers, and she cursed the pressure building behind her eyes, threatening to reveal her secret fears of losing the only good and honest thing that ever found her.

"I spoke with my mother and Gierson to inform them of my intent to assume my title as king, and it was every bit as lacking as I thought it might be." He squeezed her hand as he composed himself. "Helena doesn't think it wise to diverge from the course she and my brother set in my absence, but ultimately, the choice is mine. I pacified my mother temporarily, but I cannot abide at your cost."

"Don't risk your future successes or Calaisean prosperity for my sake." A tear slipped down Bellamy's cheek, and her voice wavered when she spoke, betraying any hope of concealing her heartbreak. The prince couldn't possibly understand why words failed her as she struggled to hold herself together.

"I will do all I can to find a way to free you from Dufoise and all its sins, but if I cannot do so before the wedding —" The faint muscles in Ffion's jaw fluttered when he paused, and Bellamy silently begged him not to finish his thought, but to no avail.

"I will demand it is me who stands before you at the altar so that you may refuse me without condemnation in the sight of those gathered."

Another tear spilled, with more pooling in its place. Bellamy could not bear a life without him. She saw the days ahead of her at his side as a gift and any spent alone as a sort of purgatory from which she would never escape. In all her loathing of the man facing her, she hadn't foreseen the hold he would claim on her soul.

"I wouldn't say no," she confessed, the words tumbling from her lips like a vow unto themselves. Confusion colored Ffion's features, his grip tightening around her hand. When he didn't speak, she continued. "I wouldn't refuse you, and I don't want to leave unless you do not want me here."

"I'd never wish for you to go," he said.

Bellamy's tears came faster as her fears began to dissipate, and Ffion's mouth tipped at the edges. "You'll be Queen of Calaise." His smile grew, warming her to her core, and Bellamy couldn't withhold one of her own.

His throat bobbed as he lowered his forehead to hers, and she nodded against him before he pulled away slightly, kissing her temple.

Bellamy was in disbelief as Ffion blotted the moisture from her face with his tunic. She couldn't stop staring at the angles of his striking face or the strength he suppressed from dawn to dusk.

"It will be done," he assured her before swallowing hard, withdrawing himself in a manner that felt as if it pained him as much as it did her.

He was gone a moment later, but she couldn't put his words from her mind. She knelt on the ground, unable to remain upright as relief overcame her, sobbing as her skirts swelled around her in a cloud of diamond white.

Ffion had chosen her, protected her. He'd offered her more than she'd ever thought to dream.

With him, she was home.

* * * *

The late King Tolliver's council gatherings were ever tedious affairs, and Gierson had neither the time nor the patience to be in attendance. But he'd been given no other option, it seemed, since *he* had arranged the meeting.

Or *Ffion* had, at least.

His blasted brother had decided he was ready to rule, and everything had changed. Gone were the days of lazing about, enjoying the company of Melis and any other available maidens. Absent was the freedom to rule as he wished, with every decision he made being observed by his ever-present shadow.

Judged. *Corrected.*

Gierson was losing his mind, with too many people trapped within too little space courtesy of the damnable winter roses, which were, incidentally, also the result of his accursed brother.

Perhaps a better ruler would've readily soothed the frayed nerves of all the courtiers and servants. Once, he was such a man, but no more.

Gierson was walking a fine line and had not yet determined what to make of his circumstances. Alas, he was the spare alone and likely to become much less if Ffion were to wear the crown.

Indeed, his brother had made him a generous offer that would allow him to help guide his twin's rule, but *only* if the heir kept his word.

But he himself would never wield the scepter — a reality that caused him no end of grief.

Nevertheless, Ffion had called their father's advisors together and presided over them as if he owned the room and everything within it. And though the advisors believed Ffion to be Gierson, they responded to him as they had to Tolliver, leaving the true Gierson feeling as though his father had risen from the grave.

The heir spoke with the authority and discernment of a leader, and though he presented himself as his younger twin, Ffion had His Majesty's council rapt.

To Gierson, his brother had effectively surrendered his birthright the day he'd abandoned Calaise, but King Tolliver had never given up hope that he would return.

The spare was never enough.

Chapter Twenty-Two

Their compatibility was utterly absurd, for never had two people been more wrong for one another. But for Ffion, perhaps that's what made it feel so right. He watched as Bellamy paced the room, having awakened long before he, leaving the other side of the bed cold.

Most mornings, Selah would hasten him from the room, rousing him long before sunrise and sending him packing into the frigid castle to fend for himself before the remainder of the palace came alive with the dawn. Her insistence was both a blessing and a curse, saving them from a contentious conversation and rumors untold, even as it frustrated him to leave Bellamy alone.

This morning was different, with the beautiful pixie assassin decidedly agitated. He hoped she hadn't changed her mind about them, or, most especially, about him.

"Are you all right?" He turned to his side, voice thick with sleep.

"I'm sorry. I didn't mean to wake you." Bellamy moved toward him, wearing an apologetic smile, threading her fingers through his hair.

He pressed himself nearer, eager for more of her touch. She wasn't running the other way, so he put his insecurities aside. "Tell me."

She shook her head as if to ward off her worrisome thoughts, but the tears in her eyes told him more than any false smile could. "I've been afraid all my life, tormented even in slumber with nightmares of my brethren coming for me. Yet, when my late-night terrors became a waking reality, you were there, and never have I experienced any sense of genuine peace. Not before you." Narrow streaks of moisture trailed over her cheeks when she looked away, seemingly collecting herself.

She was strong—so independent and brave. Her display of vulnerability was a punch to the gut for Ffion. Knowing she'd felt these things for this long, and worse, that she'd had no opportunity to express them, had him ready to shred the world apart, making the responsible parties pay for their sins.

"Feeling this way for the first time scares me more," Bellamy continued. "I'm whole. I feel *alive*, like I might now well and truly live, and the prospect of that disappearing consumes me. I don't want to sleep, couldn't sleep, because I want to enjoy the living as much as I can before it's gone."

Ffion was on his feet then, taking her in his arms. He cradled her head in one hand, tipping her face upward, taking in the never-ending depths within her gold-rimmed eyes. There was so much hidden behind her gaze that she'd refused to share, and he was grateful that he finally understood some of the long-buried pieces of her soul.

It was no wonder that she'd kept them secret, alone and at the mercy of so many elements beyond her control as she'd been, but no more.

"We'll do it all together, *ma fée*," he whispered, his breath rustling her auburn hair. "That is, if you'll still have me over my brother this very day."

Bellamy laughed, and the sound warmed Ffion to his soul, for her humor was hard-won. "There's no one better for me. I hope our plan is enough."

"I choose this," said Ffion, backing away only enough to see her face as he took her hands in his. "For our kingdom and for myself. For us." He pressed his forehead to hers, closing his eyes, and for a moment, he understood her hesitation.

It was nearly too much to ask for, and it was within their grasp.

Selah arrived, poking her head through the doorway, and Ffion and Bellamy sprung apart. Her eyes widened, likely surprised to see the pair awake at such an early hour, but she only bobbed her head with a knowing smile, ducking out and closing the door once more.

"I suppose it's time," Ffion sighed. The last thing he wanted to do was leave, to start seeing the day through, but it wouldn't be long before the palace would be bustling with the chaos of the impending wedding. He bent down, kissing her forehead, enjoying the color that filled her cheeks.

She was more lovely than he could ever deserve.

He reached for his jacket, and something thudded onto the floor. He bent, retrieving a book that had fallen from the chaise lounge. "*The Mutinous Doubles*. This was my father's favorite. He said it reminded him of my brother and me."

"It's my favorite, too. It was my next read," said Bellamy, joining him at his side. More than a few books were strewn about the room, and he wondered just how she'd had time to go through so many. But thumbing through the tome, Ffion was shocked to find that it wasn't a novel at all.

It was a journal.

"What is this?" Bellamy moved nearer, evidently having noticed the same thing.

"This looks to be my father's handwriting." Ffion paused on one of the pages. "*The man will never cease, or so he says, and even my boys are fair game in his mind. Anything at all to achieve his ends, destroying the blessed line of Calaise by whatever means necessary,*" he read aloud.

"Who?" Bellamy breathed, but the question fell from her lips with more resignation than it was curiosity.

"You must be thinking as I am." Ffion flipped to another page, convinced that they would never truly be rid of the tormentor that was Marin, though he hadn't yet confirmed his suspicion. The man continued to haunt them from beyond the grave, coloring their outlooks and plaguing their day-to-day life in untold ways.

Yet the madness Luc had described in King Tolliver, the fall from grace witnessed by the commonwealth as he descended into mania, all made more sense in the face of Marin's never-ending machinations. He was a menace who had, allegedly, tormented the sovereign of Chateau Dufoise for decades.

"Look," Bellamy breathed, directing Ffion's attention to another passage within the journal. "*It seems the kingdom of Calaise will forever be under assault, courtesy of one forsaken affair. Marin's determination to punish my mother for the transgression of duty will surely see the realm to its knees if he is not stopped.*"

"*Perhaps the serpent does have a heart,*" Ffion continued, picking up where Bellamy had left off. "*And it was broken when my mother spurned the pixie bastard in favor of her beloved husband and duties as queen, only to soon fall pregnant with me.*"

Bellamy's eyes grew wide with the revelation. "My father...*loved* your grandmother? I didn't think him capable."

"He desired her, I suppose. Love, I don't know." Ffion stifled a shudder, shocked by the gravity of their discovery. "It explains a bit about his preoccupation with my family, though, I suppose."

With a little further exploration, it was clear that the Marin had been holding a hellacious grudge, targeting the family for years in the aftermath of his falling out with Queen Alizee.

"My grandmother was wholly devoted to our family, though she had many secrets. I'm named for her favorite flower, foxglove—it's said to restore the sick of heart and spirit." Ffion smiled. "Not very beastly, perhaps, but it did infuriate my mother, and Alizee never did care for Helena."

"That might help to redeem her then," said Bellamy, drawing a laugh from the prince. "I'd just assumed your name was meant as a taunt, what with Ffion meant to draw wayward fairies wherever it's planted. It surely worked for me."

Ffion's smile grew as he reached for his pixie, tipping her chin up with one finger. "You're my cure for heartsickness."

Tears welled unexpectedly in her gaze, and he wanted nothing more than to execute their admittedly clumsy scheme, eager to move past the weight of all they'd discovered within the journal. His history was checkered, as was hers, but their future would be better, forging onward side-by-side.

"My lady, oh—"

One of the women who'd made Bellamy her pin cushion stood in the doorway, evidently having neglected to knock first. She dropped her chin, a belated apology for her error.

"A moment, please, Colette," Bellamy called, watching as her seamstress ducked out the door. She turned to Ffion, tucking the journal under her arm. "Ffion—"

"Worry not. We *will*." He took her free hand in his, kissing her knuckles, his eyes never leaving hers. "Until then."

The beautiful pixie smiled, offering only a singular nod as they parted—a simple acknowledgment of her faith in *them*, no matter how many obstacles stood in their way.

Ffion wandered from the room, moving past the attendant with a bob of his head. The woman gaped, surely shocked to have found *Prince Gierson* exchanging pleasantries with her charge in the early morning hours.

What gossip that would make.

Ffion was well beyond caring. He'd toed the line, followed orders, taken emotional shots from callous courtiers. He'd lost his father and returned to a mother with no interest in him or his well-being. He was a means to an end for her, helping her perpetrate a coup that would see him to the end of his reign before it had a chance to begin.

He ignored the sense of duty welling within, knowing that such knowledge could cause perpetual chaos. Those who wished to damage him would make him pay for the lack of discretion, but his time was coming.

C'est la vie.

Instead of covering his tracks, he headed for Gierson, undoubtedly fast asleep in the king's quarters. His brother was the other half of a false union, so what better way to pass the time leading to his faux nuptials than to pay him a visit?

Gierson's quarters were dark, with a handful of hours until sunrise. Ffion wondered absently if his brother had any reservations, knowing he hadn't been keen on the idea from the start. Still, if everything went according to plan, none of it would matter—not his mother's machinations, not his brother's aspirations, whatever they might be.

"A fine day for a wedding, is it not, brother?" Ffion bellowed, lighting the sconces lining the wall, making every effort to irritate his slumbering twin.

"Go away," Gierson groaned, burying his head beneath his pillow.

His annoyance brought Ffion some semblance of delight, prompting him to continue his efforts. He leaped onto the bed, sending his brother bouncing into the air.

"Ffion!"

"Ah, no. Alas, I'm Gierson," said Ffion, landing beside his brother on the bed, where he flipped to his back, taking vicious pleasure in hearing his given name spoken by his brother.

The games had gone on for long enough. Ffion was ready to assume his role and his reign, beginning that very day with a wedding for nobody but his bride and himself. Indeed, he couldn't think of a better way to begin his new life.

"It's a big day," Ffion continued, prodding Gierson in the ribs.

Gierson hissed, his temper flaring as he slapped his hand away. "Not for me! A mere formality. And besides, you're not being nearly strategic enough."

That brought Ffion up short. Who considered strategy in marriage? Indeed, it happened, especially amongst royalty, but never had Ffion considered that he might marry for *strategy* over love.

"A courtly match would be a more responsible approach for a king," Gierson spat, turning onto his side in a huff. "You must think of these things if you're to be king. Marrying for love is what peasants do."

Ffion balked, unnerved that his brother could be utterly dispassionate about something so important. "Careful. You're starting to sound like Mother."

"You could stand to sound more like her yourself!" Gierson rose to his elbows, looking Ffion in the face. "She is wise. While you were gone, she held this kingdom together. In fact, she was working on an alliance, petitioning the Debrecynian mountain court for the hand of one of their princesses when you showed up, not that you would care."

"So I'm ruining *your* strategy. That's what you really mean to say." Ffion moved from the bed, suppressing a spike of anger that threatened to awaken the beast within. He'd maintained control for days, or some form of it at any rate, only to have his efforts undone in a few sharp words.

"For a harlot, no less. Do not think for a moment that I'm unaware of your nightly dalliances after you return from your roving."

Ffion trembled where he stood on the bitter edge of shredding his brother to pieces, his fists clenched so tightly he thought his fingers might break. "You'll never speak those words again. Upon my word, you will meet your end if you so much as think them."

Gierson scoffed, a subtle smile forming on his face. "Your true nature will consume you, *brother*, as will mine. Now, begone." He dismissed him with a wave of his hand, rolling the other way in a flurry of kicked blankets.

An entitled bastard, hellbent upon his own way. Ffion had given him the benefit of the doubt repeatedly, dismissing his concerns and making excuses where Gierson had come up short.

No more.

Marin's curse upon his brother's lips drew him to the end of his patience.

He would execute the day as planned, playing his role to perfection.

And then he would marry his queen and take back his throne.

Chapter Twenty-Three

Though she hadn't slept a wink, Bellamy felt energized, prepared for a day that was sure to be tumultuous. It hadn't started on the greatest foot, with Colette having shown up at her door unannounced, but Bellamy could only assume the day would be full of oddities. She was determined to seize each trial as it appeared, bending it to her will.

It was worth it.

The pixie stepped aside, allowing Colette entrance to her quarters. "The prince — Prince Gierson was — "

"Your secrets are your own, Your Grace." The woman bowed low, her gaze cast toward the ground. She could not bring herself to look Bellamy in the eye when she rose. "And I'm ashamed of my behavior during your fitting. I beg your forgiveness, ma'am, and I wish to make it right."

She cast a length of fabric before her, fanning the shimmering tulle across the floor, and it was only then that Bellamy realized what she was looking at. Ivory layers in the finest of materials formed a gown truly fit for a queen. Each garment since the day she'd arrived had seemed to outdo the last, and the one before her was no exception, with the intricate scrolling embellishing the bodice nothing shy of breathtaking.

"It's lovely."

"It's yours," said Colette. "A far cry from what our dowager would approve for your purposes, but I thought, perhaps, it might be of some use if you wished to wear something your beloved had not seen before your wedding day."

Bellamy's eyes went wide with the assertion, even as she attempted to stifle her shock. The woman was unknown to her and could be up to no good with her presumptions, but something told her that she was being authentic.

"Of course, you'll wear the queen's choice for the public ceremony," Colette continued, tidying the skirt as she exposed more of its splendor. "But the second ceremony is private."

Their gazes met, and Colette's face softened, revealing a small, friendly smile. Trusting her might be a mistake, but Bellamy decided it was a risk worth taking, worth having an ally to see her through the commotion of two ceremonies even if she only cared to participate in the latter one.

"How did you know?" Bellamy couldn't help but ask, all the while wondering if she'd been too obvious in her affection for *Gierson*.

"It doesn't matter. But what does matter is a dress that suits you for the part of your day that means the most. I spent the night completing it."

"I'm in your debt," said Bellamy, brushing her hand over the sheer fabric of one of the sleeves. "Thank you."

"Fit for a worthy queen, I hope."

Bellamy nodded, stepping out of her way as Colette set about preparing for the festivities. There'd be endless work ahead as they primped and teased her into an acceptable appearance for the courtly masses, doubtless as much a distraction for the people trapped within the grounds of Dufoise as they were the fulfillment of some long-awaited rite.

To call the courtiers restless was a severe understatement. The tension inside the palace had reached a tipping point, with nobody aside from Ffion having the slightest clue what was going on beyond the rose-wrapped walls, and he hadn't left in days.

The people became panicked, unable to understand how or why they had come to be captured in the first place. More than one had been enveloped in the thorny gates, absorbed into the fencing where they'd run headlong toward them, hoping to escape, and simply ceased to be. Such horrors had only served to further frighten them, with no end in sight.

It had been a nightmare that was written off by the dowager queen as protection from the ills of the outside — a foolhardy attempt to convince her detained companions that they'd been done a favor, though they were nothing more than hostages in an otherworldy game.

Through Ffion, Bellamy was also aware of the private concerns held by the council. The kingdom was, in essence, a sitting duck, with no discernable leadership to shield the realm from takeover. Rumblings of a coup had echoed through the region for some time, with the prevailing wisdom contending that some Debrecynian mountain rebels yet plotted an overthrow.

Calaise was a shining jewel in the crown of Fayble — a wealth of rich land, healthy trade and a contented citizenry. Were they unable to defend themselves, the kingdom would be in jeopardy.

What lay beyond the walls was anybody's guess, making the reality for those confined to the castle almost too much to bear as they reconciled their separation from loved ones outside with the utter lack of information regarding their safety or condition.

It made for a dangerous environment, and not even the dowager herself was completely safe, for Bellamy had noted a growing number of knights for her protection as she daily surveyed her caged dominion with her favored son by her side.

Her stomach turned at the thought of marrying Gierson, even if it was only for show. Once, loath as she now was to admit it, Bellamy had found the spare intriguing, thinking him well-adjusted and kind. But the façade had quickly fallen away, revealing a spoiled narcissist with few redeeming qualities.

His bearing was flashy, while Ffion's was one of passive contentedness. The heir didn't seek praise, nor did he require attention. He went about the business of protecting his kingdom in silence, all the while accepting a subservient role without complaint.

Somehow, the beauty had fallen for the beast, and it was the greatest revelation of her life.

"Shall we begin, Your Grace?" said Colette, wielding an arsenal of brushes, oils and powders to prepare the future queen for her dual nuptials.

As if on cue, Selah arrived at her door alongside a handful of additional attendants, with each of the women chatting about the day to come in hushed tones.

Beginning before sunrise did not bode well for the day. With a long-suffering sigh, Bellamy followed the gaggle of handmaidens to her vanity, submitting to her fate.

* * * *

Her nerves hit all at once, as if she hadn't had the slightest idea what awaited her. The glow from the stained-glass window high above Bellamy cast radiant rainbows of color over her form while the swelling music promised the wedding would continue in earnest, regardless of her reservations. Stood at the back of the church, she paused as her numerous attendants arranged her skirts, preparing her to walk to the end of the aisle where two men waited.

One was the undisputed future of Calaise, and the other a usurper who surely had designs upon the throne that were all his own.

That Bellamy had seen Gierson as anything otherwise was to her shame. She'd imagined Helena to be the schemer behind the scenes, orchestrating deceptions to elevate her second-born to sovereignty, though he'd been complicit throughout, as eager to reign as she was to stand behind him, pulling the strings.

But none of that mattered now. Instead, Bellamy smiled, hoping she appeared as enraptured by the ceremony as her false intended, who endured patiently at the end of the aisle at the top of a small flight of stairs. An officiant was beside him, poised to oversee the blessed occasion, while Ffion stood a step below his brother.

Another insult.

Yet Ffion did not seem to care, his gaze watchful upon her as she began to move down the silken runner adorned in petals of crimson. It was a sight to behold, beautiful beyond words, but she cared naught for any of the adornments nor for any of the many courtiers, whose whispers followed her as she strode.

She moved up the steps, standing before the wrong brother, who offered her only a half-smile. Something in his eyes, in his mien, felt *off*, but she supposed it would. This was a simple civil ceremony, to be followed by the real deal where nobody who didn't matter would not be, and that, thankfully, included Gierson. Nothing about this part of the day was real, save for one thing.

Ffion put her at ease, his calm disposition like a breath of fresh air to her soul. He would see her through to the other side, where she would tie herself to the right brother before the only people she cared about in private.

While two sets of nuptials were the tradition in Calaise — an overwhelming one, at that — Bellamy was grateful that it afforded them the possibility of pulling off their most duplicitous gamble yet. The pomp and circumstance of the public wedding would provide a welcome distraction for all the people who cared, allowing Bellamy and Ffion to slip away for their own.

And though that promise filled her heart to bursting, she dared not ignore Gierson, who'd somehow agreed to it all without question, though he was not privy to what would follow their current civil professions.

The courtiers would make their way to the ballroom to begin celebrating, leaving Ffion and Bellamy to accomplish their secret quest. She didn't care what Gierson did during that in-between time as long as it didn't involve her.

The banquet that followed the second ceremony would be a trick, however, as she didn't know how she would tear herself away from her new husband...

As if he sensed the musings of her private thoughts, Gierson squeezed Bellamy's hands, drawing her back to the present. The officiant began the service, muttering some nonsense about their partnership and her duties to king and country. There was some mention of trust, of devotion, and a bit of time spent on the burden of sovereignty.

It was all rather impersonal, which wasn't a surprise given her recent arrival and how little she knew of her betrothed, but she listened nonetheless, attempting in vain to pay attention with Ffion standing one step lower.

She felt his gaze upon her, steady and sure, and eagerly awaited the moment that she could stand before him instead, pledging her devotion to a man who had blindsided her with his loyalty, with his provision. He'd nurtured her spirit in all of its darkness, leading her to a place where she could learn to accept herself as he did.

"Repeat after me," said the officiant to Gierson. "I, Ffion, take thee, Bellamy, in the eyes of the law and the privacy of my own heart. Together, we will rule, forsaking all others, 'til death parts us."

Hearing the vows was a shock, and doubly so coming from the lips of one she could never cherish. Bellamy absorbed Gierson's words, but never could they resonate.

The officiant repeated the vows for Bellamy to follow, glancing her way expectantly, but her eyes were already upon Ffion. She smiled, feeling relief when he smiled back, bringing her contentment as she found her voice.

"I, Bellamy, take thee, Ffion, in the eyes of the law and the privacy of my own heart. Together, we will rule, forsaking all others, 'til death parts us."

The last of her words hit her powerfully, with the realization of her commitment, though she was more than happy to be making it. Bellamy recovered her senses, returning her attention to Gierson, who looked less than pleased with her profession. His annoyance wouldn't be obvious to anybody else, as all those in attendance were flanking them, deprived of a direct view of his face.

The remainder of the ceremony proceeded without issue, even if the whole thing was a farce. Bellamy simply needed to look at Gierson to know how true that was, watching as he adopted a false smile, feigning his elation over signing the license.

But he didn't sign it.

The spare made a show of it, swirling his feather pen through the squatty inkpot before signing the document lain before him with a flourish and a grin. To the casual onlooker, he'd completed the job—he was the utterly euphoric, newly married husband and heir apparent. But to Bellamy, his scheming only continued, though she couldn't quite fathom what he was up to now.

And the smile upon Helena's face as he completed his faux signature only confirmed her suspicions.

Chapter Twenty-Four

The smile on his mother's face plagued him still.

Ffion briefly glanced Helena's way during the lavish performance he'd just endured, and he'd found her bearing more than a bit unnerving. She'd watched on as Gierson dipped his feather quill into the small pot of ink, his hand hovering just above the legal documents that would bind a groom to his bride in accordance with the law, and all the while, she'd beamed at the spare.

There was some reason for Ffion to doubt his twin's intentions, but his suspicions regarding their mother were worse. Too much was at stake to brush aside his wariness, and the dowager had the most to lose should he take his rightful place with Bellamy by his side. Helena was calculating and callous, and Gierson, puzzling. Whether they jointly desired to usurp the throne or not, his father declared that Ffion would take his place, and he would not fail to fulfill that desire.

The wedding was a charming distraction for those forced to attend, though it was, by and large, a sham.

While a run-of-the-mill production at best, it delighted the courtiers eager for a departure from their daily hand-wringing over their captivity within the manor walls.

If it kept the peace, Ffion supposed it was worth it. It had appeased his conniving mother, at any rate, though that was far from comforting.

Ffion arrived a little early with Luc at the extravagant chapel on the fringes of the vast grounds of Dufoise to ensure it was vacant. Per tradition, the celebrated couple would participate in a secondary ceremony intended only for them with their chosen witnesses while guests enjoyed refreshments off-site to encourage privacy.

Indeed, it could not have been more ideal. Or suspicious, given the ease with which the plan had come together, but he left his remaining concerns at the palace where they would wait, concealed until the tolling of chapel bells would resonate across Calaise in celebration of the union within its walls.

"My father would have been appalled," Ffion said, shaking his head.

"Not by your actions. This is precisely where you need to be, Your Majesty." Lucignolo's reassurance was a blessing, though it did nothing to calm the prince's nerves. He paced back and forth before the altar to prevent himself from spiraling further down a road that led to nowhere but disaster.

They would succeed, and their plan was worth it.

The bishop and his attendant entered through a rear set of doors, kneeling before the cross standing at the head of the sanctuary. Ffion and Luc inclined their heads toward the bishop as he found his place at the altar with them, splitting open the pages of the holy word in his hands. The same officiant from the previous ceremony, civil servant to the crown, Pierre, was there once more. He was a beloved confidant of Ffion's father and a member of his council. With him were the documents that would legally declare the heir and his pixie beloved as husband and wife.

Their vows would be swift, and only those present would know what transpired during the private nuptials. In the end, they'd be joined in the eyes of God and the law, and that was all that mattered to Ffion.

His focus had become singular, with Bellamy as the center of his world, and together, they would forge a path for Calaise. She would make him bolder, more just. In his mind, his kingdom could receive no better fate than to exist under the wisdom of the beautiful pixie queen.

Behind the radiant panes of stained glass adorning the impressive chapel doors, Ffion saw Bellamy's breathtaking silhouette. Selah and Kit opened the doors before her, leaving only an aisle with row upon empty row of intricate walnut seats between the heir and his future.

His heart nearly stopped at first sight of her. Bellamy's gown shimmered under the dim candlelight lining either side of her path as she moved, with her maid and halfling tag-along following several paces behind.

The heir swallowed hard, collecting his thoughts as she proceeded down the aisle. She'd changed in the brief time since he'd last seen her, and he could have wept if not for his desperation to commit to memory every detail of that moment. The pixie's unearthly presence awakened a long-slumbering calm, restoring fractured parts of Ffion he'd thought were forever broken.

Bellamy was a vision in ivory and gold, her long, auburn tresses swept back by a singular ribbon into an elegant knot at the nape of her neck. Errant bronze strands reflected the flames around her, framing her face and moving gently with each languid stride toward him. Every step echoed through the otherwise empty church, the train of Bellamy's gown trailing behind her in a waterfall of fine, silken mesh.

The light layers of her skirt, gathered at her hips with a long-lined bodice, accentuated her graceful curves, creating a devastating effect that nearly brought the prince to his knees. Winding details of delicate lace and hand-beaded embellishments sheathed Bellamy's seductive contours, while loose-fitting sleeves fell over her forearms, thin enough to see her flawless skin underneath, swelling just above her wrists before tapering into a subtle, hidden hem.

She held a single winter rose — perhaps even the one Ffion had given her at his mother's ball after they arrived in Calaise — stripped clean of its thorns. The prince smiled at her choice, however ruinous it could have proven to be. For him, Bellamy was that rose. In all her beauty, cleverness, and unparalleled resolve, his pixie was equally lethal.

Bellamy passed the bloom to Selah, who dipped into a curtsy before quietly joining Kit in a pew. The pair sat beside Luc near the front of the chapel, close enough to hear every promise exchanged.

Ffion offered a hand to his bride-to-be as she ascended the steps before the altar, and Bellamy met his gaze, her eyes a blaze in hues of glowing saffron. Long, slender fingers warmed his palm, and the prince found, at last, that he was whole.

"You are—" the heir breathed, his words failing him. Speech was beyond him as he studied her, and joy shone in Bellamy's features when she smiled softly, scrunching her nose in a way that only made her more endearing.

"I cannot leave Calaise." Ffion held her gaze, and she waited for him to continue, her calming mien dissolving his anxieties even as he spoke.

"Something is amiss. I know you feel it too, and I can't, in good conscience, desert my kingdom." He paused, hating himself for what he had to say and the threat it posed to his future contentedness. He cursed the moisture pooling in his eyes.

"Do not stay unless it's truly what you want. You've dreamed of refuge and freedom, and I offer neither. I will find a way through the gates for you if that is what you choose. I'd never think less of you."

Bellamy closed her eyes, only for tears to wet her cheeks when she opened them. She shook her head, raising a palm to cup his jaw, her featherlight fingertips brushing over the cropped ends of his hair just below his ear. "I would not find refuge after knowing the solace your selflessness sows. And what is freedom if my every thought drives me to distraction? I would think of nothing but you, tormented by what might have been had I stayed where my heart became whole." Her lower lip quivered as she spoke. "Let me be yours, Ffion. I am yours."

"I once told you that you reminded me of someone," the prince began.

It happened a short time after they met—those unsettling days in Neverwoode that felt like a lifetime past when the halfling, Wendolyne, ruled. Deranged, and a self-declared queen of those illusory lands, she was unfeeling and manipulative, and Ffion had likened Bellamy to her.

"I resented you, I think. Even though I didn't remember the details of my past or what I was, I envied your sense of self."

Bellamy sniffed in amusement, seemingly remembering the accusation as he continued.

"I was afraid of you and the way we were somehow tethered to one another from the beginning. I blamed my desperation to be near you on your relations when it was an impulse— an ache, bone-deep to follow you here. I convinced myself that it was duty that drove me back to Calaise and a thirst for vengeance, but it was you that I couldn't deny myself. I know that now, despite all my resistance."

Ffion watched his intended, his brows knitting together in contemplation. She was the blessing and anchor he'd not dared to hope for, and he needed her like the very breath in his lungs.

"Forgive me, *ma fée*," he pleaded.

She smiled again, a captivating tilt of her lips revealing that she understood. "It is nothing."

The prince chuckled once, noting his father's advisor wore a subtle smile, too.

"It is rare, is it not?" Ffion mused, addressing the bishop and his attendant.

"Indeed," they agreed uniformly.

The prince and his betrothed turned their attention to the aged reverend, whose expression suggested approval. "I do not often have the privilege of overseeing unions such as yours," he admitted, glancing between them. "With your permission, Your Majesty, I will proceed with a blessing."

The heir nodded, and the bishop spoke over the pair as they bowed their heads. His words were short but would remain branded on Ffion's soul until his dying breath.

Once he'd finished, his attendant stepped forward, holding a velvet pillow before himself with four rings, each glinting under brilliant beams of light cast through the chapel glass.

Ffion had searched for his grandmother Alizee's wedding rings the day before, once the arrangements had been made, feeling relieved when he'd found them amongst the late king's regalia and other precious pieces.

Little Ffion, she had called him. Her foxglove — an ironic name given the way that he drew pixies to himself just as the flower namesake itself was said to do.

The dowager hadn't cared what adorned her replacement's hand and would not balk at the choice apart from her dislike of her late husband's mother. But rather than having the bands delivered to Bellamy for appearance's sake alone, as was requested, Ffion had entrusted his grandmother's collection to the bishop for his secret nuptials.

"*In nomine Patris,*" said the prince, taking the first golden ring from the cushion and sliding the band onto Bellamy's thumb.

In the name of the Father.

Bellamy cocked her in curiosity, attentively observing the custom as the heir retrieved a second ring of polished gold, slipping it over the knuckle of her index finger.

"*Et filii.*"

The Son.

Ffion reached for the third ring and placed it on his bride's hand. "*Et Spiritus Sancti.*"

And the Holy Spirit.

He could not tear his gaze from Bellamy, who looked in awe at the dazzling jewels adorning her hands. She met his gaze as he took the final ring, her eyes glistening as she nodded. Her delicate hand trembled in his.

The tradition was articulated in a dead tongue, long since abandoned, though not forgotten, but the final ring was to be given in the groom's native dialect.

"*Je t'épouse*, Bellamy Rosamund Gracia," Ffion pledged.

I marry you, Bellamy.

They were the words his father and generations before him had promised, and with them, the heir and his halfling queen were forever bonded when he slipped the last ring onto her fourth finger. He ran his thumb idly over the token of his love, his heart racing when the bishop turned to Bellamy, that she might respond in kind.

"I marry you, Onfroi Tolliver Ffion Adélard," said she, and he'd not heard his full name spoken in years. The dowager despised all four of his monikers, but he adored the meaning behind each name, with Ffion the most precious of all. Each belonged in some way to someone he'd cherished and who'd treasured him in return.

"In the sight of God and these witnesses, I now pronounce you man and wife," announced Pierre, his delight plain.

The prince would no longer spend his days alone or lurking in the darkened wood each night.

Bellamy was his, and he belonged to her unequivocally.

Ffion pushed the stray locks from his pixie's brow, his knuckle grazing her temple. He tried to bury his desire and quell the rising demand to claim every part of her without success, for she was his bride.

His wife.

The prince held Bellamy's face, and his restraint evaporated as he brought his mouth to hers, a quiet groan of desperation rolling through his throat as he fought for control. Her lips were perfect, her body melting into him when she took hold of his shirt, clenching it in her fists. Ffion deepened the kiss when her lips parted, affording his tongue entry as it swept over hers. His thoughts turned feral when he felt the pixie's fingers splay on his chest, and even through his clothing, her warmth unraveled him.

The moment would come when the prince would show Bellamy the depths of his devotion, but their time was fleeting, and they were not yet alone.

While the world around them had stilled, neither could forget what awaited them when they parted. Bellamy clung to him, splintering his resolve to rejoin a celebration that was not meant for them, but he released her from his hold with a sharp exhale.

Gierson would expect her at the palace, where they would wait to be presented to their guests. The notion was vile, and Ffion's strength of will to endure the pretense faltered. He wanted to hide her.

They signed the documents, completing the ceremony. Soon, the chapel bells would sound, and they would leave separately to avoid discovery, off to find palace courtiers who would be drowning in bubbling champagne, celebrating a union that was not at all what they were led to believe.

Ffion would be with her only from a distance, standing at the edge of the room. And Gierson. Gierson would sweep her across a gleaming ballroom floor — the *bride* and *groom's* first dance for all to see. Murmurs would circulate around them, most of those in attendance believing their ruse, with the pretender prince parading his new bride about as their true sovereign kept to the shadows.

And there, Ffion would fume, dreaming of a future where he could openly love the woman who had tamed his beastly spirit.

Chapter Twenty-Five

Nothing could have prevented Bellamy's wandering gaze.

Tensions were rising amongst the confined residents, but a wedding, a celebration, was sure to pacify them, along with a reception flowing with champagne and an equal serving of ignorance and polite forbearance.

It was a preposterous notion, but then again, Helena was never known to be terribly forthright.

She was seated to one side of Bellamy, and Gierson was on the other. The dowager held her fork primly in her hand, as if another mouthwatering plate would fill the courtiers' bellies enough to make them forget the potential tribulation mounting beyond the palace gates. Five courses were on the menu, with wine poured freely for one and all, following an afternoon of celebratory toasts and sweets.

As for Ffion, he'd excused himself from the meal but Bellamy could sense that he wasn't far, his mere presence nothing shy of tempestuous. Thankfully, not a soul would wonder where the presumed second-born had gone, as the attentions of the people fell wholly upon the happily married couple at the center.

Upon their first meeting, Bellamy had thought well enough of Gierson. He'd reigned fairly in Ffion's absence, though it hadn't yet been for a sustained period. He was charming and gracious, never seeming to envy his elder twin or the title he bore. By all accounts, he'd maintained a degree of apathy in the role he'd fulfilled in the true heir's stead. But neither had he made an effort to withdraw himself from a position that was never meant for him.

"I'm sure this wasn't what you envisioned when you and my brother were engaged," Gierson said, leaning toward Bellamy, his breaths tickling her ear. He'd not touched the cake on his plate nor the glazed cranberry and maple lamb preceding it. His manner rang as sincere, but the pixie could not reconcile how he'd justified not stepping aside for the day's events or even why the nuptials had been scheduled for a time before Ffion could resume his role as their father's successor.

"I hope it doesn't grieve you too deeply. Your day of celebration will come." The spare smiled, reaching for Bellamy's hand, curving his fingers around hers on the arm of her chair. Something foul suffused Gierson's touch, forcing her to resist the impulse to recoil. They'd touched before, but never had it made her stomach turn as it did then.

"I didn't imagine anything so grand. But it's not so different from what I imagined," Bellamy lied, ignoring the anxious thoughts taking root in her mind. For one night, she, too, could pretend. "The grooms share such a likeness that I confess, I often cannot tell one from the other."

Gierson laughed, his study shifting to blatant intrigue.

Since he'd left the hall, Bellamy had searched for Ffion. She'd felt his nearness, but nowhere close enough. To have followed after him would have fueled questions they were unprepared to answer as yet, but she was familiar enough with her new husband to know when he was on the edge. Etiquette itself demanded he be seated to the right of Gierson, the supposed heir apparent, leaving him opposite to Bellamy. He'd caught her gaze once as Gierson sipped his drink, and Ffion's eyes had laid bare the chaos brewing behind them.

"Dance with me?" The spare stood, Bellamy's hand still grasped within his.

She reluctantly accepted, seeing no other reasonable response, and Gierson whisked her onto the dance floor. The music began anew as he led her around the room to a chorus of approving whispers from the gathered courtiers when she spied Ffion, watching their every step.

It was the bride and groom's first dance, by all appearances, and the wedding guests were thrilled by the spectacle. A resonating swell of stringed music filled the hall, with all eyes upon them as they danced.

But Ffion paced along the edge of the floor, cocking his head to one side and the other like he so often did in those moments when he fought for control, his darkened gaze not once straying from Bellamy.

Never had the pixie feared for herself in his times of torment, but her awareness of his anguish now was almost more than she could bear. They were uniquely bonded through Marin. Oddly enough, the affliction he'd cast upon their lives was the greatest gift he could have given her, for it had brought them together, and even if Ffion's private hell tortured them both all their days, he would not endure it alone.

As quickly as the realization struck her, another took its place. Gierson pulled her close, and she could scarcely tolerate the feel of him against her, his gentle touch like acid to her skin.

Doubtless, his sudden regard resulted from his brother's presence, leaving her at the center of a war born of flesh and blood, ever fueled by the bitterness of Helena and her wicked father.

She knew her father had somehow left his mark upon the spare, just as he had with Ffion. Every shadow Bellamy perceived behind his calm façade was a cruel reminder of Marin's vile misdeeds against the flame-haired princes.

To his credit, King Tolliver had tried to shield his sons, enshrouding the manor in iron fencing to preserve his boys from all that sought to harm them, but his efforts had occurred too late. Sympathy bloomed within Bellamy, thinking of all that the late king had endured, even unto his last desperate acts in searching for his rightful heir.

He'd been fighting a losing battle against her own father, and undoubtedly alone, for Helena cared for nobody but herself and her precious second-born.

Suddenly, Gierson's touch made the pixie's skin crawl. He was too close, and the music too loud. The false king smiled, sending her spinning away from himself before guiding her back, and it seemed he was prepared to dance until their shoes were worn through. She'd resolved to endure — it was only for the day — but she was reaching the end of her patience, eager to return to her rightful husband until, finally, she struggled to ignore the whispers stirring all around them.

Relief consumed her when she saw Ffion striding toward them with a nonchalance that exuded authority. Gierson, despite all pretense of power, acknowledged his brother with a well-practiced grin, drawing himself away from her though his arm still circled her waist.

Silence dominated the hall, the musicians having ceased their number to join in staring. But Ffion simply returned his twin's smile before inclining his head toward Bellamy, offering her his hand.

"If I'm not mistaken, it's your kingdom's custom for the bride to dance with the members of her groom's household," Ffion said, his speech loud enough for those around them to overhear.

Bellamy dipped into a polite curtsy, failing to hide her smile. "How thoughtful of you to remember." She glanced over her shoulder to Gierson, who gestured them off with a flick of his wrist, smirking as if he were simply amused by his brother's audacity.

The spare stepped away, signaling the orchestra, and a new song echoed through the room. He'd handled himself with poise, but Bellamy was too wise to view Gierson's tact as anything less than careful diplomacy.

Ffion spun Bellamy elegantly toward himself, and she relaxed in his embrace. She didn't know the song or the steps to match the pretty melody that played, but she'd not soon forget how she felt when he took her into his arms.

Every distraction faded from her mind as the heir spun one of the four bands he'd given her around her finger, turning her to face him, and when their eyes met, Bellamy lost all sense of reason or decorum. She was carrying on, moving nearer to a supposed brother-in-law than she ought. And while she knew her rapture to be unbecoming, she didn't care.

"I couldn't help myself," Ffion murmured in her ear. His voice was deliciously low, his breath skimming over her flesh as he drew her nearer. "When can I see you?"

His question ignited an urgency within her that would demand her husband's ministrations if they didn't part, but she couldn't allow him such an easy victory.

"Come to my chambers when you know you'll not be seen." Bellamy's cheeks warmed when she met her husband's gaze, his possessive study summoning an overwhelming ache for him that a lifetime would not satisfy.

The heir leaned into her, his nose grazing over the curve of her neck. He inhaled her scent, a wolf if ever there were one, his boldness nearly incapacitating her resolve to remain polite. "I can smell your desire."

He withdrew slightly, wearing a fiendish grin, the soft glow of the chandeliers above highlighting the divinely cut angles of his face and collarbones. His cravat hung loosely beneath two unfastened shirt buttons, making him beautifully disheveled, and the mayhem in his gaze called her to him.

Indeed, rumors of their unseemly turn about the hall would spread quickly. Bellamy knew how it must look, what with her flushed cheeks, their scandalous proximity. But she was enthralled by the one who could inspire goodness in her while somehow encouraging matchless abandon. He was reckless and commanding in a way that effortlessly eclipsed his younger brother. Ffion was a born leader and would have been no matter the circumstances of his birth.

Every eye was upon them as Ffion extended his arm, twirling Bellamy elegantly by his lead. Her gown dusted the floor with a gentle hiss, swirling about her legs before he led her back to himself, her palm landing upon his chest.

"Let them watch," he said, when her gaze met his. "One day, they will learn the truth and realize the love their king has for his queen."

"And that is the truth?" Bellamy dared press herself nearer, her fingers twisting the ends of Ffion's cravat.

"That I'm in love with you?" He smirked, placing his hand over hers. His lips hovered over her knuckles, his eyes exposing his soul's profession. "I do not think it much of a secret." Ffion kissed Bellamy's hand, and she returned his smile as he repeated the gesture, pressing his mouth to the other. His admission was not hushed, though he didn't seem concerned if anybody were to overhear.

Deafening quiet fell over the grand hall when their dance came to an end. Retreating a step, Ffion's gaze lingered upon Bellamy before he glanced in Gierson's direction, who approached as if his brother had not again outdone him.

Wearing a devilish grin, the rightful heir bowed only to his bride before departing, the promise of untold passion lingering in his wake.

Another hour had passed when, at last, Gierson agreed to see Bellamy to her chambers. Lords and ladies were given baskets of wheat to toss upon their departure, leaving the spare plucking bits of the grain from his formalwear as they made their way through the private corridors. Every sconce along the walls was lit, warming their walk and illuminating papered panels, which, Kit had learned from a castle attendant, were hand-painted by a handful of local Calaisean artists.

At the end of the long hall, where it diverged into separate wings, Gierson guided Bellamy toward the king's quarters, down a passage where none but His and Her Majesty were to reside in connected suites. Her steps halted when it became clear where he planned to take her, and she refused to move an inch further on his arm.

"I will spend the night in my own room," she said, realizing she'd not spoken a word to him since leaving the banquet. The halfling removed her palm from Gierson's elbow, and he took her hand in his just before it fell to her side. It was evident in his gaze that he understood her meaning.

"This won't end well for him. You must know that."

With a few errant words, Gierson confirmed her suspicions regarding his loyalties. Bellamy pulled away, unable to endure his treacherous touch any longer, and when Gierson reached for her, she put more distance between them. "I know that what you say is treason," she spat. "And I will have no part in it." She turned from him, but his blurred form remained in her periphery as she continued. "What makes you think yourself better? Do you believe you understand the world better than your brother does?"

Gierson closed the gap with a single stride, disregarding her desire for space. Picking a small piece of grain from the hair framing her face, he flicked it aside onto the crimson runner underfoot. "He can barely hold himself together in front of his people without risking tearing Dufoise and everyone in it apart. He cannot be trusted to rule them. He's not meant to rule anything." Gierson scoffed, shaking his head in disbelief. "His eyes reflect the instability of our father, but at least *he* had sense enough to lock himself away most of his days. Until he went after Ffion."

"Are you finished?" Bellamy refused to meet his eyes, her posture stiff. She felt his study searing over every inch of her body as he sniffed in irritation.

It was answer enough.

Bellamy left Gierson standing alone in the empty passageway, dressed in a king's finery that belonged to another, and fading footsteps indicated that he did not mean to follow her. She took a fortifying breath despite her corset's attempts to prevent air from entering her lungs. A door slammed at Bellamy's back, and the walls shuddered.

For all his pretending, it seemed Gierson had never eluded his curse.

Chapter Twenty-Six

The halfling who would be queen was not one to preen. On the contrary, she was much more likely to be stippled with sweat than any sort of cosmetics. While Bellamy was growing more accustomed to the latter, she had reached her limit for one day.

Because it was her wedding night, Selah would not attend the bride until morning, but had laid aside a set of white silk unmentionables trimmed with delicate eyelet lace on Bellamy's bed. Beside them was a floor-length robe of gossamer with flowing sleeves.

She shimmied free from Colette's sensational gown, dropping it in a billowing whisper to the cold floor before changing into Selah's gift. The robe enveloped her, gliding over her skin like water.

Padding across the room to her vanity, Bellamy seated herself before the large mirror. She picked at her hair, still swept neatly away from her face, finding bits of grain hidden within it when the hinges of her door creaked almost inaudibly.

Her heart skipped, thinking of Ffion as he revealed the need he'd sensed in her. She'd not expected him so soon, and she'd been right. The hair rose on her arms when she confirmed her suspicions that it was not her husband in the doorway, for she'd have felt his nearness.

Bellamy breathed deeply, steadying her nerves. *He* would feel her alarm, with her own awareness of him twisting in her stomach as she reached for the hand mirror from the desk in front of her.

She slid the hilt of her stiletto into her palm, but not before eyeing what lurked behind her in the mysterious looking glass. She might've retched had the inky tendrils of her nightmares not seeped into her room with every step Gierson took toward her. Shadows wended and coiled around him, the reflection within Marin's mirror unveiling the tainted essence Bellamy had felt in his company but had never *seen*.

Her blade, concealed on her person, was flush with her forearm, hidden away as well as she could manage from beneath the wispy sleeve when she rose from her vanity.

"I've missed you," said Gierson, sounding nothing like himself. Bellamy willed herself to turn, to face the roiling darkness awaiting her, but it was gone when she did. She felt it, her body alert to its presence without taking shape as it had in the glass.

The spare looked and sounded like Ffion. Anyone else would not know the difference, save for perhaps their mother, but Bellamy wasn't sure even the dowager could've. Gierson's hair was mussed like his older twin's, his jaw shadowed with stubble. The wildness in his eyes mirrored her husband's as well, but where Ffion's were always shrewd, the spare's were hollow, like staring into a blackened well.

"You shouldn't be here." Bellamy measured her words, and though a chill chased down her spine, her voice didn't waver.

"Is this not what you wanted?" Gierson asked, pacing closer to where she stood, her chambers seemingly shrinking with each purposeful tread. He was undoubtedly determining Bellamy's familiarity with him, playing a dubious game that would be idiotic to anyone who'd ever been in love, for never could she mistake him for her beloved.

She only prayed Ffion would not discover them.

Bellamy didn't fear for her husband's love or trust, only that his restraint would fail if he found Gierson attempting to take more that was not his to have.

And what, then, if the spare was realized to be dead?

Wearing a flirtatious smile, Bellamy made her way to the exit, passing him by when she did. Ignoring Gierson's salacious surveyal was not for the faint of heart, his gaze passing over her scantily clad body causing her stomach to lurch. "Not like this, Ffion," she purred. "We both agreed."

Had she not already been convinced, the false king's hefty sigh would have given him away—a stark and spiteful contrast to his brother, who met Bellamy's needs before his own, even when he was lost to himself.

They were nothing alike.

Bellamy watched while Gierson's eyes traveled the length of her body, every inch of her visible through her flimsy covering. "You need to leave."

He curled his lip, sneering. "He was a fool to bring you into this palace."

No more pretense, then.

It was just as well, as it was wearisome to feign anything but revulsion now that Gierson had made plain the sort of faithless lech he was. She wanted nothing more than to be free of him.

Yet, even as Bellamy pleaded with the heavens that he would go, that something would cut through the sinister haze shrouding the prince, he advanced slowly toward her, heedless to her visible discomfort. He was more demon than man, more shackled to damnation than any of her forsaken kin.

Would that he might deem her unworthy of the wrath that would surely follow an attempt to harm, for Ffion would spare no mercy when it came to redeeming her.

Armed only with her stiletto, Bellamy felt her palm begin to sweat where she gripped the blessed little dagger behind her back, the blade a godsend. She would, at the very least, leave a hell of a wicked mark.

"I won't act as though I've not appreciated the distraction you've created," said Gierson at last, inching closer with each word until he was before her, tipping her chin so she could not miss the lust within his gaze.

"You would jeopardize so much?" Bellamy could not withhold her disgust, cursing herself as she trembled under his study. "You come here, pretending to be the brother you will never be, and for what? The rapture of my touch?" She scoffed, looking him dead in the eye. "It would be for *him* alone. *Never* for you."

His hold tightened, his fingers digging into her cheeks as he leaned nearer. "What difference is it to me if you wish it were him? I think of you often — what it would be like to taste the salt on your skin." He closed his eyes, inhaling deeply as if he savored the thought itself. Gierson met her gaze again, running his tongue lazily over his bottom lip before brushing his nose over Bellamy's.

She clutched the steel in her hand, prepared to strike if she had to, and each second she waited felt like a lifetime. If he was anything like Ffion, it would but maim him. Even so, it would give her a chance to run. Or scream.

Gierson jerked her head to the side, kissing the flesh of her slender neck, and she had enough, adjusting her weapon in her hand, determining where best to strike when something clattered on the ground at the end of the hall from outside her open door.

A huff of unadulterated fury broke through the prince's blind savagery. "Some other time then," Gierson spat, shoving her away, and Bellamy stumbled backward, the wall breaking her fall as she clung to it.

She waited for him to change his mind, to slam the door behind him and take her for himself, but the moment never came. He stood silently for a beat with his back to her, his frame rigid as if he considered it, before he left without another word.

Bellamy closed and latched the door, sinking to the floor. To say she was relieved would not have come close to describing what she felt as moisture filled her eyes. She'd heard of miracles beyond reason, and Gierson relenting felt like one such wonder after seeing firsthand the depravity oozing forth from him.

Never would she forget the answer to her quiet petition, for mercy had found her.

While Gierson deserved whatever end would meet him should Ffion find Bellamy so affected, she wanted nothing more than to purge the memory from her mind. She was well and would not give Gierson a foothold over the peace his failings granted.

Wiping the tears from her face, Bellamy rose from the marble floor. Her chambers had only served as a secondary prison disguised as a generous accommodation, and she couldn't stand to be there any longer. Ffion made her quarters feel like home, but without him, the room was everything foul. It reeked of the pixies she'd killed, regardless of Selah's efforts to wash them away.

As if it was not enough to have a reminder of their malevolence forever a part of her...

Bellamy scribbled a note to her maid, informing her to have her things relocated to the queen's suites, serving as a message to anyone who might be watching, though she'd not yet been coronated. If Helena could play games, then so might she, especially given the added benefit of displacing the nasty dowager.

She was unfamiliar with the protocol, but it seemed plain enough that sovereigns were not expected to share a bed for love but, rather, to further the royal line. It was not her objective to reside separately from her husband, but she did mean to make her intentions to rule at his side known. Ffion would assume his throne in short order, whether with his family's blessing or not, and Bellamy crowned Queen of Calaise along with him.

Her husband had promised that soon their people would know the truth. Until then, she cared not about what rumors might take root.

* * * *

Nervous tension prevented Ffion from thinking of anything but his wife. He told himself to give her time to settle before going to her, that too many guests were still wandering the halls, soused with drink, to solicit his bride's attention.

He hated every second that passed, loathing the circumstances that made him feel as though he had something to hide, expected to sneak around an estate that was his by law.

Ffion would have no more of it. The charade would be put to rest, strategy and scandal be damned.

Throwing a wrinkled tunic over his head, he started for the door, failing to consider how unkempt he might appear, navigating the halls to Bellamy's chambers in linen trousers worn only for sleep and nothing on his feet.

His temper had piqued earlier that evening as he'd watched his brother peacock about the celebration, leaving Ffion so incensed that he'd had no other option but to return to his room, where he'd requested his bath filled with ice water. He'd sunk into the copper tub, fully clothed in his formalwear, soaking himself from head to toe. His body had shuddered from the cold, but he'd forced himself to submerge again and again until his beast was silenced.

Fanciful musings of his wife had aided the calm that came in due course as he shocked his system into submission. She'd unwittingly upset every misconception he'd held as truth from their first meeting when she brought him back to life, triggering echoes of what had led him to Neverwoode in the first place.

She made him believe he could be good.

The prince stopped short of his doorway when his pulse quickened, recognizing Bellamy's rousing scent well before she stood at his door. She didn't have time to knock upon her arrival, as Ffion was already opening the door to greet her, but nothing could have prepared him for what he saw.

Countless times that day, she'd robbed him of all sense, but clad in a wispy robe of pure white, Bellamy was a creature of staggering elegance.

Anyone might have seen her walking the halls that way, and some corrupt part of Ffion reveled at the thought of them watching him usher her into his room.

They didn't speak as he closed the door behind them, bolting it shut.

"I've asked for my things to be moved to the queen's chambers." Her eyes danced with mischief, her shameless smirk suggesting she knew he would give anything to have her.

Of course, she was right.

Often, he wondered which half of her looked back at him, but the answer was not so complicated. Bellamy was uncommon perfection, with each half making her whole in her own right. Indeed, he would have it no other way.

"My mother will be delighted that you've seen fit to evict her," said Ffion, doing nothing to mask his amusement. He chuckled at her irreverence, unsurprised that she would so boldly move against the dowager.

"Indeed, she will." The exquisite halfling raised a slender finger, beringed with one of the promises he'd made. Pressing it to her full lips, she quirked a brow. "*Shh...* It's a surprise."

Moving farther into the room, she surveyed their surroundings, tracing the brass inlay gilding an end table beside her. "And I can only assume Gierson has missed his former lodgings. They're quite beautiful."

Beauty. Ffion could think of but one thing consistent with that description at the moment, despite him finding the term profoundly lacking. "I should think he would like to resume this more modest apartment as early as tomorrow. My brother isn't one to prefer grandeur, humble as he is."

Bellamy laughed, and he prowled toward her, teasing the seam of her covering with his knuckles.

"I confess, I shall miss this," she admitted. "When we were simply Ffion and Bellamy."

"You speak as if we were ever normal, *mon cœur.*"

Ffion closed the distance, threading his fingers through the silken hair at the base of her neck before gently taking her earlobe between his teeth. Bellamy sighed, shrugging her robe from her shoulders, and the prince left a trail of kisses in its wake, feeling her pulse quicken beneath his lips. She plunged her fingers into his tousled hair, forcing him to meet her gaze as she reached for the hem of his tunic, and he groaned. Her touch, the warmth of her hands on his stomach, and her lithe body pressed against his sett him alight with longing. Lifting his shirt over his head, she cast it aside.

Rising to her toes, Bellamy kissed the corner of his mouth, hooking her finger around the waist of his trousers. "*Viens avec moi, mon amour.*"

Come with me, my love.

The sound of his native, lyrical language on her lips had him wholly under her command. Step after devastating step, Bellamy retreated toward the bed, and her cover fell to the ground, revealing the delicates underneath.

"So then, is that the truth?" Ffion asked, repeating the question she'd asked him only a short while earlier, and she smiled — a merciless provocation to his wavering self-control.

"I have loved you longer than my heart dared to admit," she said at last, hypnotizing him with her eyes in the color of the rising sun. "My soul begged me to find you."

Ffion inhaled slowly, her confession breaking and healing him at once, feeling unworthy of such fortune. She moved nearer to him, taking the chain circling the prince's neck between her fingertips, letting the gold filter through her splayed fingers. A question formed in her eyes as she examined the ring dangling from it.

"It's my seal. A signet ring given to me by my father and passed down from one generation to the next. When he declared me as heir apparent, my name was etched within it, just like my father's and his father's before him.

"Ffion." He pointed to the tiny etching with his finger, tipping the ring so that Bellamy might see. "It's the only moniker I carry that's unique to me alone. Or was, rather, before my mother and brother saw fit to take it for themselves. I've kept it around my neck all this time, clung to it even, when I'd forgotten who I was."

"Because it is yours." Bellamy opened the clasp of his thin chain, slipping the ring free. "It signifies who you are and who you were always meant to be. You're the High King of Calaise."

Taking his hand, she slid his father's signet onto his finger. "Never believe the lies of your enemy. *Ffion.*

Foxglove. You drew me to you just as the flower is said to draw pixies."

"And you are my queen." He pulled her closer, tipping her chin up toward his face, brushing his mouth over hers. "My love. My *wife*. You're a trial and an angel, and you are mine."

Bellamy smiled, and he was defeated, their mouths colliding in a frenzy of withheld need that demanded satisfaction. Ffion loosed her hair from the ribbon that held it, letting it cascade in a deep, burnished bronze stream down her back before lifting her onto the bed, the feel of her body trembling with anticipation wrecking him as he climbed on top of her. "Not yet," he whispered, his voice rough with desire.

The fairy lightly ran her nails over his abdomen, stopping at the buttons of his pants. "You've forgotten, my love, that I relish a game."

Chapter Twenty-Seven

The love of women had always kept Gierson well, and never did they spurn his attention. Eventually, his brother's pretty little diversion would warm his bed as well—only a matter of time.

It wasn't often Gierson was denied anything by anyone. And that, without question, only made him crave the beguiling she-devil that much more. Her protestations would have ended eventually had their moment alone not been interrupted. He'd imagined it countless times, his name on her lips. *His*, not Ffion's, that she would whisper when he showed her bliss.

Most nights, he'd have found a beautiful servant to relieve of her household chores or, more likely, would have already found gratification with one of the dowager's many ladies. But alas, it was his wedding night, and discretion was…favorable.

Gierson scoffed to himself.

Nights such as this were when he appreciated his understanding with Melis. At times, she was wearisome, but she was agreeable enough when their desires aligned.

As a valued member of the royal guard, there were few days their paths did not cross. It was enjoyable enough to seize the opportunities they were given, even convenient.

Best of all, neither wanted more from the other. Both were content to go their separate ways and neither had asked questions until recently. Even then, Gierson thought Melis' possessiveness to be a result of her own ambition rather than jealousy over Bellamy. She hadn't even blinked when he'd told her of his plans to arrange a strategic union between Calaise and Debrecyn through their fair, firstborn daughter. Indeed, it would not be a burden to bless her with many heirs.

Melis' room was on the highest floor of the palace, a bid she'd made two years prior when they were young and angling for the very most in their respective stations. It was more a loft, and Gierson thought it drafty and unremarkable, but she'd fallen in love with its view of Loch Apsaras, nestled just beside the heart of their kingdom.

Her features expressed her surprise. "What—"

"Close it," he said, pushing through the door, and she did, though she seemed unsettled as she turned to him.

Gierson didn't wait, pulling her to himself, his mouth claiming hers as he scrunched her thin shift in his hands. Melis tensed in his embrace, her own hands upon his chest to force him away, but he was not in a mood for games.

"Don't play as if you're suddenly coy," the spare mumbled, nipping at the tip of her chin as he lowered himself to better reach the hem of the nightgown now raised to her thighs.

Melis pushed him harder. "*Stop.*"

Stepping away, he released her, arms raised in forfeit. "My apologies," Gierson groused, his breath heavy with desire. He was well beyond irritated, his self-control teetering on the bitter edge.

"What's happened to you?" While her words conveyed anger, there was no small bit of alarm in them. "Don't let him affect you this way."

The spare clenched his jaw. She didn't need to say who she meant. "Do not speak of my brother in my presence."

Melis moved several paces away from him, though her eyes never strayed, as if she saw something in him that could not be trusted.

"I was there when you told Queen Helena about the demon fairy's curse," she admitted.

Gierson matched each backward step the lady knight took, maintaining their close proximity.

She averted her gaze under his scrutiny, and the devil in him loved watching her squirm. He hadn't known Melis was aware of Marin or how the pixie had forever changed him with a few malicious words.

Gierson had been a child when he'd awakened to a suffocating golden haze. In the dead of night, his room had shone like the sun, his lungs desperate for air only to be suffused with fine, luminescent dust.

Simultaneous tranquility and havoc had seemed to tear him apart when he'd heard a voice. He'd thought it another night walking incident, like those that had driven him and Ffion that much further apart in their early years.

His growing disdain for Ffion had spiraled out of control from there, betraying the depths of his hostility in the form of a dagger held above his twin's heart while both were fast asleep. While Gierson had awakened to a gentle hand over his, keeping him from plunging the knife into the older boy's chest, he'd been wholly alert to every word spoken over him by the figure that had emerged from the gilded vapor surrounding his bed the following month.

Marin hadn't revealed himself fully — not even after the tiny flecks of gold had settled onto the floor. He'd been hollowed darkness with wings tucked at his back, illuminated by a silvery crescent moon hung low outside Gierson's bedroom window.

The faceless pixie had secured Gierson's damnation with a serpent's tongue. The spare was sure of it, and if he were hell-bound, he would not waste his days toiling in the shadow of his brother's crown.

After the incident, he'd gone to the queen's chambers and told her everything. She'd been the one to awaken him at his brother's bedside, and only she knew the breadth of his contempt for Ffion. She hadn't judged him then, or when he'd shared every unsavory detail of Marin's curse.

In him, she saw the zeal his twin lacked.

Gierson would never forget that night, nor the panic that had seized him when they'd realized they were not alone.

"I couldn't sleep that night with the winds howling as they were, and my mother brought me with her to tend to Queen Helena's fire," Melis said after a brief pause. "Mother cracked the door open so as not to wake Her Majesty when we overheard you telling her what happened, how you were to prove yourself before the kingdom. I dropped the fire prod when I heard her say Calaise would be yours — that everything pronounced over you was a gift and your destiny. Mother sent me back to our quarters downstairs, and I ran all the way there. And when she returned, she told me never to speak of it, so I have not."

"So, you have not," Gierson repeated, taking in all that he'd learned. Surely, he'd known the maid had been there, but not her daughter. The dowager's maid had died only days later, leaving Melis alone.

There'd been no other way.

"But neither did I question what Queen Helena told you about your destiny. And soon after, Ffion left Calaise without saying goodbye, leaving you to prove yourself fit for the throne," Melis continued, her voice trembling as she revealed her truth.

Perhaps it should've helped, but hearing that she thought him worthy of the throne did him little good. "You should not have been listening."

Something shifted in her posture when he spoke. She blanched, putting more distance between them, eyes widening with understanding. No color flushed her cheeks as it so often did when they met in private.

"How did my mother really die?" asked Melis after a moment had passed, though it was clear in the set of her jaw that she already knew.

Gierson saw no purpose in dignifying her question with a response, and she did not press it further, with his silence confirmation enough.

The dame nodded, the truth settling over her so many years later. "Leave me," she ordered, moving farther away, but Gierson was losing his patience. He'd not sought her company to rehash the past, to uncover long-forgotten traumas.

Still, it could not be undone.

"*You* tell me *nothing!*" he shouted, lunging toward her with a heavy tread.

Gierson always favored order, and Melis disrupted the tenuous symmetry he'd achieved in balancing his roles with soundness of mind.

She was a stumbling block he could not abide, and he never left loose ends.

* * * *

Bellamy awakened, enveloped in a tangle of silken sheets. Ffion kissed her bare neck and shoulders, his breath rustling her hair as he turned her toward himself.

"Good morning, Belles," he said, grinning when he saw the smile he brought to her lips.

Morning filtered through the window, bathing their bed in warmth as it highlighted the subtle freckles sprinkling Ffion's nose, making him look more youthful than the man Bellamy had come to know.

Twisting a lock of his bronzed hair between her fingers, the pixie fitted her mouth to his. Deepening the kiss, his hands wandered over her body, rediscovering every inch of her, and she could not stop the sigh of sheer bliss that escaped from her with his rambling touch.

Bellamy hitched her leg around his, rolling him to his side and wrapping her arms around his neck, eliciting a heartbreaking smile from her beloved. He traced the length of her spine, his eyes glinting with mischief when she shivered, causing her flesh to rise.

"Again," he growled, kissing her once more before a quiet rap on the door drew them out of their reverie.

Ffion groaned. "What good is it to be king if I'm to be interrupted just as my morning is becoming interesting?" Flipping Bellamy to her back, he pressed his lips to her jaw before raising his voice to address whoever waited outside. "Begone! And tell anyone else who might require my attention that I mustn't be bothered until noon, or perhaps eventide."

But the messenger slid something through the small opening under the door, followed by retreating footsteps that echoed down the corridor.

Bellamy pecked the prince on the cheek before pushing him off her. She tucked a white sheet under her arms to cover herself and padded over to the entryway to find a sealed note.

"From your mother," Bellamy said, showing Ffion what she'd discovered. He nodded for her to open it, and she broke the wax seal, unfolding the note carefully as she made her way back to her husband.

"She wishes to tell you that I'm to attend a brunch this morning," the pixie continued, tossing her mother-in-law's communication onto the bed for Ffion to see.

He read the short message—an order, not a request. Folding it neatly into its original shape, he set it on the bedside table.

"Very well." Ffion rose, ringing for an attendant. "We shall not keep our guests waiting."

It was Ffion's idea to be the first to arrive.

They entered the dowager's formal brunch hand-in-hand, bringing about a flutter of excitement amongst the servants that remained in the dining hall.

Together, Bellamy and Ffion greeted them, one by one. Each lowered themselves before their sovereigns, the couple urging them to rise each time they did.

If they knew the prince apart from his twin, few showed it, but Ffion made no effort to style himself as Gierson surely would. His hair was a mess of copper waves that fell to his brow, his angled face shadowed with stubble.

He was mesmerizing to observe, for not only was he imposing but his manner with his people did not change based on anything so trivial as one's title. The prince spoke with his palace staff as if there were no social differences between them, and Bellamy adored him all the more for it.

Fayble would never know a more gracious king. The continent was familiar with great leaders, but none so merciful or selfless as he.

It wasn't long before courtiers began to arrive, with the wedding having done little to allay their concerns over what might be happening beyond the gates. But as they entered the banquet, Ffion and Bellamy addressed them at once, though neither pretended all was well, listening attentively as their people poured their hearts out to the soon-to-be king and queen.

The pair mingled freely with guests, enjoying the solace afforded them in the absence of Gierson and Helena, but that was not to last. Bellamy watched as a statuesque form approached the archway to enter, alerting her husband with a winged elbow to the ribs.

"The Dowager Queen, Helena!" announced a stout footman.

Conversation dulled as she made her way through the gathered attendants. They parted for their former queen, nodding when she passed them by without acknowledgment. Her lips formed a thin line of fury though she maintained a stately air.

Ffion beamed at his mother, pressing a kiss to her knuckles when she stood before them. "Mother."

Helena did not lower herself before him or Bellamy in a blatant display of defiance. She knew the nobility of Calaise was watching, and that more so than usual, with tensions heightened as they were, yet she remained as scornful as ever.

Officer d'État Civil, Pierre, cleared his throat, proceeding toward the trio from behind the dowager. His timing could not have been more prescient as a man so staunchly loyal to the Crown and late friend of King Tolliver's. He, too, was observing every move the royals made, and the halfling grew to like him more every day.

"It must be strange to see your son and his bride ascend to your once-held position," he began. The officer had already greeted his sovereigns, offering a slight bow to both Ffion and Bellamy before returning his attention to Helena. "I imagine it might be difficult in the beginning to remember yourself."

The dowager narrowed her gaze, a contemptuous sneer wrinkling her painted lips. "Ah, yes." She dropped into a deep curtsy. "How very humiliating."

Her focus shifted, her gray eyes lifting to the pair's adjoined hands. She straightened, tidying her skirts as she met Bellamy's gaze. "Might I beg a moment alone with His Majesty?"

"No," Ffion snarled, instinctively stepping nearer to Bellamy. "Anything you wish to say can be shared with the present company. In fact, once my brother arrives, I wish to relieve us all of these secrets we've been keeping."

Pierre smirked, observing Helena with apparent amusement. It was easy to forget the history many of those gathered shared. The revelation could have been intimidating if the people's love for Ffion's father had not been so evident.

Further, King Tolliver had *chosen* his successor. Despite the heir's four years away, he was one of them, made obvious in the way they responded to him. He was beloved, and they had only just begun to know him.

Helena resumed her haughty air, her features pinched with irritation. "It is not wise to — "

"Prince Gierson!" the footman bellowed, cutting the dowager off.

She abandoned Ffion and Bellamy at once, moving for Gierson as he entered, his countenance grim. He shoved past Helena, moving directly toward his twin.

The darkness emanating from him was worse than that of Marin. Bellamy was nauseated from it, and though she'd not told her husband what the spare had attempted the night before, Ffion seemed to see the disease rotting Gierson's soul.

His eyes were furious and wild, as they had been when last Bellamy had seen him. He was utterly bewildered, as if he could not prevent himself from stalking toward them for all to see.

He was nearly to there when Helena hastened her steps, reaching for him and pleading in vain, when a woman's scream rang through the dining hall.

"Help!" she cried, stumbling into the gathering, her apron stained with crimson. "Help, *please!*"

Without hesitation, Ffion and Bellamy followed her outside to the palace lawn, where she attempted unsuccessfully to hold herself together. Courtiers and staff alike tailed them as they moved out of doors, watching on as sobs wracked her slight form.

Bellamy rushed to her side to help keep her from falling to the ground, and the woman raised a trembling finger, but Ffion had already discovered what had broken her, his storm-filled gaze fixed on something several meters beyond where Bellamy held the shaking servant.

Sprawled upon the stone patio, with hair dark as pitch shrouding her face, was Melis. Clothed in nothing but a sheer nightgown, she lay in a heap of shattered limbs, leaving the gray stonework painted red with blood.

Bellamy shuddered, remembering how Gierson's eyes had promised violence before he'd left her chambers.

It could have been her.

Chapter Twenty-Eight

Something about Ffion's calm in the face of chaos had Gierson fuming, and watching on as the people responded to his leadership only made it worse.

For four years, Gierson had managed the kingdom. He'd lived under his mother's thumb and worked to honor his father's wishes both while Tolliver was alive and afterward in his death. He had led not one but two separate lives, attending functions as the blessed prince and heir apparent, Ffion, while living privately as himself.

A divided mind had he, and all the ills that came along with such disharmony plagued his spirit.

In the end, he was being cast aside. It didn't take a genius to see what was happening as Ffion orchestrated order, soothing people's terror over something so insignificant. Bellamy was close by his side, and Gierson knew he'd been frozen out, with his brother rapidly rising to take his place alongside his beautiful betrothed.

Together, they'd be a force for the reckoning.

The brunch had come to a standstill. A handful of women cried, and at least one had fainted. A few brave men took to the courtyard to examine the fallout, attempting in vain to piece together the events that had led to such a bright, vibrant knight meeting her end upon a cold stone floor.

But only Gierson knew what had happened, and try as he might, he couldn't bring himself to care. Perhaps it should've concerned him that he felt so little, but really, Melis should've known better than to test his patience.

She'd driven him mad, going from a woman he could depend upon to one readily lobbing flaming arrows of accusation, some of which were largely accurate, making him seethe.

He hadn't seen the end of their arrangement coming. And while that had undoubtedly caught him off guard, he was more bothered still by the secrets she'd carried for so long. Melis could've derailed all his carefully laid plans with a few words, revealing the origins of the division between the heir and the spare.

She might've exposed the curse, establishing once and for all the inadequacy of both brothers, dominated by their truest nature with neither worthy of their sovereign duty. Instead, she'd found herself at odds with her lover, who craved power more than he would ever desire any woman.

Gierson hadn't been aiming for the balcony and had been temporarily bothered when Melis had toppled over the edge in their struggle, but he'd quickly found peace in the knowledge that his secret was safe, choosing instead to make the best of her misfortune.

He would rule.

And not with some halfling abomination as his queen though, somehow, she satisfied his wretched brother. He would wed a Debrecynian princess, unifying the mountain region and all its myriad resources and able-bodied countrymen with his own prosperous kingdom, effectively conquering the majority of eastern Fayble.

Gierson watched a moment longer, his irritation rising with each reassuring word Ffion spoke over the people. His brother was naive and far too optimistic, with the thought of marrying for love utterly foreign to the spare. Ffion lacked the cunning and ruthlessness required of any monarch. Surely, he would crumble under the pressure of the Crown.

He could take it no more. Gierson stormed from the hall, eager to be free of the chatter. The courtiers had been on edge since the whole of Dufoise became trapped within the hideous winter bloom barricade, but that was no excuse to fall apart as they had.

It was not within Gierson to coddle and pacify at any rate. Let his brother handle the ever-frayed nerves of the fragile people, whose fears grew with each turn of fate. Let Bellamy tend to the teary maidens, who surely cried as much for Melis' demise as they did for their own fortunes, for none would become queen.

Doubtless, Ffion would wed Bellamy soon if he hadn't already. Gierson didn't know and didn't care what they'd done the day before in the in-between amid the civil ceremony and the celebration, but he had his suspicions.

Ultimately, he'd underestimated the pixie halfling, with Bellamy's arrival a not uncommon diversion for him — an exquisite plaything to lure into his bed. Indeed, he'd imagined her to be nothing more than a passing fancy for Ffion, who'd eventually see her off with a palace-fabricated excuse, only to settle for a more suitable bride.

But he had not, nor had he shown any inclination to step aside despite Gierson's many attempts to waylay him. He hadn't begun his double life longing to reign, only coveting the status in time, having sent pixies to accost his brother — to end him, if necessary. Yet Ffion had proven too strong, and while the spare hadn't wanted to dirty his hands, he'd soon be left with no other choice.

Gierson made for the king's quarters, his body trembling with pent-up anger, seeking a release. Knowing he was meant to set things straight with his brother for his kingdom, he'd never felt so preoccupied by his need to right wrongs. Powerful strength gripped his limbs, burning within his core and aching for an outlet.

But his quarters were far from empty. Indeed, they were fuller than ever, laden with the contents of Ffion's and Bellamy's rooms. Dresses. Trinkets. Regalia.

He was being displaced.

As if on cue, Luc arrived with an armload of personal items from Ffion's quarters, with the little nuisance Kit on his heels. Kit grinned, his arms overburdened with fluffy gowns that Gierson quickly recognized as Bellamy's.

"Sire," said Luc, offering a half bow that was nowhere near deferential before entering the room. He slipped past Gierson in all his scarcely contained fury, and Kit followed suit, though he said nothing.

He could sense their mockery. It was in their eyes, in their smiles. It was all over the room, lain with the belongings of not one but *two* people who cared not a whit about him as they carved him out of their lives and out of his own.

"*Leave me!*" Gierson roared, stomping into the room like a petulant, punished child.

Luc shuddered as his voice echoed through the chamber, and Kit stumbled over his feet from the sound, though neither was genuinely impacted by the tantrum. Instead, they returned to their work, emptying drawers only to fill them again with Ffion's belongings.

Gierson observed the display, his temper on the edge of becoming uncontrollable. But control was his way and always had been. It's what had seen him through the curse and every measure of duplicity. If he lost his hold now, he might never recover.

"*Get out.*" His voice was low, his breaths coming in heavy spurts as he worked to recover himself. The pressure in his chest was staggering as he nearly gave into the mania consuming his soul.

"We've orders, Your Grace," said Luc. "And they aren't from you."

Kit stood beside him, eyeing the spare as though he were crazy, and perhaps he was. He didn't want to stick around and prove them right. Instead, he fled, leaving the king's quarters as quickly as he'd arrived. It was his only means of self-preservation as the walls around him closed in.

The shift within the palace was palpable, though he was, for all intents and purposes, still *Ffion*. Yet orders that were not from him were being given in the name of the king and accepted as gospel. How and when it had happened was another matter, with Gierson feeling nothing shy of ambushed.

He ran to the rooms that once were his, finding that they were no longer the refuge they had been. These, too, had his brother's possessions strewn about, though Ffion seemed to be abandoning his time spent as Gierson in favor of a return to heir apparent.

Taking his head in his hands, he breathed deeply, desperate to recover some shreds of who he used to be. Before the curse, he'd been free, full of life.

Your true nature will consume you.

He'd embraced the plague spoken over him by Marin, believing that, at long last, he would be strong and courageous like the brother he so despised. Somehow, he would be found as an equal, not the younger, the spare, lacking in everything from intellect to seniority. But giving into it had not produced any benefits, leaving him to conclude that he'd fallen short of his ambitions.

He let go.

"Ffion—"

"No!" said Gierson, rounding on his mother, Helena. The queen stood before him, dressed in blues and golds, every inch the royal. She'd been steadfast in her insistence, pushing him to reign, pushing him for *more*.

"*Ffion* is in the great hall leading his people. *Gierson* is licking his wounds in his old quarters with his conniving mother!" the spare spat, his anger spiking over her maddening calm in the face of his juvenile tirade.

Helena folded her hands, her patience never waning. "I fear that you're becoming complacent. What's gotten into you?"

"You should be grateful, for I may be the only thing that keeps us afloat when we're banished from the castle." He began to pace, his thoughts running in vicious circles. "There's no going back from here, not with Ffion's return."

"You've become sloppy," Helena sneered, eyeing him sideways without an ounce of empathy. "The girl—"

"She jumped." It was a simple lie meant for a simple woman. She would never understand the burdens he bore, nor did she likely care. Still, the accusations flowing from her lips were beginning to grate.

But Helena only smiled, narrowing her eyes. "I was speaking about Bellamy, not Melis." She stepped nearer, disapproval coloring her features. "How did you know what befell her? You left the brunch so quickly."

His silence was answer enough. Helena sighed, wearing her displeasure like an overwhelming fragrance. "You were not to sully your hands in this. The pixies—"

"The *pixies* are as useless as that half-breed interloper taking *your* crown!"

Helena slapped his face, leaving his cheek stinging. He pressed his fingers to his flesh, utterly blind with rage. Moving without warning, he gripped her by the shoulders, and though he looked upon her, he could not see her through his madness. "I'll no longer be your puppet."

Gierson shoved her with all the strength he could muster, ignoring the way that her body buckled under the force of his weight. Her head hit the marble floor first, the sickening crack echoing through his chambers as her skull fractured.

A crimson pool seeped from beneath her graying hair, her eyes round with impending terror even as they dimmed before him. Returning to himself, he watched on as her pallor faded moment by moment, feeling eerily composed when he realized he was finally free from her machinations.

She'd been no better than Marin in the end, manipulating her circumstances for her benefit even as she convinced him of his necessity, his value.

Lies.

Crude as it had been to become the beastly version of himself he'd always suppressed, Gierson finally felt *alive*, full to bursting in the freedom of his inner-monster. It had always been there, lurking beneath the surface, offering mild directives for years, biding its time for an opportunity to take control.

He only wondered why it had taken him so long.

Gierson smiled, filling his lungs with what felt like his first full breath in years, wiping his hands of the nagging dowager as he moved to begin covering his tracks.

But he wasn't alone, for the damned kid, Kit, stood in the doorway. The boy squared his shoulders as their eyes met, a halfling rat much like Bellamy, though he was nowhere near as brave as he pretended to be.

Gierson could smell his fear, and when he turned to run, the spare was delighted, for he loved a good chase.

Chapter Twenty-Nine

No one could be foolish enough to think Melis' death was accidental. High above where she lay, the curtains from the tower she resided within streamed over the balcony balustrade with the quiet, late-morning breeze.

When Ffion had known her in their youth, she'd been one of his dearest confidants. The lady knight was clever and capable. Ambitious. He didn't believe for a moment that it was a tragic mistake, or even that it might have been intentional on Melis' part.

No.

It was the result of something more heinous than all that, the revelation casting a chill over the day that had little to do with the changing seasons.

Bellamy urged Ffion to take the time needed to say goodbye and collect himself, so he carried Melis' fractured body away with tears in his eyes, incredulous that somebody so vital could be gone in a blink.

Even if the woman she'd become was far from who he'd known her to be as a girl, she'd still seemed to care for him. Indeed, she'd warned him to be cautious when he'd arrived in Calaise, though even then, she'd seemed hardened, if not a bit crestfallen, in the few interactions they'd shared since his return.

He would regret never learning the heartache that changed her or the things that brought her joy but hoped she was at peace.

The prince delivered his old friend's lifeless shell to her chambers only to find the doors had been left open. Evidence of a struggle littered the room, and Ffion recognized an all too familiar fetid odor amongst her things. Her body was cold when she was discovered, and Melis' blood had long since dried where she'd fallen. The one who had courted the dame's gruesome end had done nothing to cover his tracks, remarkably unconcerned with being found out.

Her bed was unmade on one side, and Ffion laid Melis there, covering her with the plush duvet. He would send someone to care for her, but could not linger. Glancing around her quarters, his fury piqued when he thought about the encounter that had led to his friend's sickening final moments. She'd deserved so much more.

Kissing his fingertips, Ffion pressed them to the dame's forehead, her eyes closed as if simply asleep.

"Forgive me." The prince did not withhold his tears. "Forgive me for not seeing the truth sooner. His crimes will not go unpunished."

He left, closing the door behind him to return to the gallery, bent on locating his wife. Certainly, she could handle herself, but thoughts of Melis' end plagued his mind, hastening his pace.

Ffion spotted her instantly, surrounded by their guests on every side. His entrance, while unannounced, caused a stir through the crowded hall, those in attendance parting as he made his way through them to his beloved.

She was well. Thank heaven she was well, for he'd seen the bloodlust in Gierson's eyes before Melis had been found.

Ffion had recognized the murderous gleam when he'd stormed toward them in the dining hall but always thought his twin more controlled, if not wholly unaffected by the curse that had altered every facet of their lives. It pained him to see Gierson that way, despite the danger he posed, because he knew the misery of his affliction.

But nothing would have pushed Ffion so far as to see their childhood companion to an unspeakable demise, to leave her then exposed to be discovered. It was inconceivable.

The prince embraced Bellamy, holding her to himself, unsure when he might ever see fit to let go. He took her face in his hands and kissed her before she gently broke away from him, her study filled with questions.

Ffion slipped his arm around her waist as he turned his attention to their people. She'd done wonders to calm them in the time he was away. Many cheeks were stained with tears, several ladies blotting their eyes with handkerchiefs as they stared back at them, but among them, Gierson and Helena were nowhere to be found.

"At this time, we would ask that everyone remain in the gallery," Ffion began. Bellamy laced her fingers through his, and he wondered if some part of her already puzzled out what had transpired. "If you must leave for any reason, we suggest it not be alone, for until we have concluded with certainty what took place, we encourage vigilance."

No words of dissension followed his request, though alarm persisted throughout the room. A grand portrait of King Tolliver hung proudly near the entryway, like a stalwart guardian looking after his court. Ffion knew that he would have reminded him to trust his instincts, which told him that his mother and brother's absence meant worse things awaited Calaise if he did not find them quickly.

While Helena was likely trapped along with the rest of the palace residents, the prince could only assume that like him, Gierson was not.

"My brother's scent was all over Melis' chambers," Ffion said into Bellamy's ear. She turned to meet his gaze with anger etched in her features, ever the vengeful creature he'd met in Neverwoode.

"We can't allow him to leave the grounds, but I've not seen him or your mother since Melis was discovered. It may already be too late." Bellamy paused, her face draining of color. "He will do it again, Ffion. I felt it when he was near. He's lost any sense of reason, and we've sent Luc and Kit to relocate our belongings."

The prince inclined his head toward the exit, and Bellamy nodded. They skirted the outer walls of the gallery, picking up their pace as they ventured down the eerily quiet hall, her gown swishing lightly against the floor.

"Here," said Ffion, ducking into a darkened stairwell. "It's the fastest way to Gierson's quarters."

The prince led them as they ascended the steps, his beast roused by the promise of eminent discord, for Gierson had been there. Ffion felt his twin's nearness, sensing his lurking presence in the air around them. The prince bristled when they reached the doorway. Something stomach-churning awaited them on the other side, a metallic aroma pervading his nostrils.

Ffion cast a wary look over his shoulder to Bellamy, and she inclined her head, prepared for whatever awaited them on the other side of the door. "We have to," she persisted, though her eyes shone with the fear of what they might find.

Twisting the knob, Ffion slowly pushed through the archway. The heady stench of blood hit him immediately. Gierson's apartment seemed to be fully his once more after Lucignolo and Kit's efforts to oust him from the king's suite, but it was the shining ruby pool on the ground opposite the bed that caught Ffion's notice. Veins of red flowed from it, seeping into thin hairline cracks of the stone floor.

"*Ffion,*" Bellamy whispered as if she'd read his thoughts. Tightening her grip on his hand, she forced him to wait, to brace himself before taking that final step that would reveal his twin's next victim.

He knew. Her perfume had endured in Ffion's memory — a thick floral fragrance imported from Sundsvaile.

He moved into the room, spying white-gray hair stained with red stuck to the ground, confirming what the prince had already concluded. Ffion sucked in a breath, taking in the sight of his mother dead at his feet.

He choked on a sob, letting go of every bit of loathing he'd felt for the woman who had never loved him in return. Kneeling, he pulled her into his arms.

She was still warm, her vacant eyes staring up at the ceiling. Grief overwhelmed him, accompanied by a healthy dose of fury and fear as he closed her eyes, rising to lay her upon the bed beside him as he'd done for Melis not an hour past.

A prayer passed his lips, though he scarcely registered what he said—not hardly words, but mere groans from the spirit that had carried him through every trial he'd faced.

The dowager was cruel and unfeeling, but his mother, nonetheless. He'd known nothing different, and now she, too, had perished along with his father and Melis.

It was more than enough.

Ffion felt himself slipping, that relentless tug that seduced him into mayhem. Soon, but not yet, he would answer.

"He's still here at the palace." Ffion's words were rough, his throat tight with suppressed emotion that had the power to break a man or sharpen a warrior.

Ffion rummaged through one of the wardrobe drawers, snatching a pair of slacks from within. He tossed them to Bellamy, who shimmied free of her dress, folding and cinching the waist in the next breath. The prince threw a buttoned shirt her way, grateful she'd opted for silk flats rather than heels. Tying the long flaps of the top into a knot at her lower back, they left without a word, sprinting headlong for the king's chambers, hoping to find Luc and their halfing nuisance.

Lucignolo met them halfway, a look of confusion plain on his face. His partial smile faded when he saw the blood on his friend's hands and sleeves. "What's happened?"

"Where is Kit?" Bellamy pressed, her words teetering on the verge of panic.

"I was just looking for him." Luc's gaze darted between the halfling and Ffion, concern evident in his speech. "Please, somebody tell me what's happened."

"Melis and the Dowager Queen are dead. Gierson is unwell, and we need to find Kit before—" Bellamy paused when something caught her eye at the end of the hall. "Find Selah and tell her to hide!" she ordered before taking off toward whatever she'd seen.

Ffion followed at her heels, catching up with long, fleet-footed strides. A strip of white linen snagged on the railing caught their attention, leading them up another stairwell.

The prince could smell both Kit and Gierson, their sweat and blood. Dread gripped Ffion, but he refused to give it any power, instead sprinting up the steps. Ever higher, they tracked them, finding mild hints of struggle that had the pair pushing themselves up flight after flight.

"*Quickly!*" Bellamy cried, whether more to herself or the heavens, he didn't know, but the word echoed through him like the tolling of cathedral bells.

The beast beckoned as they approached the highest point of Dufoise, and at long last, Ffion did not resist its demand. Tremors coursed through his muscles, his pulse thrumming with nervous anticipation when he looked out over Calaise. The sun was at its peak, reflecting off the castle rooftop like tongues of flame.

It was the worst possible place for a battle with his brother, but when Ffion saw Gierson trudging toward Kit, he had to commit. Sloped panels of gleaming copper cascaded downward in a waterfall of hammered metal, making for a precarious pursuit. The lad was agile and beyond clever to have coaxed Gierson there. He'd given himself a fighting chance, for while he could not fly like his wicked brethren, he wouldn't plummet.

"So, this is who you are?" Ffion shouted across the rooftop. "Your true nature has bested you, brother!"

Gierson whirled around to face him, and all facets of the strategic socialite he had been were gone, replaced by an inhuman, cold-blooded fiend. He glanced between the young halfling and Ffion, with Bellamy stood beside him, her hair whipping around her as the winds picked up. She moved forward, and Ffion resisted the inclination to hold her back. She hadn't survived in a world wrought with horrors by being reckless.

"Choose," she demanded of Gierson. "Which of the three of us will you pick? The boy has done nothing, so perhaps I'm a better option. After all, I did reject your advances last night."

Ffion knew nothing of such information. She'd known he would kill Gierson for it.

"Go!" Kit pleaded, looking first to Bellamy and then to Ffion. The desperation in his words was heartbreaking, his readiness to sacrifice himself without a thought for himself reminding Ffion of the days he'd spent believing he, too, was somehow less valuable than those he sought to protect.

Courageux est le sacrifice.

Kit was the very definition of the motto so beloved by his father, by his predecessors, both sacrificial and brave. Likewise, the prince would lay down his own life for anyone he loved or served as king, just as he was willing to do for the boy who was prepared to face the devil in Gierson for their sake.

The spare turned his attention back to the boy, who remained several strides out of his reach, and Ffion braced to run. They were not far, but enough distance and gaps lay between them that Gierson would have Kit flayed before he could reach them.

Ffion leaped once he'd gained enough speed, hurling himself over a cavernous void and onto an angled turret as Kit retreated further from the spare, so near the roofline that a sudden gale would send him over. It would be a favor for the boy in truth, putting him out of reach for the beastly usurper, enabling him to glide to the ground below.

But the look in Kit's eyes suggested he meant for Gierson to follow him over the parapet's edge, even as his tunic was already torn from an earlier encounter, its jagged edges revealing broken flesh.

The spare didn't disappoint, slipping down over the copper panel in pursuit of Kit, a move Ffion was sure he'd made for spite. Nothing Gierson did followed expectation, not when he was cornered as he was now.

It was a maneuver meant to inflict pain.

The turret's ledge was barely wide enough to find footing with nothing else to take hold of, leaving Ffion teetering precariously until he found his next mark, vaulting over a matching opening that would see him hurtling into the courtyard flights below if he missed.

"*Jump!*" Bellamy screamed to Kit, having gone the other direction. She was nearing Kit from the other side, clinging to a similarly angled turret, though she would have more of a fighting chance if she lost her footing, given her lineage. Still, she was too near to Gierson for Ffion's liking.

He leaped again, landing paces behind Gierson. His brother turned, eyeing the heir with a murderous glare before again advancing toward the kid.

From his nearer vantage, Ffion could see another gash across Kit's ribcage, leaving him barely in control of himself in all his righteous anger, knowing that his brother had dared to injure a helpless child.

"Jump, Kit!" Bellamy called once more, and this time, he did, throwing his arms out to either side and dropping into the nothingness behind him.

"Find him, Belles!" Ffion yelled, meeting his pixie's gaze. Her features were pinched with worry. She'd have seen the boy's blood-soaked shirt and shredded trousers, and Ffion needed her as far from the palace as her legs would carry her.

"Oh, yes. *Go*," Gierson chided, twitching as he narrowed his focus upon Ffion. No longer did he acknowledge Bellamy's presence, his mind set on his brother alone, even as he muttered unintelligibly from before him.

Indeed, Ffion had once thought himself mad, but this, *this* was madness. This was what it meant to be utterly spent.

With one final nod, the heir sent Bellamy on her way, praying for the preservation of his wife and his kingdom as he turned his attention to Gierson, whose eyes were black with the promise of death.

Chapter Thirty

It had been a while since Bellamy had jumped from such a height. Perhaps she never had, for the way down looked much farther than she'd ever attempted before, but time was wasting.

Everything from the beginning of her journey had been against her better judgment, from her travels to Wylewoode to her trek into Calaise. Within a handful of years, she'd gone from her work mining sift to a queen in wait, and nothing she'd done to reach her station had come through any force of her own will.

Yet, despite her struggles, she'd have done it all again, for in the end, it led her to Ffion.

His insistence that she run for Kit did not sit well with her, but again, she had little choice. Ffion held his own against his rabid brother for now, though that could change at any moment. She took her chance, leaping from the heights with her eyes pinched shut, uttering an earnest prayer as she drifted to the ground below where, God willing, she would find the boy unharmed.

She reached the earthen floor in a matter of seconds, her legs buckling from the impact. Halflings had few of the graces possessed by full-blooded pixies, with the gift of flight just out of reach given their lack of wings. Even so, gliding was better than falling.

Bellamy picked herself up, scanning her surroundings, finding Kit huddled beside a short hedge. He, too, seemed to have had a challenging impact, brushing his hands over his trousers to remove the dirt and grime. One of his knees was also exposed, and the pant leg split open where his skin was rubbed raw.

She moved to his side, squeezing his shoulders. "Are you all right?"

"I'm fine. The princes—what happened?" He glanced above, and Bellamy followed his line of sight, seeing only brief glimpses of the two men as they grappled. Kit rose to his feet, and she helped to steady him, but he shook her off. "We need to help."

It was true, but offering aid would be easier said than done from where they now found themselves at the castle's base. They moved several paces away from the fortress, and Bellamy counted floors while attempting to discern which wing and rooms were immediately above the brothers.

Bellamy didn't yet know the palace well enough to readily guess, and the time she was squandering in her efforts had her near panic. Grunts of frustration and cries of pain trickled down to where they lingered, leaving her wishing that she had a sling.

Or wings.

Rather than guess and be wrong, she decided to climb, running for the castle's stone walls, hoping there'd be enough of a lip on which to find purchase.

"Be careful," called Kit from behind as she made her way upward, though she hadn't moved far. The bricks were nearly flush with little mortar to speak of, making for an arduous climb. But it soon became clear she would not meet with success as she slid down the face.

"We'll have to try our luck inside," she fumed, only to change her mind again when, some four stories up, she saw Ffion dangling from the parapet.

Gierson stood over him as Ffion attempted in vain to regain his footing, hoisting himself upward. The spare gesticulated wildly, undoubtedly spewing abuse in his perceived triumph until he swung a thick metal rod, crushing Ffion's fingers.

His hold faltered, but Gierson didn't back down. He took another shot at his brother, this time smacking him in the head.

It was too much.

Ffion dropped from the ledge, appearing unconscious from the blow as he slid down the side of the turret, and Bellamy gasped, feeling utterly helpless as she watched his limp body fall in what felt like slow motion. He stalled a bit when he hit a dormer set just above an open window, but he continued his descent, rolling from there only to glance off another dormer before toppling unimpeded to a tangle of brush below.

Bellamy ran before he touched the earth, heedless of the monster lingering above. Her heart was in her throat, with the uncertainty of what awaited her in the thorny brush eating her alive.

She'd only just reached her beloved when Gierson plunged toward them, his delusion evident in his eyes as he moved with a grace that only an otherworldly creature could possess.

"Ffion!" Bellamy cried, taking his face in her hands. He wasn't conscious, but he was breathing. She patted his face, tipping his head backward in desperation, but there was no response. "Pull!" She grabbed one of his arms, Kit taking the other, and they dragged him with all their might, but he was far too heavy.

He didn't budge, surrounded by brambles in the thick of the hedging. Gierson reached them a moment later, batting Kit away with a wicked swing of his arm before turning his attention to Bellamy. "No wonder your father abandoned you."

With a swift backhand across her face, Gierson sent Bellamy flying, her vision briefly disappearing. He was strong, so strong, inflicting untold damage with a thoughtless sweep of his hand. She felt the sting in her cheeks as much as she did his words. They were callous, brandished to harm, and they'd hit their mark. She'd never loved her father, never needed him, but neither did that stop her from feeling the depths of his indifference toward her.

Recovering her senses, she flicked her wrist, but her stiletto wasn't there, leaving her no means of protecting herself or Ffion. It was too late for that at any rate, as Gierson had somehow managed to hoist his brother's inert body onto his shoulders.

He was leaving, well on his way to the perimeter of the estate. Bellamy climbed to her feet before drawing Kit up alongside her, preparing to give chase.

"Wait!" Luc approached, jogging toward them. "I've been searching everywhere for you." He paused, bending at the waist with his hands on his knees to catch his breath.

"We're wasting time," Bellamy snapped, her head throbbing from Gierson's jab. "He'll kill Ffion."

Luc watched the escaping beast, following his departure with narrowed eyes. "I saw what happened. If you chase him, he'll kill you too. It would take less than nothing to do so."

As much as it irritated Bellamy to hear it, she knew Luc wasn't wrong. But with every second that passed, Ffion was further out of reach. "What do we do, then? Where will they go?"

"I think Gierson's gone to prove himself." Luc reached into his tailcoat, withdrawing a dagger and handing it to Kit, who held it with awe. He then girded himself, drawing his sword from the sheath at his side before presenting Bellamy with her stiletto. "I found this when I was moving your things."

"Prove himself? What do you mean?" She tucked the stiletto into her sleeve, grateful to be armed as she fought to suppress her growing panic.

"The journal." Luc paused, as if he was measuring his next words carefully. "King Tolliver's journal declared that to be part of the curse levied by Marin, and while I don't believe *prove yourself* to mean publicly, I think Gierson does."

Bellamy balked, following the only person who might know Gierson as well as Helena or Ffion. "Public?" she demanded as they ran. "Why is he running away from all the courtiers in the castle then?"

"Doubtless, he believes them to be on his side. He'll be headed for the wharf to plead his case to the people."

The trio followed at a distance, and Bellamy worked to suppress the nagging sense of foreboding. She'd seen enough of Luc, and Ffion seemed to trust him unequivocally. But, she'd been burned too many times before to blindly accompany the man. "You know about the journal?"

"I helped Tolliver write it. Watched him descend into hysteria as we searched for his lost son," said Luc, his breaths coming in fitful bursts. "Ffion is the rightful heir, and I will not see him waylaid by an unworthy demon."

"Why the wharf?" Bellamy demanded. "What's to stop him from killing Ffion just outside these forsaken walls?"

"Killing an incapacitated man wouldn't be much proof of your worth, now, would it? He'll want an audience," Luc wheezed. "You sure have a lot of questions for someone running at breakneck speed," he added, his subtle humor helping to ease her reservations.

He didn't have all the answers, but he knew more than she about the history of Calaise, about the brothers and their curse, and his loyalty felt true enough.

Luc stopped dead in his tracks, bringing Bellamy up short. Kit nearly bowled her over as he reached them, gasping for air as they observed Gierson from afar. Much as the winter roses had obeyed Ffion in his presence, they parted for his brother as he moved nearer, making a hole in their barbed barrier for him to pass through unharmed as Ffion bounced on his back with each stride.

As quickly as the poisonous blooms had moved aside, they reunified, forming a deadly obstacle that none could surmount.

Bellamy had seen it before, observed as dedicated knights had attempted to breach the boundary, only to disappear within the vines, poisoned and suffocated. No weapon wielded against them, from torch to blade, had successfully seen anybody through.

Only the flame-haired princes and their armor formed of curses could so boldly command their way through.

Bellamy fell to her knees, taking her head in her hands, though she refused to fall apart. No good would come of breaking now. If there were any way to breach the wall of lethal weeds, it was through sheer force of will.

"What do we do?" asked Kit, his small hand resting on her shoulder.

"We go through," she decided. "*I* go through." She rose to her feet, ignoring the little voice within that begged her to preserve herself. It was the only way to reach her husband, and she would not leave him to the hands of fate alone.

"I made it through once with Ffion's aid, but I'm no halfling," said Luc, drawing looks of horror from Bellamy and Kit. He shook his head, dismissing their incredulity. "I know more than I let on, and I know with certainty that doing what you're thinking of doing could be devastating given your heritage."

"There's no other way for me. Left to Gierson's designs, Calaise will no longer have the rightful king." Bellamy glanced at the wall, seeking the least dense avenue by which she could climb. "If I fail, do not let Gierson ascend, for he is not worthy."

She proceeded without looking back, eager to meet the challenge head-on. Reservations abounded in her mind, but there was no better way. Yet even her nearness to the otherworldy blooms made her feel faint and panicked.

Without another thought, she ran for the wall, ignoring the tightness in her chest. Cold sweat swept over her when she touched the deadly vines, a breathless whimper escaping her lungs when she saw them slither toward her like a serpent with its prey in sight. She could feel their evil, their venomous touch on her skin, causing spikes of pain that started in her fingertips, moving down her limbs toward her heart.

This was it. She was going to die, bound within the constricting coils left in place by her malevolent father. She could almost hear him laugh.

From beside her, she saw Kit and Luc, each joining her in her quest to overcome the infernal winter roses. She opened her mouth to scream, to warn them away from the agony that wracked her own body, but no sound emerged, with the growing tension in her chest threatening to squeeze until she burst.

Higher, Bellamy climbed, side-by-side with the halfling boy and Luc, ignoring the pain with only the thought of Ffion holding her together. Kit was a wonder, fearless in the face of certain danger, shoving through the chaos that had likely seized his mind to help recover the rightful king, while Luc had proven to be a truer friend than ever she could've imagined.

Indeed, she was beginning to hope...

An errant spike sliced the tender skin of her forearm, leaving a deep wound that bled freely, streaming over her flesh and dripping from her elbow. She bit her lip, pushing onward as she pulled herself to the peak of the wall.

She straddled the top, reaching for Kit to assist him, only to nearly topple from the edge when she momentarily blacked out, a wave of nausea overcoming her when she recovered herself. The discomfort began to subside, replaced with a sense of euphoria as she grew more vital moment by moment.

She could *breathe*, her peace returning little by little when, at last, she realized why.

All of the vines were dying around them, shriveling and blackening along with the flowers. The creepers became crisp before her eyes as if they were drying out, and when Bellamy reached to touch one, it crumbled between her fingers.

"It seems the cure is in the disease," said Luc, nodding toward her wound, and he was right, for as her blood slipped down her forearm and landed upon one of the blooms beneath her, the flower withered on the spot.

Up and down the ramparts, the greenery shrank, fading as if it had been blighted. It was astonishing to watch, like a wave of visible illness flowing down the walls.

"If only we'd tried that days ago," Kit mused, the color returning to his pale face.

"You'll be a blessing to the kingdom, indeed, milady, but we must return your husband to the throne." Luc scaled his way down the iron fencing, catching Kit when he leaped from halfway and settling him on the earth below.

Bellamy was next, making for the ground and recovering her breath, grateful to begin feeling like herself again. She'd address the arm injury later, too eager to find her husband to think of anything else at the moment.

They took off, following the trail left behind by Gierson and his heavy tread. Signs of his manic escape from Dufoise were everywhere, easy enough to follow through the shaded woods. His scent, too, and his essence were everywhere, and that was a godsend, given the emerging mist rolling through the trees.

"Something is very wrong," Bellamy breathed, the statement nothing but evident on its face. Yet she felt something more in the air, something deeper that called to her very soul.

But it wasn't until she *heard* the call that she began to run.

Chapter Thirty-One

Ffion came to with a raging headache and several swollen fingers, bruised and purple from where they'd been struck with a metal rod. He didn't remember much from before he'd blacked out, but he did remember that as much as the look of utter contempt covering his brother's face.

Gierson had rained blows upon him, absorbed as he was by his true nature, and had seemingly lost any sense of reason. He'd murdered Melis in cold blood before doing the same to Helena, leaving him bereft of any humanity so far as Ffion was concerned.

Once, he had worried over his own nature, convinced that he was losing himself to the curse and all the ills it meant for his future and kingdom. But Ffion had realized of late that he had a say in the direction he chose, and he wouldn't allow the loose lips of a wily pixie to dictate his decisions any longer.

But none of that would help him in his current predicament, held at the whims of his manic brother as he worked to come to terms with his beastly soul. The haunting melody running through his head wasn't doing him any favors as he tried to regain his wits, leaving him wondering how significant the blow to his head had been.

Gierson dragged his listless body behind him by the collar of his jerkin, and Ffion did his best not to alert him that he'd awakened, even as his bare skin grated over the rubble beneath him. He flexed his hands, testing the strength of his fingers. The ones that weren't injured would have to do, though he hadn't a clue how he'd free himself.

Through narrowed eyes, he watched as they entered the town square, though his surroundings were obscured by a creeping mist, thick and pearly, as it rolled into the town along with him. The whole scene felt off, but there was naught to be done at the moment. Ffion was forced to bide his time, assessing the next move of his deranged kin.

Concerned whispers accompanied the pair into town as people watched, with mutterings of the flame-haired twins following them to the dais, where Gierson towed him up the stairs before dropping him altogether at the center of the wooden podium.

Sea spray scented the air around Ffion, filling his senses as reveries from his past invaded his mind. His head lolled to the side, and he fought against unconsciousness, drawn by the fog toward oblivion alongside the enduring siren song echoing through his spirit.

As if they were called to attention, the people assembled before the dais, watching on as Gierson paced, his energy nothing shy of frantic as he gathered his thoughts. Any semblance of prestige or composure he'd once had as the acting heir had vanished in an instant.

The balance of power was a precarious dance, lost as quickly as it was claimed. And sovereignty gained through dishonesty left a void wherein truth and honor met their end.

"Good people of Calaise," Gierson began, adopting the haughty air their mother had always worn. "I come before you as a broken man, for I've been betrayed in the worst possible way by none other than my own flesh and blood."

That got Ffion's attention, even if he couldn't show it. Instead, he slowly positioned himself to make his move, flipping to his side, where he observed his brother's performance. Gierson was always at his best when playing the pitiful, overlooked spare.

But he'd added a new act to his repertoire.

"Gierson's return has brought much discord to our sacred kingdom," he continued, gesturing toward Ffion where he lay still at his feet. "He returned to us with a thirst for power, eager to unseat me from the throne, and worse..." Gierson paused, his dramatic delivery having the desired effect as the crowd held their collective breath.

The spare shook his head, his countenance grim. "Worse...in his zeal, hellbent upon rule, Gierson has killed — our beloved mother as well as the indomitable Dame Melis, who sought only to prevent further destruction before losing her life."

Cries of anguish rose from the people while Ffion fumed in silence. Never had he seen such absurdity, yet the gathering was ready to have his head, with demands for *Gierson's* life reaching a fevered pitch, blending seamlessly with the persistent melody that, Ffion realized belatedly, was not within his head alone.

"Gierson has become a beast!" howled the spare. "Owned by an otherworldy presence of which we've only just become aware, beholden to a pixie populace that would rule through him. I tell you, he will stop at nothing for control!"

Fear.

It was evident upon every face in the crowd as Gierson's musings became more dire, more frenzied, fostering a growing panic amongst the citizenry as they attempted to decode his madness. Pixies were fantasy and beasts the epitome of lore, or so they believed. Understanding the reality that lurked beneath the surface would take time to come to terms with, if it ever happened at all.

Shifting slightly, Ffion managed to draw his dagger from its sheath at his waist, concealing it in his palm as his brother pleaded with the people in earnest. The shreds of sanity Gierson was clinging to were beginning to fray, his eyes wide with desperation.

His breaths became heavy as he rubbed his eyes with the heels of his hands, his internal anguish more evident with each passing moment. If Ffion didn't know him better, he might've felt sorry for him, in all of his power-hungry misery.

But Ffion *did* feel for him, much as he wished to ignore such sentiments. Gierson's lust for domination and control had left him bereft of any other purpose in his life. Jealousy had colored every facet of his relationship with his twin, and he'd readily pitted himself against Ffion in counterfeit competitions for everything from hunts to women.

He'd been used for his title, too, with their own mother having seen him as a means of acquiring authority. She'd loved him, too—certainly more than she'd ever cared for her older son, but love didn't exploit. Much like Ffion, his life had never been his own, and even less so after Marin had seen fit to inflict his curse.

Gierson paced the length of the dais, grasping for control, his hands opening and closing at his sides with each step. Ffion prepared to make his move despite the haze clouding his vision. The pervasive melody, too, was setting him on edge, filling him with urgency. He was running out of time, likely to meet his end at his brother's hand, else by the will of the crowd the spare had whipped into a panicked frenzy.

"My brother has killed not once, but twice!" Gierson continued in vain. "Should he not be punished?"

His ambitions to prove himself worthy of being king were an unmitigated irony, for every offense he'd mentioned had, indeed, been committed by Gierson. But Ffion was beginning to wonder if his brother had, at long last, finally lost track of who he was.

If his protestations were any indication, he well and truly had.

"Good people of Calaise," said Gierson, looking down his nose at his lifeless brother. "We must kill the beast!" With his proclamation, he pointed an accusatory finger toward Ffion, leaving no room for error over whom he believed to be the villain of the story.

But while the people made no move to action, Ffion did, swinging his body around as he kicked Gierson's legs out from under him. His brother landed with a heavy thud on the wooden platform, leaving him gasping for air upon his back. Though every movement Ffion made came with unbearable pain in his head, he knew he'd never have a better chance to save his kingdom from his destructive brother than now.

He willed himself forward, leaping on top of his prone twin, pressing his knees into the spare's arms as he crouched on his chest, holding a dagger to his throat. "You're right, brother. *Gierson* did do all of those things, and he should not be permitted to rule."

Ffion didn't see fear in his double's eyes — only hatred, which he would never understand. Their lives had been largely content until Marin had stepped in, their parents attentive enough. And the role that envy surely played was, for Ffion, moot, as he'd have involved Gierson in the upper echelons of the kingdom at his right hand until his end of days.

There'd been no need for such strife. The utter contempt between them would always be beyond the heir's understanding, but that wouldn't keep it from breaking his heart.

"Favor smiled upon you when you somehow managed to enter this forsaken world first," Gierson spat. "It was an error of fate, not some divine intervention. That you seem to think as much tells me just how lost you are."

He rolled, disorienting Ffion as his head swam in pain. But the older son would not surrender so easily. He fought back, stabbing Gierson in the shoulder with his blade before shoving him away and springing to his feet. The spare followed suit, matching Ffion move for move, somehow unbothered by the seeping wound on his upper arm.

A howl of anguish whirled around them as they sparred, the voice familiar to Ffion though he could not place its origins. The sorrowful tune ebbed and flowed with the fog, like melodic fingers beckoning them toward peace that would never be had until one of them was dead.

Gierson narrowed his eyes, a growl rumbling forth from his throat. He'd lost all sense of reason, his feral presence revealing the depths of his true nature. He moved for his brother, wrapping his arms around the heir's midsection and throwing him into the ground, knocking the dagger from his tenuous grasp even as it stole their breath from their lungs.

Ffion's anger spiked as he struggled for air, slamming his knee into Gierson's groin. Yet what would incapacitate any other man only made the spare more violent. He took the heir's neck between his hands, squeezing the life out of his gullet.

Still, the king refused to die at the hands of his corrupt twin. Darkness tinged the edges of his vision, but his arms were free. He thrust his palm up, driving it into Gierson's face, his brother keening as his nose bled heavily.

Ffion bucked, knocking his brother from atop him, finding his feet again, and plucking his dagger from the dais. He was unsteady, exhausted beyond words, but never would he yield. Bellamy waited, along with a kingdom in desperate need of direction and decency. He would rule like Tolliver, exterminating the evil that dwelled within his borders.

It was time for this blood war to end.

Chapter Thirty-Two

Calaise nearly lost both heirs that day.

Bellamy feared she would not reach them quickly enough, hastening her pace when she laid eyes upon her beloved. Ffion was on his feet, lunging for Gierson with a blade in his hand, wielding the knife as an extension of himself. They were an even match in size and skill, but her husband was faster than she remembered, his movement fluid despite the blood trailing down his head and neck.

Ffion struck his brother again, cutting a long, currant-red slash at the back of Gierson's knee, dropping him to the platform as he bellowed profanities into the growing mist rolling off Loch Apsaras' rocky shore.

Gierson's face contorted with rage, but never would he surrender. He spun away from Ffion, wobbling on his feet before recovering himself enough to strike, swinging at his brother's stomach. Ffion recoiled from the blow, but bounced back, locking his arms around

Gierson's neck. They clung to each other, like two prizefighters who were running out of steam but refused to submit.

Their countrymen seized the opportunity, setting about breaking them apart, even if Gierson's lies had fostered much uncertainty amongst those gathered regarding their allegiance.

Though Bellamy could see plainly in Ffion that he'd embraced his strength, he wasn't nearly as hostile as Gierson was when the residents attempted to restrain him. His brother flailed with the hands of five men holding him back, sending a sixth off the dais after connecting his fist with the man's jaw. Bellamy heard his bone crunch even from where she was, still some ten yards from them.

A tendril of fog whipped toward Gierson, his eyes wide and searching as it slithered around him like an eel disorienting its prey. The lagoon beyond them sang with outstretched arms, a ballad of perilous seduction written by the Mistress of the Undersea herself. Wonder filled the spare's features, the tension in his body easing for long enough to bind him before the mist drifted elsewhere.

Bellamy ached, wheezing a bit as she caught her breath. The infernal winter roses had taken a toll on her, and Kit and Luc likely felt the same. Luc was not far behind Bellamy and the boy, the trio arriving at the inland port along the westernmost perimeter of Calaise, one after the other. The air was thick with sea mist, making it difficult to see, accompanied by a soulful melody wending through the haze.

Unforgettable, eerie notes filled the billowing salty gray that reached out like tentacles through the streets and into the town square where the citizenry had begun to gather. Few could resist the lure of a siren song, but this was unlike anything Bellamy had ever seen. She knew not to answer a summoning from the deep, but this call did not seem to appeal to all.

A vaporous limb of ocean mixed with sun-drenched sky coiled around a young woman, altering her course away from the man beside her. The female's eyes glazed over as fog seemed to swallow her up. Her silhouette was barely visible, but through the haze, she could be seen walking toward the water.

Others did the same, spellbound by the chilling tune. Some tried in vain to stop those who were entranced from finding their way into the heart of Loch Apsaras, but its pull proved too powerful.

"You would restrain your king?" Gierson roared from the podium, where he and Ffion had been bound with ropes from the ships docked within the wharf. "You will release me at once or pay the consequences!" He strained against his cords, muscles taut as he attempted to break loose.

Bellamy made for the dais where Ffion looked as if he was struggling to keep conscious, his injuries and exhaustion catching up to him. Luc and Kit kept close, weaving through the bewildered spectators who could not seem to look away.

Lucignolo hoisted the halfling onto the platform, her heart lurching when she saw the extent of her beloved's wounds. The men who had restrained the princes stood in her path until Luc joined her at her side. Two of the men seemed to recognize their late sovereign's aide, curiosity in their eyes.

"Do not stand in the way of your queen," Lucignolo ordered, allowing him to push through the barricade they'd formed with their bodies. "Can you not see the truth for yourselves?"

Bellamy shoved past them as murmurs circulated through the crowd, the deep's melody softening but not fading entirely. Mist crept over the platform as she ran to her husband, carefully lifting his chin. His eyes were barely open, the Mistress's hum melting into something all too familiar.

Selah.

Ffion must have realized it, too, as he recovered some of his awareness, his gaze meeting Bellamy's.

She didn't know how it was possible, or even when Selah had left, recalling her wedding as the last time she'd seen her friend. Since'd they met, Bellamy had known she was different, but never could she have anticipated something so mesmerizing or frightening as this.

Selah's song circled around Gierson, vaporous and breathy. He began to sob, whispering to himself words that made sense only to him. It was like watching a man splitting in two, one part overwhelming the other in a long-fought battle for the spare's lost and wearied soul.

Bellamy and Luc removed the ropes from Ffion's wrists where they were tied at his back and anchored to the balustrade surrounding the dais. And even then, in all his pain and frustration, concern etched his features as he examined his bride.

"I'm all right," she assured him, and to her own surprise, she was. Despite the gash upon her arm from a winter thorn and the breathlessness born of her foray into the poisonous vines, she was whole, and Ffion was alive before her. "We're all right."

He nodded, his lips twitching into a slight smile as he took her hand in his, but his eyes betrayed the profound sadness burdening his spirit.

He rolled his shoulders and, righting himself, stood tall beside Bellamy, though she heard his breath hitch as he did so. "What my brother said is true," Ffion said, drawing gasps and cries of outrage throughout the square, but he went on undeterred. "Only I am not Gierson."

He allowed his words to settle over the people, breathing in then releasing a sharp exhale. Bellamy squeezed his hand and took a step forward, commanding the attention of their countrymen.

"Do you hear the call of the deep?" Bellamy began, raising her voice above the crowd. "Though her song can be heard throughout the land, the truly wicked cannot evade her bidding. So, tell me then, who would you have as your king? And, if you cannot distinguish between them who your true sovereign is, tell me which of the princes before you do you trust?"

Across the platform, Gierson moaned and sobbed, his head jerking from side to side as he struggled against his restraints. Blood pooled around his ankle, flowing freely from the back of his leg where Ffion cut him, but it seemed the least of his worries. His mouth was moving, words falling from his tongue as he stared longingly at Loch Apsaras through the fog.

Ffion stiffened, his grip on Bellamy's hand tightening around her fingers before he released them. "I've not heard it aloud since Marin spoke his malediction over me those years ago," he said, moving toward his brother.

No one held him off as the evidence of his people's understanding began to wash over the gathering. He was deliberate in his steps, approaching Gierson with no apparent reservations. Complete and utter desolation enveloped the spare, and it was more than Selah's persisting melody, engrossing him with her spellbinding harmonies as he wept.

Taking his twin's face between his palms, Ffion forced Gierson to look back at him, their once uncanny likeness replaced by stark contrast — the rightful king's compassion measured against his brother's demons. "You do not have to yield," Ffion pleaded, meeting Gierson's vacant eyes as he spoke.

Sobs wracked Gierson's body, but he made no effort to intimidate his twin, his voice cracking and desperate. "*Please.*"

Ffion shook his head. "Hold on to yourself, brother."

Gierson's life lay within the hands of the king. One sharp twist and it would be over, but the true sovereign's empathy was too vast. Bellamy watched as Ffion's hands trembled, his throat bobbing as he waited for Gierson's reply like some part of him clung to hope of redemption for his broken sibling.

Gierson closed his eyes, a tear slipping down his cheek and over Ffion's fingers. "This is me," he sighed as if the admission relieved a fraction of his torment. "I would have killed you even before the fairy cursed us. Father knew who I was. He felt it and preserved you. I have not lost myself."

Ffion dropped his arms to his sides, and Gierson's gaze followed, falling to the signet ring on his pinky. Ffion lifted his hand to examine it, several of his fingers shockingly bruised and swollen.

"He had one made," said Lucignolo, nodding toward the ring Gierson wore. He patted Ffion's shoulder, addressing him directly. "I never believed he was you to begin with, mind you. But remove the replica from his finger, and you'll find that one is not like the other."

Sliding the ring from Ffion's hand, Bellamy examined it. "*Courageux est le sacrifice,*" she whispered, reading the inscription scrawled within the signet's band before meeting Ffion's gaze, recognizing in him the embodiment of the motto. He was strong. Fearless.

And sometimes, the truest form of bravery was manifest in acts of surrender — something she readily perceived in her husband. Leaving the comforts of home for the wilds of Neverwoode to protect his kingdom and giving of his daily life to shield his people from the affliction of the pixies in his night wanderings had him living for more than himself at every turn.

To Bellamy, he had the makings of a fine leader and a dedicated ruler. His people would be blessed.

Luc plucked the ring from Gierson's finger with no resistance from the imposter king. He examined its interior, running his fingertip over the smooth metal. "No inscription. I suppose he didn't realize." He tossed the false ring to a nearby townsperson, who inspected it in much the same way.

Nobody would doubt Lucignolo's knowledge, so indispensable to King Tolliver as he had been. "The heir apparent stands before you," he continued. "Handpicked by the late king himself. Who better to serve in his place than Prince Ffion?"

Growing ascent echoed through the crowd, even as the sea mist around them slowly dissipated, save for a singular coil circling Gierson, tethering him to Selah's lagoon. Her song was carried with the breeze, beckoning him to follow as he inhaled the hazy caress of salt, sea, and sky.

"The deep—" Gierson hissed through his teeth. "She's calling. Who are you to stand in my way?"

Ffion appraised his brother, the famed flame-haired heirs anything but united as they clashed before Calaise. With longing, Gierson looked out upon Loch Apsaras, the sea's winding tendrils embracing him like a lover.

"Release me," the spare demanded, and Ffion clenched his jaw, considering his brother's plea.

"If you answer, you'll not return." Ffion looked to be struggling against himself, bewildered by his twin's desire to disappear into the deep. But Gierson appeared acutely aware of the fate he wished to pursue, having watched dozens of others seeking the same as they journeyed into the mist.

"*Please.*"

Without another word, Ffion nodded to Luc, who promptly assisted him with Gierson's bindings.

Brave is the sacrifice.

Again, Bellamy's beloved embraced the ancient Calaisean adage, even if he was riddled with reservations. The crease of Ffion's brow revealed his hesitancy even as his posture conveyed his resolve. Gierson was not the brother Ffion deserved, but he was the only family he had left, and it took courage to willingly be left alone.

Bellamy understood the feeling well. Blood bonds could not be undone, no matter the vulgarity of one's relations. They were not unlike invisible shackles that burdened some while blessing others, but she'd never met anyone who didn't crave some sense of family or belonging.

It was the inane reason she'd kept the mirror from her father for so many years.

Regardless, Ffion would never live out his days apart from those who loved him. She would see to it that he wasn't bereft of affection or family, for that matter. She would stand in the gap, ensuring that he would find fulfillment and happiness for all his days.

Ffion and Lucignolo dropped Gierson's cords to the platform as vaporous fingers motioned him forward. There were no goodbyes for, or from, the one who moments earlier meant to destroy. Gierson was rapt, wandering into the surf as though he were one with the sea. Entranced. Fearless.

Free.

Bellamy took her husband by the hand, reading sorrow in his eyes as he watched Loch Apsaras swallow his twin and several other erring lives into her fathomless, swirling pool. The tides swelled alongside the billowing fog, making it impossible to see anything beyond the shimmering gray until, at long last, the siren's song waned.

All at once, the waters calmed, giving way to pristine, aquamarine waters as tranquil as a secluded spring. The sun above warmed away the remaining chill of the mist, leaving behind a people disoriented by so many mystifying phenomena.

It was a world none had been privy to until now, causing silence to fall in its wake. All of Calaise looked to the dais for explanations, and though they would not come easily, somehow Ffion would answer the call. He turned toward Bellamy, extending his hand, and she took it, their fingers laced together for all to see.

"My father, the great King Tolliver, had the misfortune of meeting a creature of lore given flesh, who revealed himself to my brother and me in the night—a pixie who meant to threaten the whole of

Calaise and beyond for his own pleasure." He paused, seemingly measuring his words. "We were cursed. Damned. Or at least so we thought. But my father built a fortification around Chateau Dufoise, doing everything in his power to save us, his sons and heirs, from the ills of these otherworldly beings."

The citizenry watched with bated breath – a people wholly hypnotized with their attention focused irrevocably upon the heir as he continued.

"For my own safety, I ran away, knowing the perils seeking to harm me at home. I fought demons each night in the thickets of Neverwoode where no one would find me, and for four years, I was not a prince but a lost, reckless boy. I sought nothing more than to protect those who did not know the nightmares that lurked outside their doors. I learned that I had a choice in who I would become, though I did not see it that way then."

He was strong, though the memories looked to be taking their toll upon his mind, his throat bobbing with suppressed emotion. "I could cower and preserve my life or challenge death itself every night so that others might never have to look evil in the eye. I chose to fight, and will do so for Calaise and all of Fayble until I die.

"I am Prince Onfroi Tolliver Ffion Adélard, and heir apparent to my father's throne, if you will have me," said he, his words spoken with humility, as if he were not set apart from birth. "And beside me stands Lady Bellamy Rosamund Gracia, my wife and future queen of these lands, should you accept us as such."

Bellamy made no effort to withhold the tears flowing freely over her cheeks, and she was not the only one so moved by her husband's transparency. For a time, quiet gripped the square as his promise found rest with his countrymen until a small voice was raised from below.

"All hail the king!
King Ffion, he shall be — "

The voice belonged to Kit, who stood amongst the crowd, beaming up at Ffion and Bellamy as he continued the song sung in the streets the day they'd first arrived in Calaise.

"No greater reigns beyond the sea,
our future rests on thee!"

Kit finished the song alone, and the air around them was silent once more before several others began the refrain again. Bellamy squeezed her husband's hand, his eyes welling with moisture at the resounding sound of acceptance.

"All hail the king!
All hail the king!"

The chant grew into a thunderous roar of support for the pauper prince as the people sang in earnest, with cheers and applause filling the void left behind by the siren of songs. And though nothing about where they were now had come easily, Bellamy knew that the kingdom would thrive. Ffion's true nature *had* consumed him, leaving him stronger and more merciful — more than capable of leading a nation.

He was destined for it.

Chapter Thirty-Three

Bellamy refused to leave the closet first, pressing a kiss to Ffion's brow before shoving him out of the door.

A pair of maids giggled from the other end of the corridor, averting their eyes as their newly minted king rearranged himself after tripping into the hallway. They hurried along, cheeks flushed with pink, dipping into synchronized curtsies.

"Your Majesty," they said, neither willing to look him in the eye, as if somehow they were the ones who should be embarrassed.

Ffion inclined his head to the young women. "Good day," said he, smoothing the wrinkled hem of his tunic into his trousers.

They continued walking, one whispering to the other as she glanced over her shoulder toward the king and the closet from which he'd stumbled. Something crashed against the door from within, likely the result of his wife putting herself back together.

"Oh, I beg your pardon," Ffion called after them. "But might you assist my queen?"

Bellamy spat his name like a curse from inside the closet as the young women obliged, their footsteps nearing. He made haste, not wishing to be anywhere near the scene when the door was opened. Ffion's grin spread when he thought of what fun he would have later. Oh, she'd be angry with him, but the reconciliation was always worthwhile.

They were similar in ways he couldn't count, which made Ffion treasure his wife all the more. Maddening, impetuous, a vicious tease. But beyond that, she was his joy, his safe place. She balanced him, an equal in every way that mattered and a treasure he could never do without.

Bellamy was a piece of his life that he knew he didn't deserve, yet somehow, she was his. Through all the chaos, through the pain and tumult of curses and coups, she was there, and never would he take her for granted.

Months had passed since the coronation, and the king and queen had adjusted to the rigors of their reign in exquisite fashion. They were naturals, empathizing with the plights of their people even as they would readily provide thoughtful solutions to the most puzzling of dilemmas.

The people of Calaise were happy.

It was a peaceful existence within the walls of Chateaux Dufoise, as well. Ffion would love his queen, with the pair neglecting their duties for hours at a time, sneaking away to all corners of the estate to steal a handful of breathless moments, only to work through the dedicated mealtimes to make up the difference.

He could not get enough.

It was the life Ffion thought he'd never have and a far cry from the unpredictability of Neverwoode. They were surrounded by blessings, from dedicated courtiers to productive stewards. Everybody offered their talents and gifts, making for a smoothly running routine built on trust.

His council was a godsend, and he was grateful for its members' wisdom every day. Their experience was unparalleled, and having them was, in many ways, like having pieces of his father to guide him in matters of state.

The king had met with the council more frequently than usual of late. Word from Debrecyn communicating their disappointment regarding the abandoned agreement between their eldest princess and Geirson made for a tenuous state of affairs. But the accord had been struck under false pretenses, as the Debrecynians believed themselves to be negotiating for their daughter's betrothal with Prince Ffion himself.

The fallout was ugly, making for tense relations along their borders. The mountain nation felt they'd been had, particularly as rumors of the supernatural chaos within Calaise made their way Fayble wide. Doubtless, they believed it all to be nothing but duplicitous—a means by which the Calaiseans might relieve themselves of their obligations to Debrecyn.

Ffion had always been vaguely aware of the mountain kingdom's designs, even as a young boy, knowing that they'd like nothing more than to waylay his family and install their own. Calaise was a prize, fertile and productive.

Impending war was in the air.

The king sent correspondence to Chamelaute, knowing well the limitations of his own forces and knowledge. The kingdom was renowned as the most powerful in all of Fayble, and Ffion trusted its sovereigns unequivocally. Their time together had been brief and unusual in every conceivable way, but if the rumors were true about Chamelaute's vaunted *round table* of advisors, their insights would prove exceedingly valuable.

Ffion was set to meet with a Chamelautean emissary upon the hour. His wife's insistency had delayed him longer than expected, but he was not one to disregard punctuality. In short order, Bellamy would join him for their introductions, assuming she'd forgiven him for giving the maids more to gossip about.

Still, there were worse things to learn of their monarchs than their fervid devotion to one another.

Lucignolo greeted Ffion outside the drawing room, bending at the waist in a manner all too formal for old friends, but so it was. No matter how often he'd told Luc how unnecessary it was for him to do so, his friend had persisted.

"They're early." The aide kept his voice low as he nodded to the doorman, who entered before his king.

Ffion brushed his hands over his tunic again, realizing he'd left his jacket behind with his pixie in the closet.

Hell. These receptions always made him nervous.

"His Majesty, King Ffion," announced the doorman, ushering his sovereign inside with Lucignolo following close behind. Ffion wondered if he would ever grow accustomed to hearing it.

As it turned out, that was amongst the least of his concerns, for when he entered the room, he was entirely unprepared for the company that awaited him.

Hair black as pitch cascaded over Queen Aurora's shoulders, braided into thin rows above her ears on both sides. Her eyes were just as he remembered, the most striking crystalline blue, though they softened as they took him in. Beside her was His Majesty, King Artyrus, broad and stalwart, ever his beloved's ardent guardian.

Rory pushed past him, approaching Ffion without pause, pinching his chin between her fingers as she examined his face.

"It's him, Artyrus. The rumors were true, indeed!" she exclaimed, turning slightly to see her companion's reaction before returning her attention to Ffion.

"I'm not sure if that explains anything," Artyrus mused, studying the young king's face for himself as he moved to Rory's side.

Ffion laughed, the pair observing him as if he'd lost his mind, or perhaps as if they'd lost their own, for much had changed since last he'd seen them.

"I didn't expect it to be you who answered my request, but I'm grateful, nonetheless," Ffion began, unable to keep from smiling.

"We searched for you for months." Rory's eyes pooled with tears as she wrapped her arms around him, releasing him like she still couldn't believe he was right in front of her. "We only stopped when we received your letter, but we had to see you for ourselves."

"You would not have found me in slumber." Ffion understood where first they might've hoped to find him. They would've searched their dreams—where they'd met so fortuitously in Otherlande, in the poison-induced dreamscape that had brought them together only to wrench them apart.

"While Fayble slept, I hunted."

Thus began Ffion's story. For the next hour, he told them everything, from the origin of his curse and why he'd left Calaise to all that happened once he returned.

Not once did they look at him like he was anything other than the ally they'd known before they'd awakened, though they were mystified by the change in his appearance.

"I used the strangeness afforded by subconsciousness to conceal my age and face," Ffion explained. "I did so in Neverwoode also, where sift clouded the lawless citizenry's perception of reality so much that no one questioned how it was that I never grew up, even as those around me matured."

"James mentioned as much in his letters," said Aurora. "The sea captain, you might've known as Captain Hook."

Ffion nodded. "I know him well. We owe him a debt of gratitude for what he did alongside Petra, the halfling piratess. I correspond with them regularly. We parted ways after the destruction of the sift supply and the demise of the self-appointed Queen of Neverwoode, Wendolyne."

"So it's all true," Rory began, coming to terms with the otherwordly elements of what otherwise sounded like a fantastical story. "The sift, the...*pixies?*"

"Real. Strange, but true," Ffion confirmed with a chuckle. "James was surprised, too."

"Did he know you were a *prince?*" Rory smacked the Calaisean king playfully, and he laughed again.

"No. Not a soul in Neverwoode or Otherlande was so aware."

"Now, I do not feel so guilty." Artyrus smirked, squeezing Ffion's shoulder. "I knew you were a peculiar nuisance, but never would I have guessed the reason you seemed so beyond your years. You were not a mere boy, nor were you a penniless pauper."

Aurora shook her head, sighing contentedly when Artyrus pulled her closer. "We wouldn't have believed it without seeing you with our own eyes," she said, taking Ffion's hand in hers. "Of course, we knew of the flame-haired twins of Calaise, but assumed you were simply named after the heir."

Ffion nodded. It only made sense, and he understood how his story would confuse them as it did.

A knock sounded at the door, and Luc crossed the room, ushering Bellamy in to meet their guests.

The doorman rose, bellowing, "Her Majesty —"

"Thank you, Andre," said Bellamy, patting the strapping man on the chest to excuse him. She stood before the trio, wearing a beautiful smile as Ffion took to her side, drawing her toward the cozy setees.

"My wife, Bellamy," said he by way of introduction, and soon she was enveloped in the arms of Rory, drawn forth into their circle of friendship.

For hours, they talked, sharing the challenges and responsibilities of their stations and enjoying one another's company. Ffion watched as his beloved bonded with his dear friends, enjoying the way that Rory's eyes widened throughout each harrowing story shared by his bride. Tales of her halfling origins fascinated the Chamelautean royals, leaving them awed by her fortitude.

Alas, he was home, blessed beyond measure to be surrounded by his chosen family.

* * * *

Winter came and went, and still the dead man's bells tolled.

The violent blossoms that had caged Dufoise had long since died, their poison seeping into the soil and bringing life to the king's namesake.

Foxglove grew in place of the winter roses, bordering the palace grounds with toxic bell-shaped flowers, standing as a warning to any remaining pixies nearby. The sunset-hued perennials survived the Calaisean winter months, blooming when they should've faded.

Dead man's bells were aptly named, for ancient lore proved, once again, to be true as the flora called to the pixies. They were a trap, a lure to coax the demons out of hiding, but the fairies learned quickly that none would survive long within Calaisean borders.

When all was well, the flowers chimed faintly like a distant melody, heard only by those who knew what their silence warned.

Spring was in bloom, and the late King Tolliver's garden was thriving and vibrant with color. It was there where Ffion found his wife, her nose buried in a book Kit had left out for her the day before.

"Just one more chapter," she said, aware of Ffion's presence well before he'd made himself known.

"If you say so." The king prowled toward her, sitting on the bench beside her. She rested her head on his shoulder, sinking into him, flipping to the next page of her story.

Peace.

It was all they'd ever wanted, and somehow, they'd found it in one another. At times, Ffion still couldn't believe it was real.

They sat in companionable silence as the birds trilled around them, the sun illuminating cracks and imperfections of the pavers lining the walkway leading into the palace. It was beautiful and tranquil in a way that could only be achieved through brokenness.

Bellamy closed her book, turning in Ffion's arms, "Do you ever think about what might've happened had Selah not been there that day at the wharf?"

He tried and failed not to remember the look in his brother's eyes, both tragic and vile.

"No," said Ffion, because the answer was that simple.

Bellamy's brow creased, her fingers idly twisting the tousled ends of his hair as she considered his naked honesty.

Ffion lifted her chin, her eyes shining like the sun above, golden and full of life.

"I don't think of it because it would've meant *this* would not be, and I cannot imagine a world where we are not together."

His response seemed to pacify her, but instead of relaxing in his hold, she rose to her feet. "Their song reminds me of her," Bellamy said, indicating the quiet refrain of the foxglove.

She held out her hand, and Ffion stood, her slender fingers slipping into his palm. The king swept his beauty over the cobbled ground. Graceful as ever, Bellamy spun around him to music heard only by them. It was not the first time and would not be the last, for there were few things Ffion loved more than to watch his wife dance.

The world was nothing, and their pasts insignificant in these stolen moments when their hearts beat as one.

It was a song without end that changed with the seasons, with the wind, and the hour. On those days when time allowed it, they were known to dance well into the night.

Ffion's beast had all but abandoned him, though he'd come to welcome it when trouble sought them, and Bellamy reminded him that he was not less because of it. They were much the same that way, and always had been.

Cursed, the king had been, and his pixie, half wicked, or so they'd once convinced themselves. For both, the opposite was true, as the former were nothing more than deceptions spun by an enemy that no longer had authority over either.

Near where the pair moved, enveloped in one another, mind and body, a handful of servants watched. Ffion dipped Bellamy, her back bent elegantly over his arm before she drew nearer to him. She was perfection against him, made for him.

"Let them watch." He grinned before kissing her forehead, and she smiled. These were the same words he'd said the night they were wed when their people observed him guiding her across the dance floor.

Bellamy melted into him, tugging him closer as Ffion wrapped his arm around her waist, twining his fingers through her hair before tipping her face upward. Indeed, she was capable of far more than he could've imagined, taming not only wild creatures, but beasts and monsters of the darkest order. And while she didn't bend woodland creatures to her will, she'd controlled Gierson and befriended the Mistress of the Deep feared by all. She'd humbled Ffion and ruined him with her fury and beauty while healing him just the same.

"*Je suis à vous,*" said she, meeting his gaze. "I am yours, always, my love."

His.

And so, they would live for the remainder of their days, swaying as one alongside the foxglove that was everything lethal, everything lovely. Would that it could always be until the last bell tolled.

Want to see more like this?
Here's a taster for you to enjoy!

Cursed Fates: Isle of Wolves
Tiffany Daune

Excerpt

It's too sunny to celebrate death. I shield my eyes from the piercing rays illuminating our kill.

"Ready?" Luba huffs, blowing her sweep of bangs from her eyes as she hoists the *vovkulaka's* bloodied head from the back of the truck.

"Don't drag it by the ears." Yeva shoves her arm under the beast's head, and it slides to her chest, knocking her back. "Some help here." She shoots Luba a pointed stare. "We need balance, so the rocks don't tumble out before we get it in the boat."

I shift to her side, and brace my hand at the base of the skull, my fingers digging deep into the fur.

Luba rolls her eyes and distributes some weight from my arms to hers. We shuffle side by side, none of us daring to look the beast in the eyes even though the *vidmy* have already scooped them out and there's nothing more than spell-sewn sockets filled with smooth black soul stones.

Looking made us what we are.

Every hunt, with my finger steady on the trigger of my crossbow, the image of my pregnant mother, the crimson blindfold torn from her eyes, drives my courage to kill. The ancient magic of my *vidma* ancestors burrows in the marrow of her bones. That's why the *vovkulaka* captured my mother's stare and lured her into eating its kill. And why I'm now damned to hunting and afternoons of burial drownings instead of careless summer days without blood on my hands.

As we wade into the water, my foot catches in the silt. My ankle rolls, but I bite back the pain. "*The mind must be clear of emotion,*" my captain's warning whispers through my mind. Spirits are listening.

Ahead, the others in our hunting party rock the boat from side to side as we make our way out to them. I wanted to be in the boat this time instead of waist deep in stinking reeds.

Until Valentyn offered to row.

Like the *vovkulaka*, I don't dare look at him either.

He's my curse.

But I shove those thoughts away, too. I don't need the spirits to hear about the boy who broke my heart.

"Lift, Olena." Luba nudges me. "I can't hold it much longer."

"Sorry." I prop the head up. Its wet fur tickles my arms, making me itch. I imagine my body sprouting with the same wiry fur. Seeds in my pores growing thorny and thick, breaking through my flesh. Not today, though. Today we bury another, a soul who couldn't keep the *vovk* from rising within them. I'm thankful it's not one of us. "Never," I whisper, hoping the gods hear my prayer.

"She shouldn't be here," Yeva says between forced breaths.

"I'm right beside you," I say, though she's spoken little to me since the night of the fires. Not even when the others jumped and cheered when I aimed my crossbow and struck the iron rod through the *vovkulaka's* heart with one hit. Yeva won't let me forget the past.

"It's Olena's kill." Luba hoists the head higher. "She must be the one to bring it to the lake. That is the way of the *zhnetsy.*"

Yeva huffs, her energy thick with anger as she wades farther into the water. She has nothing to worry about. I don't want Valentyn back. He belongs with her now.

The head weighted with rocks tugs at my muscles. I wish now it hadn't been my kill and that I'm not wading out to give it to my ex, who I vowed never to speak to again until hell froze over. Cliché, I know. But I meant it.

Valentyn, Haru and the new hunter Nyx reach for the head, taking it by the ears until Yeva shoots them an icy glare.

Valentyn slides his arms into the water, his face inches from mine as he scoops the head from my grip. His languid gaze meets mine. "Hey, O."

My breath catches as the name only he calls me falls from his lips. I try to avert my gaze from his mouth, but I'm drawn to the secret inside.

Most look at Valentyn and count six scars crisscrossing his face.

There are seven.

The other raised mark hides along his tongue, a jagged line cut by claws. Valentyn wears our demons on his face. It's hard for the *vidmy* to forget who we are, what we can become. It's impossible for me to forget how he feels next to me.

My stupid heart beats faster, not from the weight straining my arms, but with the thought of Valentyn's hidden scar I've kissed a thousand times.

I slip back against the water, floating away from the pull of the boy and the intoxicating spell he has over me. I hate this feeling of me without him. I hate myself for wanting him despite what he did. His gaze lingers seconds too long and Yeva shoves the head into him, splashing water in his face.

Haru too gives me a look. His dark eyes cut with concern. We have plans later. He's my heartbreak distraction, a friend who knows how to help me forget. Did he see how Valentyn looked at me? Did he witness the way my gaze fell over Valentyn's sun-kissed arms—how if there weren't blood and bone between us, nothing could keep us apart?

The new hunter is oblivious to what Valentyn and I shared, how we burned what we had to ash. And I'm thankful for one person who doesn't know every detail of my life—who hasn't been on the isle long enough to be tainted by all the lies—who wasn't there the night of the fires.

But Luba saw my awkward exchange with Valentyn. This I know by the death grip she has on my arm as she drags me to the shore.

I don't dare glance back at Yeva. I'm sure her hex would sting.

"What the hell was that?" Luba hisses at my ear. She hasn't forgiven him. Good friends hold grudges in your name.

"Nothing." I turn away so she can't read the lie on my face.

Valentyn's laughter echoes across the lake as Haru breaks out in song.

Three hours before they return to shore. Three hours before the head of the *vovkulaka* settles in the sand. Three hours and the *rusalky* will sing their death song.

"Well, it sure as hell didn't look like nothing." Luba interrupts my thoughts of the ravenous maidens who guard the lake and the boy who's rowing out to offer them the beast's head.

"I can't wait to see Haru tonight." I lean into Luba like I'm being confidential but speak loud enough to catch Yeva's attention. I don't need new rumors circulating. I can barely get through the weeds of my family's sins.

When Yeva slams the tailgate of her truck and hops inside, Luba says, "You still love him."

Yeva revs the engine of the truck and takes off, leaving us in a cloud of dirt and sand.

"Do not," I say as casually as possible, but the lie cuts deep into my soul.

She shoots me a sly grin. "Hate to love him."

"What were those super-intense vibes you were sending Nyx's way?" I divert the conversation to her.

"No vibes. And besides, I didn't think you could see anything while under Valentyn's trance." She wriggles her fingers like she's casting a spell.

"So, you *were* checking out the new hunter!" I nudge her.

"Busted." She grins. "She's hot—right? I mean, did you see the way the sun turned her eyes an amber gold color? And those abs… Who has abs like that?"

"I'm pretty cut." I pull up my shirt.

Luba slaps my stomach. "You don't count."

"Gee, thanks. I guess all those crunches were for nothing." I pull down my shirt, laughing. Luba was my first kiss. We've loved each other forever—before we kissed on her thirteenth birthday—and long after. But we discovered two things that day—one, Luba only wanted to kiss girls, and two, I still wanted to kiss Valentyn Alexandrov.

Luba shrugs off her wet shorts and T-shirt and tosses them into the back of her four-by-four. She towels off and throws it at me. "You're not riding wet in my new truck."

I dig in the back and pull out my jeans and sweatshirt, aptly printed with a growling wolf. I dress and hop in the passenger seat. Before I even fasten my belt, she takes off into the forest like we're being chased by Veles' minions. If they caught us, I'd be dragged to the underworld for sure. No trial is needed. I'm guilty of everything they say.

A series of quick chimes fill the truck. Luba doesn't even slow as she twists her bracelet to the left, pops out a tiny tablet and places it under her tongue.

I do the same before the last chime sounds. The tablet fizzes with a bitter taste.

Luba's face puckers. "Gross." She digs through the backseat, pulls out a canteen and takes a swig. She blows out, fanning her tongue.

The staunch scent of alcohol fills the air.

"What the hell? You're drinking?" I grip the roll bar as she barrels over a log, tossing us from side to side.

Luba takes another sip. "I need to wash the tablets down with something. The shine doesn't taste right since your mom —"

No one ever finishes that sentence. Maybe they're afraid there's a curse attached to *vidmy* whose cars fly off bridges.

"Hey, look, I'm sorry I brought her up," Luba says.

"No. Fair. This shine is bitter. I don't know what they're doing up in the labs, but it's not from my mom's grimoire. Give me some of that."

She hands me the canteen and I take a sip.

"Oh, that's nasty. You're cut off from day drinking, my friend." I joke, but I'm concerned. Luba isn't a drinker. Then again, her sister Tetyana was alive the last time we drowned a head in the lake.

"My mom uses it for healing," Luba says. "Kills the demons in your nightmares."

Tetyana, growling with fanged teeth, haunts my nightmares, too... My captain who taught me how to aim, how to prop the crossbow on my shoulder and steady my feet on the ground before releasing the trigger—how to kill with one shot the monsters we'll become. I tuck the canteen into Luba's backpack. "Keep us on the road."

"Hey, we just drowned a *vovkulaka*. One less demon. Let's go to my house and celebrate. My parents are on some grieving retreat up the mountain. We have the place to ourselves. We can skinny-dip and binge eighties movies."

"Can't tonight." Can't and won't ever step foot in her house again. I swallow hard. I couldn't walk into their home, knowing I'm the reason her parents grieve. The others believe our captain took her own life when she turned. But I see Tetyana so clearly with my bolt in her chest, blood seeping through her shirt and the waves crashing below... Then nothing. Only stars over an endless ocean.

My phone vibrates. My stomach knots at the thought of it being from the infirmary. Inhaling a deep breath, I prepare for the worst. I never know if it will be *the* call—the one that says they turned off the haunting machine that mimics my mom's breath. The healers need my permission, but I know they want her out. Same as they pushed me to the fringe, far from town and my old life. It's funny how one can wake up and have everything and go to bed the same day with nothing at all.

I take a deep breath before swiping the message. The alcohol in my stomach churns when I read who it's from.

"What's wrong?" Luba asks.

"Professor Svitlana's summoned me to the academy."

"I'll go in with you."

"No need for us both to get punished." I scan the trees, searching for spying drones.

Luba leans forward, peering toward the sky. "They didn't see us drinking."

"They're looking for any reason to cite my ass. And I just gave them a reason."

"Maybe they have an update on your mom?" She gives me a hopeful smile.

"I love your optimism, my friend, but we both know what it means when they call me in." I should have known better than to drink. I shouldn't have come at all. I could have faked a stomach bug. No one would blame me. I'm the girl whose mom stole shine, torched the labs then struck a match to our family home, all while she was busy driving an iron rod through her best friend's sister. Oh, and maybe happened to catch her boyfriend cheating. Since that cursed night, I have had a permanent stomachache—a deep and gnarled knot in the pit of my gut that will never unwind.

My phone vibrates again.

"What now?" I huff under my breath.

Stay away from Valentyn, the message reads.

Seriously? I roll my eyes at Yeva's drama. I'm about to reply with some choice emojis when I notice the number is unknown. Yeva would want me to know it's her.

Who is this? I type.

Another message illuminates the screen.

The book didn't burn.

My breath hitches. The book. A flash of flames flickers in my memories—lips sealed—secrets curling with smoke. My hand trembles over the screen. I'm not sure how to reply when the next message pops up.

I've read your secrets.

About the Authors

Britt Cooper

Brittany has been a cosmetologist for over a decade, an occupation that continuously explores fresh avenues of creativity and beauty. She is a new mother, learning to balance the reality of what it means to be a mom, wife, stylist, and author. Reading has always been one of her passions and writing an endeavor she refuses to leave behind.

Erin Dulin

Erin is a wife and mother who loves spending time with family. She's an enthusiastic fan of all things sports, experimental baker/chef, and amateur gamer in her free time. Writing has been a passion since her childhood, and while finding peace and quiet in which to write never comes easily, she knows it worth every ounce of chaos when the stories take shape.

Britt and Erin love to hear from readers. You can find their contact information, website details and author profile page at https://www.firstforromance.com

Sign up for our newsletter and find out about all our romance book releases, eBook sales and promotions, sneak peeks and FREE romance books!